A Cat in Hell's Chance

Samantha Elmhirst

© Samantha Elmhirst 2021

No part of this book may be reproduced, or stored in a retrieval system, or transmitted in any form or by any means, electronic, mechanical, photocopying, recording, or otherwise, except for the use of brief quotations in a book review, without express written permission of the publisher Synergy and Light, and the Author, Samantha Elmhirst.

Synergy and Light
info@synergyandlight.com

Cover design by: Samantha Elmhirst
Illustrations by: Samantha Elmhirst
Publicist: Leah Maloney
Typesetting: SuziSavanah Hogan

Published by Synergy and Light
Printed in the United Kingdom 2021

Content

DEDICATION 5
Chapter 1 6
Chapter 2 10
Chapter 3 24
Chapter 4 33
Chapter 5 41
Chapter 6 47
Chapter 7 54
Chapter 8 66
Chapter 9 75
Chapter 10 83
Chapter 11 90
Chapter 12 99
Chapter 13 110
Chapter 14 118
Chapter 15 126
Chapter 16 134
Chapter 17 145
Chapter 18 157
Chapter 19 169
Chapter 21 207
Chapter 22 227
Chapter 23 237
EPILOGUE 239

...and Today	248
The Animal Angels	250
A Day in the Life of an Animal Angel	254
Acknowledgements:	263
About the Author	266

DEDICATION

To Simon, Louie, Mimi and Street Cat Bob,

and Christina.

With my love and respect.

And if you are the sort of person that cannot pass a cat by without first stooping down to say hello to him or her, then this book is *definitely* for you.

Chapter 1

We flew out of Glasgow International Airport at six-fifty am, having been at the airport for half past three in the morning.

We had arrived by taxi, bleary eyed and exhausted as we hadn't been to bed. I had thought there wasn't much point in sleeping. We had to be up at one o'clock in the morning, washed and dressed and ready for the taxi to pick us up an hour or so later. I'd learned from experience that sometimes, grabbing just a couple of hours of sleep at that time of night only to be up shortly afterwards, was the worst thing you could do. You just can't seem to shake off the feeling of waking up almost minutes later. Besides, we would have been far too excited to sleep.

As the plane took off in the half-light, we were glad to be leaving the wet and windy weather behind in Glasgow. Gathering speed on the runway, then slowing down to turn into take-off position, engines louder as we raced along the tarmac and finally that sudden, weightless sensation of taking off and leaving the ground behind us. It was quite euphoric, the butterflies doing dances in the pits of our stomachs. Lucy gripped my hand as we were launched through the low cloud almost vertically, and tiredness temporarily overcome, we were beaming with joy at the sensation and the excitement. We were both thinking the very same thing at that split second during take-off….

Paradise here we come!

We didn't actually see much as we flew out of Glasgow as it was so misty and cloudy, Scottish weather being mainly rain, rain and more rain. As we gradually climbed higher and higher through the grey clouds, the wisps of white cotton wool rushing past the little cabin windows like smoke suddenly gave way to that beautiful blue which is always there behind them. When the alarm chimed to take off our seat belts, I relaxed back into my seat and started to daydream a little. To think about how far we have come. I wanted to give Lucy happy memories of this holiday. I had so many happy memories of my own childhood holidays and at the end of the day, when you have lost both of your parents, that is all that you have left. I was determined to fill every nanosecond of this holiday with happiness, love and laughter, and to make it the most memorable holiday of all.

* * *

When I had originally asked Lucy where she wanted to go on this very special holiday we were planning, I really hadn't been expecting the reply she gave me. I had been mentally preparing for her to be beside herself with excitement, jumping for joy eagerly saying 'Disney world!' Up until this point in my mind's eye, I had been seeing us at *Big Thunder Mountain* on the Runaway Train, hurtling down the rickety tracks, laughing and shrieking with excitement and fear in equal measures, as we dipped, turned and plummeted. Then we would be blasting off on the high speed roller-coaster into the darkest reaches of the cosmos, even the men screaming, on *Space Mountain*. Lastly, I had seen myself holding Lucy's hand as we stood in awestruck wonder watching the spectacular night time fireworks over Sleeping Beauty's castle, the reflections of light shining on her excited but tired face.

These myriad images, just momentary fragments of an imagined future at Disney world, quickly dissolved and disappeared into Disney fairy dust as Lucy replied,

"I want to go to Corfu."

I wasn't sure whether I was disappointed or relieved, but it was definitely a reply I hadn't reckoned on. Just sun, sand and sea. It seemed like a soft option, easy and stress free. I had underestimated her thinking she would want a Disney world holiday when all this beautiful, sensitive child wanted was the peace and tranquillity of a small Greek island. Before I even gave my reply, I saw an alternative Disney world. The nine hour flight journey and turbulence; queueing for hours for each ride in the heat of the Florida sun; crowds, the constant noise and seething mass of humanity in all its shapes and guises. How many times can illusions be shattered? I really didn't want this, of all holidays, to be spoiled in any way. There was a real risk of a Disney holiday being a shattered dream in reality. Too many of those already in Lucy's mere fifteen years of life, and mine too.

I had quickly snapped back to the present. Wrapping my hands around the mug of thick, sweet hot chocolate that Lucy had made me as soon as I had got back from work, I sat back on the sofa. Louie, one of my white cats, immediately jumped up onto my lap, head butted the mug just as I had taken a sip from it, which was more annoying than painful (why do cats *always* do this?), and then padded around a bit more for good measure to make himself comfy. Lucy was animated, saying that one of her school friends had been to Corfu last year and she had seen her holiday photos. She told me that Corfu looked amazing and was really keen to go there.

"Mum, it just looks like Paradise", she'd finished.

It would also be the hottest and busiest time of year I thought to myself, and that doubting little voice inside my head told me that any popular holiday destination abroad in the middle of July would be the same. So, why not Corfu then? All I could do though was explain to Lucy that if we did go to Corfu, we would be stuck there for two weeks, even if she didn't like it. The previous year we had been to a farm house in St Andrews, which was ruined by the fact that it had rained solidly for the full week we were there. We certainly would not be repeating a 'home from home' style holiday again, and weather-wise, it certainly had been that. No. This was going to be our special holiday, for so many different reasons, and if anyone deserved one then it surely was us. We had had too many years of heartbreak, suffering and loss, and Lucy especially had had more than her fair share of the fall-out, with things she should never have been exposed to for one so young. I was also determined to have some real quality mother and daughter time, not least because she was growing up fast.

Despite my partner Stephen offering to come with us, which of course would have been nice, this was the time that Lucy and I had been subconsciously craving for I think; to just be able to shut the rest of the world out and be left to please ourselves. Selfish, indulgent, lovely, and a prize that together we had truly deserved and won, against so many odds. And so eventually, in the April that followed, I went to the travel agents and flicked through some Greece brochures. Lucy was right, it did look like a truly beautiful island and just like paradise. The sun, sand and sea was just what we needed for a relaxing time, so there and then I booked a two week package deal flying out from Glasgow Airport to Corfu. Lucy would not have coped well at one of the larger, more commercial hotels as she can find large crowds and noise quite overwhelming, so I picked a small family run hotel set beside the beach called Smartline Nasos in Moraitika Resort.

So. Corfu it was. What could possibly go wrong?

Chapter 2

Originally from the south side of Glasgow, Lucy and I had moved to our cosy two-bedroomed bungalow where we live now, in Bishopbriggs, in 2012. I had lost both my parents very suddenly in 2010 and then not long afterwards I separated from my ex-husband after years of domestic abuse. We had to endure six months in homeless accommodation before getting here and, as you can imagine, those were very dark days indeed.

Two years after my separation I met Alan, who I felt was the true love of my life. We met through an on-line dating site and I only clicked on his profile picture because he had a ginger cat sitting on his shoulder and I thought to myself, now there's a man after my own heart. We spent just a few short glorious years together until Alan suddenly became unwell in January of 2014. I could feel an old familiar feeling of portent, of icy fingers creeping up and reaching out to engulf me in a shroud of black again, as history started to repeat itself. Sick with worry, we went through the next few days back and forward between doctors and hospital appointments and within a short space of time he was diagnosed with pancreatic cancer. Just four months later, as the useless Spring gave way to the first tentative hint of warmth of May, Alan died. He had left some funds for me in his Will as he had wanted me to take Lucy on a special holiday. He also left me with his cat, Mimi.

Before I met Alan I had never really thought of myself as a cat person, and actually used to feel I had a fear of these somewhat aloof, independent and disdainful creatures. I think this had its roots in the fact that when I was a toddler, my grandmother had a cat that she had taken in as a stray. He was called Ginger, and whenever I went to visit my Grandma, he would eye me from his perch on top of the coat rack, give that funny little bum wiggle and then pounce on me. As a three year old, I looked at him as a wily, scary cat, who was out to get me and so of course that made me distrustful of his kind. I grew up feeling I was more of a dog person.

My parents had always had cocker spaniels who were playful and loving and had no hidden agenda. I also had when I was a child a beautiful fluffy white rabbit who I named Mr Snow, and a goldfish, imaginatively called Jaws. It was not until Lucy was a bit older, after losing her beloved little Syrian hamster just before Easter in 2012, that she started going on and on at me about getting a cat. Her relentless cries of 'Please, Mummy?' had started to wear a bit thin and so eventually, like most parents, I gave in.

In our area there was a local Cat's Protection (formerly the Cats Protection League) rehoming centre in Glasgow, and it had an Open Day coming up. So I promised Lucy that we would go and have a look to see what cats were needing a home. I say cats plural, but I was only planning on re-homing one cat. Not so according to fate, because Lucy fell in love with *two* white cats who were brothers. We were given the chance to spend some time with them and handle them and they were both very affectionate; nothing at all like the so-called 'ginger terror' of my childhood. However, the lady at the centre explained that they had to be re-homed together because they were brothers and at five years old were now inseparable. I told her that I really was only looking for one cat, having never had a cat before, and I really did not want to jump in at the deep end by having two. I had no experience of them, apart from the wily ginger, and homing two felt like unnecessary hard work.

However, perhaps subconsciously I could relate to both these little creatures, who would potentially grieve at being separated from each other after losing a life-long sibling and companion; and then when Lucy became upset and tearful, I reluctantly agreed to adopt both cats. So, after the necessary form filling and house-checks we collected Simon and Louie (so named by us, after the X-factor), and brought them home just after Easter in 2012; instead of Easter bunnies everyone joked and told us that we had Easter Kitties instead!

Arriving home, we carried the two boys indoors to show them their new home and in the years that have followed they have proved to be the most loving and affectionate cats that I have ever known, especially Louie who is so laid back and doesn't seem to mind Lucy carrying him around all the time. We can tell them apart because Louie has much larger eyes and a very loud meow, whilst Simon cannot meow very loud at all and is very timid.

After Alan died I took in his beloved cat Mimi as I had promised I would. It would have broken Alan's heart if Mimi had had to go into a cat shelter. He had been a stray kitten when he had taken him in and spent most of his time outdoors when he was with Alan. I cannot say that taking Mimi in had been easy because at first all he would do was hiss and spit at my own cats. Eventually though Mimi did settle, and when I had a conservatory built a few years later, Mimi quickly claimed that as his own space. I would say Mimi just tolerates my cats now but he does get annoyed if they get too close.

In 2015 I thought we were going to lose Louie. He started to lose a lot of weight and our vet diagnosed hyperthyroidism, which was caused by a tumour on his thyroid gland. The vet tried him on various medications but nothing seemed to work for him at first so he was referred to the small animal hospital, which is part of the Glasgow Veterinary school, for radioactive iodine treatment. This would cost £1,500, but at that time I would have paid anything to have Louie well again as I didn't want Lucy to have to endure any more loss in her life. We managed to scrape together enough money, some of which Alan had left to me, so I thought it was money well spent; you can't put a price on love. He had to be kept at the hospital for six weeks because he literally was radioactive with all the treatment he had been receiving but we were allowed to have him back just a few days before Christmas.

We brought him home just as the first few flakes of snow had started to fall, and that eerie quiet that always goes with the onset of new snow suited the sombre occasion, as we quietly and reverently carried Louie inside the house. He was just skin and bone, struggling to walk and a secondary problem of respiratory distress had set in. So during that Christmas I had to prepare Lucy for the fact that we might lose him. Louie had always been 'her' cat really and loved to snuggle up with her in her bed at night. He then had another month on iodine-free cat food and was afterwards asked to come back for more radioactive iodine treatment.

Unfortunately, the treatment failed the first time round and on hearing this news Lucy and I were both in tears. She had told me that all she wanted for Christmas was for Louie to be well again but with fingers still crossed for a recovery, he went for a second bout of treatment, despite my being convinced that this wouldn't work. Perhaps because it was Christmas and the season of goodwill, the hospital provided this second lot of treatment for free; and then by some miracle he pulled through and got better.

The head vet had been confident that his second treatment would be successful and Louie was photographed and used as a case study at a conference later on. Meanwhile during all this, poor Simon had been lost without his brother, as Louie was away for six weeks each time for the radioactive iodine treatment, and although the vet nurse telephoned me every day to give me an update on Louie, Simon of course didn't understand what was going on. Since then, apart from some minor surgery earlier in the year to remove a couple of malignant lumps, Louie is now the picture of health. Out of the nine lives he was given as part of his feline birthright, although he may have used a couple up already, he still has plenty left.

* * *

The build up to our holiday had been filled with days together with Lucy, and days without, as her father and I have a shared care arrangement. I was very busy at work at the clinic. As a Community Nurse, my job can be very stressful. We work in environments which change from day to day and which lack many of the resources that are available in hospitals. It is a demanding job providing educational and advisory services to both patients and families as well as involving the more practical nursing skills, such as dressing wounds, setting up drips and monitoring on-going care. The days tend to pass very quickly, despite being on my feet all day, and so from booking the holiday, to it finally arriving, came in no time at all, or so it felt like. I had worked the day before, on Tuesday, until five o'clock in the afternoon and had taken the Wednesday off to pack. Later on in the afternoon I picked Lucy up from her Dad's and as we drove back home we couldn't contain our excitement, singing at the top of our voices to songs on the radio, laughing, and just enjoying the general pre-holiday high spirits.

Now, just twelve hours later, we were in the sky. The flight took just under four hours and was quite smooth going, apart from some turbulence towards the end of our journey. Lucy had fallen asleep with her head on my shoulder about an hour into the flight. She looked peaceful and serene and I wondered what she might have been dreaming about. I was reading a book called *Blood Sisters* by Jane Corry that I'd picked up earlier that day and also had a few Corfu pocket guides that Lucy and I had already had a browse through. A little later on into the journey, I had to very gently wake Lucy as the stewards came round to each seat and served us up a cooked breakfast. The little in-flight meal perked us up a bit and after that Lucy stayed awake.

At around 1100 hrs Corfu time (Corfu is two hours ahead of the UK), the pilot announced that we would soon be landing, and gave us a breakdown of air speed, land temperature and the local time. People started to return to their seats as the seat-belt light pinged on and the stewards started to fasten their own seat belts at the back as we prepared to land. We gasped as we looked out of the windows as the plane was starting to descend, very quickly, not a cloud in the sky. It was so bright and sunny, almost dreamlike. We looked down at clear turquoise waters, the sea pennies sparkling on the surface of the sea and little white yachts bobbing about. We could see white sandy beaches and palm trees, and terracotta and cream coloured houses sitting close to the beach and Oh, it looked so beautiful!

We landed on the runway very suddenly with a jolt and then a bumpity-bumpity-bump along the scorching tarmac. The brakes were pulled hard and screeched as the pilot decelerated very quickly and masterfully, normal landing practice in Corfu because the runway is so short. Lucy and I couldn't wait to get off the plane. Standing up in our seats we gathered our hand luggage from the lockers above our heads and waited for a gap in the queue to leave the cool, air conditioned plane.

We made our way slowly down the aisle to the exit, said our goodbyes to the stewards who were wishing everyone a happy holiday, and stepped out into the daylight. Feeling the instant warmth of the sunshine on my face, was like opening the door of a fan oven with that sudden rush of intense heat. It wasn't even midday yet but already the sun was making our skin start to tingle and the shimmering heat haze, like a mirage, hung over the tarmac making the horizon wobble.

It didn't take us long to collect our suitcases and board the tour operator's bus that would take us to our hotel. It was an exciting journey, it felt like the bus was a voyage of discovery once we had reached the main road after leaving the airport complex that would take us to Moraitika. Our heads felt like they were on swivels, there was so much to see. We passed by olive trees set in neat groves and the most beautiful garden centres. I just could not believe the size and vibrant colours of the geraniums that seemed to be all around us; they certainly don't grow like that in Scotland, I thought to myself wryly. Lucy pointed out what looked like little fortresses set high up above the rocky landscape and rugged mountains which were just in view from our vantage point. You could definitely see the Venetian, French and British influence on a lot of the older architecture. Set against the backdrop of a peerless blue sky, it looked more like a film-set from a Bond movie and hard to believe it was real, as if it had been fabricated just for us tourists, a clever, artistic deception.

It wasn't long until the bus turned off the main road and started to descend and follow the coastal road. We could see the beach umbrellas dotted along the shore line and cheerful, colourful bars and cafés overlooking the beach. We passed tourists on mopeds, the bus slowing down to get around them as they put-putted along, unhurried and with not a care in the world. We both thought that Corfu certainly was like paradise.

Lucy squeezed my hand and smiled at me then asked if we could go to the beach as soon as we arrived at the hotel. I could not refuse, despite feeling quite hot and drowsy, as the child in me wanted to kick off my shoes and do exactly the same. It didn't take long to get to our destination as we were the third hotel drop-off for the bus. It slowed to a halt just outside Smartline Nasos and the driver jumped out to help us get our suitcases. Calling out our thanks and goodbyes, we made our way up to the hotel's reception.

The hotel looked lovely, it was very fresh, light and clean. Brightly coloured chairs and pictures in shocking pinks, bright yellows and deep turquoise set against the white tiles and walls made it feel very modern and quite chic. The reception was very busy as many other guests had just arrived but it didn't take long to check in. The lady on the desk told us that the hotel rooms were still being cleaned and would be ready in a few hours. She suggested that Lucy and I visit the hotel's restaurant for some lunch while we waited. We agreed but decided to have a quick look around the hotel to get our bearings first. The pool outside looked a good size, with wooden sun loungers all around it and bright yellow and turquoise sun umbrellas. We took our seats in the pool bar and ordered a bowl of chips and a glass of Coke each. The waiter served us with a welcoming smile and a really friendly manner, cheerfully asking us where we were from.

When I told him that we were from 'sunny Scotland' we all laughed. It was hard to imagine the dreary mist and rain that we had left behind us, and rather like *Alice Through The Looking Glass*, it all seemed to belong to a different world. We tucked into our chips and just as we drained the last dregs of Coke from our high ball glasses, the lady from reception came to tell us that our rooms were ready now. She gave me the key and brief directions on how to find our room and Lucy and I set off with our suitcases in suspense.

Our room was lovely and was situated on the ground floor overlooking the gardens at the front of the hotel. The sliding doors which led onto our balcony were partially open, letting in the most heavenly, heady scents of the many flowers and blossoms that were in full bloom in the surrounding gardens. We opened the doors fully and stepped out onto the balcony where a table and two chairs had been placed, shaded by the tall trees which were welcoming in the heat of the afternoon. Back inside our room, there were two twin beds, covers neatly folded down and an en suite toilet and shower room. The floors were tiled throughout and felt deliciously cool on our feet. I noticed a large television mounted on one of the walls and my first thought was, why on earth would anyone want to watch TV in such a beautiful idyllic setting?

I knew Lucy was eager to be outside again so I quickly unpacked our clothes and hung them up in the wardrobes. Lucy had already changed into a bikini and shorts and announced that 'we' were going to the beach. I felt exhausted. The energy of the young! I was torn because all I wanted to do was lie down on the bed with the balcony doors open and drift off for an hour or so. After all, Lucy had had some sleep on the plane whereas I had stayed awake. Torn between selfish and selfless, the latter won the day of course. And so I agreed to go to the beach as Lucy seemed so excited about it, her face radiant with happiness. Her enthusiasm was infectious and that gave me my second wind of energy.

I quickly changed and then Lucy and I made our way back through the hotel's lobby to start the five minute journey to the beach. The warm earth scents mingled with the smells of food being served in the cafés and restaurants which were nestled between shops selling clothes and beach goods, and they all seemed to be doing a roaring trade. The beach itself was busy and hot as the temperature had now hit 40ºC and the sweat was dripping off us.

Unfortunately all the sun loungers on the beach were full, which were owned by the bars on the seafront and you had to pay extra when buying drinks if you wanted one. All around us other holiday makers seemed like they had had a bit too much to drink. It was rowdy and quite boisterous and I could see that Lucy was feeling a bit overwhelmed by it all. The heat, the noise, the overcrowding on the beach, it was all becoming too much for her, and actually I was beginning to feel the same. We were after a more gentle introduction to our holiday really, as we both still felt a little frail with this sudden change of climate, travelling and having no proper sleep. She said she wanted to go back to the hotel. I agreed, then suggested that maybe we should come back to the beach later on in the evening when it would be cooler and hopefully not so busy.

We turned around and made our way back the way we had come, past the still heaving beach cafés, the strains of music from each one giving us an eclectic mix from Golden Oldies to disco beats but once we arrived back at the hotel it was more peaceful. We headed straight for the pool and had a glorious swim in the cool water, enjoying the refreshing change of temperature on our skin which was already starting to turn pink from the relentless sun. We were tired of swimming and feeling much more relaxed. Now we left the pool and sunbathed on the sun loungers to dry off, positioning the parasols so that we were shaded.

I half dozed, going over the whole journey again. Lucy looked shattered but happy as she lay there listening to music on her phone through headphones. Hard to believe that the rain was probably falling at home, vastly different from last year's holiday in St Andrews. No parallels to be drawn there at all. It was all quite blissful and unhurried with the thought of two weeks here stretching out ahead of us to do as we pleased and when we felt like it. I felt like a child again on the first day of the school holidays. We were feeling quite hungry by now. The breakfast that we'd had on the plane earlier felt more like days ago than just mere hours and the chips at lunch time, although very good and at the time quite filling, I was looking forward to a proper evening meal. We both were. I had booked us in for half-board accommodation which meant that we had both breakfast and an evening meal included, which seemed a sensible plan. We could start each day with a good meal and end it too with another one and just snack during the day as I knew that we probably wouldn't have much of an appetite during the heat of the day.

Dinner was served between 6.30 and 8pm and as it was just coming up to 6 o'clock we decided we would go back to the room and have a shower and change for the evening meal. I was a little concerned that Lucy might not be able to find any food that she liked at dinner as she is a vegetarian but once we arrived at the restaurant I realised I need not have worried.

A huge delicious buffet spread with a wide selection of foods, which certainly catered for all tastes, was set out in front of us. There was everything from classic Greek dishes to the more traditional fare and so she was able to choose fish and rice which she really enjoyed. I was looking forward to sampling some of the Greek specialities and chose a Greek feta salad. It tasted amazing, the olives fat and fresh and the feta creamy, drizzled with olive oil on a luscious bed of green salad and tomatoes. It really did hit the spot. All this good food started to make us both feel very sleepy, which was not surprising seeing as we had now been awake for over 24 hours. Pushing our seats back into the table we drifted back to our room to get an early night. It felt good to be back in the quiet of our own personal space. Lucy fell asleep as soon as her head hit the pillow.

I was almost too tired to sleep by now so I decided to sit out on the balcony for a little while. I opened the doors very quietly, although I doubted that Lucy would be woken, she was in such a deep sleep already, her arms thrown back against the pillow like a baby's. However, I still crept out very quietly and lowered myself down into one of the chairs to enjoy the sunset. I sat back and relaxed, bare legs stretched out in front of me, feet cool on the tiles just drinking in the atmosphere. The cicadas were humming in the trees still and, mixed with the distant chatter and general bonhomie of the other guests some way off, it was quite soothing. I looked at my watch. Nearly nine o'clock. No great rush just yet, I can have a few more minutes out here and then turn in. No sooner had I made this decision, I heard another sound which at first I couldn't place. It seemed both strangely familiar and yet alien too in these surroundings. It was a faint mewing sound and I realised that it sounded like a cat. I turned to where I thought the sound was coming from, and there on the neighbouring balcony sat indeed the cat in question, quietly mewing.

She looked a delicate little thing, with a few tabby markings on her otherwise all white body. I watched as a lady came out onto the balcony with a saucer of milk and what looked like some cold meat on a plate for the cat. She bent down and placed the dishes at the edge of the balcony and stood back as the cat jumped up and hungrily started eating the food. The lady appeared to be on the telephone. I heard her telling whoever she was talking to that she had been feeding a lovely cat every day while she was on holiday and would be sad to leave the cat behind. I wondered if this was perhaps the hotel's cat, as she seemed very confident and knew her way about. I assumed she was female as she was quite small and compared to my three males, she was half their size.

A little while later, both the saucer and the plate now empty, she made her way over to my balcony and sat and stared at me. I felt bad because I didn't have anything to give her. I grabbed the ashtray off the table, filled it with some water and placed it down outside at the balcony's edge. I also apologised to the cat that I didn't have any food. The cat didn't move at first, probably wondering who this 'new person' was. She must have decided that I was alright though as very timidly she came over to drink from the ashtray. After she had taken a few laps of water she continued to sit and stare at me.

She was a beautiful little cat with the most stunning and mystical blue eyes. She had a slender body which made me think perhaps she had some Siamese in her. There was something definitely quite pedigree about her. Thinking that I had gained her confidence, I reached out in an attempt to stroke her. She was gone in a flash, running away into the night. I went back inside, quietly sliding the doors shut as I heard Lucy stirring. Sleep had finally caught up with me and, as I laid back on the pillow, the last thought I had was the sight of those piercing blue eyes, and I wondered what secrets might lay behind them.

Chapter 3

The following morning Lucy and I still felt quite tired from the flight so we decided that we would just take it easy today and stay around the hotel. The Tour Rep was coming over to the hotel at 4pm anyway, and I didn't want to miss him. I wanted to book some day trips and Lucy was keen to go on some boat trips around the island and go snorkelling.

After we had finished breakfast we gathered our bags and went to the local supermarket which was just a five minute walk from the hotel. We stocked up on snacks and bottled water as it was not advised to drink the tap water in Corfu. The shop had a very limited selection of pet foods but I was able to buy some wet and dry cat food and some feeding bowls. I had already told Lucy about our little feline visitor last night, who had popped around while she had been asleep, and I hoped that the cat with the mystical blue eyes would visit us again today so that Lucy could meet her too.

We paid for our shopping and just as we were leaving through the side of the supermarket we noticed a lady feeding a black and white cat. Across the road from us was a car and moped hire centre, and on the wall outside it, sat a long haired ginger and white cat. He certainly didn't look like a stray as he appeared to be very well kept and beautifully groomed. I assumed that he belonged to the hire centre as there was a bowl of cat food and water outside their office. It really was reassuring to see that all these cats were being well looked after. Food and water in bowls seemed to be in plentiful supply and never far from any of the cats we had seen.

Back at the hotel I unpacked our groceries while Lucy changed into her swimwear. I loaded up our little fridge in the room with bottles of water and cans of drink, put the biscuits and crisps away and then got changed into a bikini and shorts. Following Lucy out to the pool area it was surprisingly quiet, as we were the only ones about and so we had the pick of the best sun loungers. It was very hot and I didn't think that we would be able to do much else today in this heat. I quickly slapped on some sun protection cream and asked Lucy to do the same. I had just laid on the sun lounger when I heard a mewing from behind me. I quickly turned around and there was a little white cat with the blue eyes from the night before.

"Lucy, quickly look, there's Misty!" I whispered as loudly as I dared as I didn't want to scare her off before she had a chance to see her.

"Who's Misty, Mum?" she replied, sitting up on the sun lounger. I had decided then and there to call her Misty because of her incredible eyes. Lucy asked me who she belonged to.

"Maybe she's the hotel cat," I answered, as she sat on, just staring at us from in front of the bushes.

Lucy thought she was a stunning little cat too and agreed that she had never seen eyes so intensely blue before. Misty ran back towards the gardens at the back of the hotel just then where the owners stayed so I decided that yes, she must belong to the hotel. Having sorted that out in my mind, we spent a relaxing afternoon together. When we got too hot we just took a dip in the pool to cool off. When we got tired of that, we went back to our sun loungers and dried off in the sun, the afternoon passing peacefully, just lazing away the day. Much later on I met with the holiday rep. and booked a few day trips for the coming days. The boat trip from Pargo-Paxos and Antipaxos looked exciting. Set in the Ionian sea, they are the smallest of the islands, the azure blue crystal clear waters being apparently ideal for snorkelling. There was also a bus trip which promised a tour of the 'Highlights of Corfu' which I thought sounded fascinating, and seemed a very good way to get to see other parts of the island.

After we had had our evening meal in the restaurant, Lucy was keen to try the beach again. Thankfully by now it was a lot cooler so we took a gentle stroll down to the sea shore in the pleasant balminess of the evening. On our way we passed a group of about six or seven German tourists who were all crowded around something on the other side of the road from us. It made me wonder if someone had perhaps collapsed in the heat as the tourists seemed upset and concerned. Being a nurse I went over to investigate, just in case I could offer some assistance. As I got closer I could see something small and white lying next to a storm drain by the roadside. It was a kitten. Its matted fur looked dirty and it's eyes looked sticky. A can of half-eaten tuna was lying next to this pathetic little scrap.

The group seemed very smartly dressed and I assumed that they had been on their way out to dinner. I asked one of the women what was happening but she just couldn't understand my accent. A young girl stood next to her, who I thought must be her daughter because they looked so similar. She could only have been about ten years old and standing there, in her pretty floral dress, I could see that she had been crying. She appeared to be very distressed about the kitten. One of the men in the group was on his mobile phone and I thought he was trying to get help for the little mite. Lucy was standing behind me and was starting to become upset. She thought the kitten looked so sad and helpless, but thinking that the Germans had everything under control we went on our way to the beach.

It was fairly quiet by this time. One of the restaurants had moved their tables and chairs onto the beach and there were several couples having candlelit dinners. I must say I thought it looked very romantic sitting there as the sun was going down. A few people were still swimming in the sea and Lucy wanted to do the same, but I decided that I would just paddle. The water was still warm as I let it gently lap around my ankles. Behind us further up the beach I could hear holiday makers laughing and having fun at one of the beach-side bars and I turned round to see where these happy, carefree sounds were coming from. At first I thought I had stumbled upon a fancy dress party as some of the men had their hair slicked back and were sporting quiffs, and the women were wearing full skirts.

It was like something out of the *Grease* movie. Even the bar itself had been decked out in retro 1950's American memorabilia, with Elvis (and only Elvis) posters from floor to ceiling. It looked fun and inviting; someone has put a lot of effort into this party I thought but as I peered closer, squinting against the sun, I could see that it was only the serving staff who had dressed up. I realised then that I had been mistaken and it was in fact an Elvis Presley tribute bar. The small crowd which had started to assemble outside the bar suddenly turned as one as a guitar started to gently thrum and an Elvis lookalike started to sing 'Love Me Tender'. In an instant I felt my eyes filling up with hot tears as memories started flooding in. It was my mother's favourite song.

How evocative music can be; reminding us of times past, people and places. Times I would have preferred to forget, of life ebbing away from the people I loved as I watched in helpless panic and horror, and of places that I never want to revisit. This innocent little song had immediately taken me back to some very dark days indeed. Days when all light, love and laughter had, I thought, been extinguished for good, and that I'd never feel anything ever again other than constant fear, sadness and loneliness and above all, failure. I felt I had failed as a wife and mother, and also as a daughter. After my separation and meeting Alan, who had given me hope that life was improving, the days were to become even blacker.

My mother developed cancer of the oesophagus shortly afterwards. It was a slow, painful and cruel death and being a nurse, I understood the agonising months she had to endure before she finally succumbed to the disease and died in August 2010. It was the day of my fortieth birthday. My father was devastated as they had been together for almost fifty years and, as the brutal twist of fate would have it, they were denied the chance of celebrating their golden wedding anniversary. Just twelve weeks later my father suffered a massive heart attack and died. I am sure he died of a broken heart, and losing both my parents in such a short space of time I felt as if the ground had been taken away from under me.

It could have been just yesterday, all those memories suddenly feeling fresh and painful. Sadness welled deep inside, all over again. Why now? I asked myself. Why couldn't they have played Hound Dog, or at least something a bit more upbeat. Anything but this of all songs. Maybe the sight of that poor kitten had triggered something deep down in my subconscious. I really had to fight back the tears now that were threatening to spill, and more than anything I didn't want Lucy to see me like this.

I cupped my hands in the sea and splashed my face with the warm, salty water to mask the hot salty tears. Get a grip on yourself I thought to myself. Don't spoil the holiday, for Lucy's sake.

I tried to shut out the song, took a deep breath and concentrated on the ripples around my feet. I concentrated so hard as if my life depended on it, watching the slowly setting sun making flecks on the water's surface as it glittered one minute, and darkened the next. Lucy, who had tired of swimming, wanted to go back to the hotel and of course by this point, I was more than happy to leave the sea. We left the water's edge and walked back along the road to the hotel. By now there was no sign of the German tourists, or the kitten at the drain. I felt a huge sense of relief then thinking that they must have sorted something out for it. It was a good start to the holiday then, I thought, comfortable in the knowledge that we seemed to be among animal lovers.

We got back to the hotel at about half past nine. Lucy had a quick shower and went straight to bed. I took a can of diet coke from the fridge and went outside to sit on the balcony and watch the dying embers of the day. I had literally just sat down when I noticed that Misty was sitting at the edge of the balcony, watching me and I suddenly remembered the cat food and bowls that I had bought earlier. I quickly slipped back inside to prepare a meal and saucer of milk for her. Carrying these carefully back outside, I put both dishes down at the edge of the balcony. It didn't take long for her to decide that it was safe to venture over. Misty started eating the food hungrily and it wasn't long until both bowls were empty. They were licked completely clean. Once she had finished, she gave a luxurious stretch and went to sit under a bush a few feet away from me. She looked very content as she started to wash herself all over. The peace of this quiet little ritual was strangely soothing to watch. Hypnotic. It made me feel quite sleepy. I quietly got up from the chair and went back inside and, just like last night, as soon as my head touched the pillow I drifted off remembering those beguiling and impossibly blue, mystical eyes.

* * *

The following morning I was awoken by a faint mewing sound. At first I thought I was dreaming; where was I? Was I at home? Simon? Louie? As I came fully too I remembered that I was on holiday here in Corfu, Greece. The mewing was coming from the balcony. I turned over in bed and reached out for my phone from the bedside cabinet to check the time. It was early, only 6.30am. I stretched and yawned. Already the sun was streaming through the chinks in the curtains. Another beautiful day I thought to myself. I decided that I would get up, as I didn't want these plaintive mewing sounds to wake Lucy. She is not a morning person and to be woken this early would make her extremely grumpy. I very quietly lifted the covers up and pulled them aside and CRASH! There went my phone, splat on the tiles. I hadn't realised it had still been lying on the sheets on top of me. I looked over to Lucy, half expecting her to wake and curse me. But no, she slept soundly. She looked very peaceful, the sounds of her gentle, steady breathing being the only clue as to her presence at all; well, that with her head turned away from me so that all I could see was her hair brushed back away from her face on the pillow. Luckily not a movement. Not even an ear twitch!

I tiptoed (why I don't know, seeing as it was a tiled floor), over to the patio doors and very gently unlocked and slid them back slightly, just allowing enough space for me to creep through. Stepping out into the sun I immediately spied Misty. She was sitting in that very correct and upright, expectant looking way that cats do. She watched me, those blue eyes were boring deep into me. I remembered to lower my gaze and look away in classic cat whisperer style, so as not to appear a threat to her. Quickly and quietly I removed the empty bowls from the night before and carried them back into the room. I gave them a quick wash being mindful not to wake Lucy with the swish-slosh of the whole routine. I wiped them dry and filled them up with biscuits in one bowl and a sachet of wet food in the other.

Moving quickly, stealthily back outside onto the balcony I set them down at the very edge, then stepped back some distance. No sooner had I reached a safe distance, to Misty's mind, than she jumped up onto the balcony and started wolfing down the wet food first. She seemed ravenous and emptied the bowl within seconds. Even my own greedy monster cats at home never ate that fast. Misty looked up at me, licking her lips, continuing to stare at me. I suspected that she was still hungry. I was always able to read cat's telepathic food related thoughts very well. I went back inside and split open another wet food pouch and tipped it onto a saucer. Misty had meanwhile retreated to a polite distance while her second helping was being prepared. Placing the fresh new saucer of food back down outside again, she was almost on it before I had taken a few steps back. I watched her devour it just as quickly as she had at the first sitting. This time though she decided that enough was enough and that she was thirsty now.

The glass ashtray was still quite full from the night before so she lapped at that while I crept back inside to grab myself a bottle of water from the fridge. I took it outside with me and sat down on one of the chairs away from Misty's feeding station. She had moved a little way along under the bushes now and was carrying out her morning washing routine. She started with her ears, then her shoulders, her back, her tail. Every inch of her little body got the benefit of that sandpaper tongue, nature's natural de-tangler. She certainly took pride in her appearance. However, in scrutinising her this way, I realised that actually she was very thin. The bones on her back stood out in bobbles down her spine and were very visible, and her shoulder blades seemed accentuated more than on any other cats I had seen.

It made me wonder if she really was the hotel's cat. Surely she wouldn't be that thin and continually crying out for food if she was someone's house pet? Mind you I thought again, cats in hot countries are always quite lean looking and also, I'd heard of cats that had several 'homes' and would go from one person to the next glibly eating whatever they were offered as if they were a starving little waif and stray. The cunning, guileless cat, a creature with no shame, with about six or seven people who all thought they owned him or her! Mulling things over though I decided that I would make enquiries at the Reception later on and find out more about her. There was something quite proud about her but at the same time she looked neglected. I wondered what I could do though if the hotel told me that she *was* their own cat. If she did indeed have an owner then I was really tempted to give them a piece of my mind about their ideas of cat care. I didn't want to upset the locals but something had to be said. I wasn't entirely looking forward to finding out though.

Chapter 4

It was still early. I leaned back in my chair watching from afar Misty's quiet, concentrated toilette regime. My eyelids started to feel heavy and I felt myself gradually drifting off. I must have dozed off for half an hour or so because by the time I woke again, Misty was long gone. It was as if I had dreamed of her being there at all. All the bowls were empty, and not a trace of her anywhere. All quiet and looking exactly as I had left things last night. I got up out of the chair and realised that the hotel and its grounds were slowly coming awake. I stepped back inside to have a shower and then Lucy woke. We went down to breakfast. Helping ourselves to the cereals and pastries and pouring ourselves cups of tea and coffee, we planned how we were going to spend the day.

We decided that we would get a bus into Corfu Town. Lucy wanted to see the shops and go to McDonald's, which I didn't mind but as I was still full from breakfast, I didn't want to argue about Big Macs and Big Tasties versus fresh, local cuisine at that time of day. We popped by the Reception Desk on the way back to our room to find out about bus times into town. The receptionist pointed out a bus timetable that was pinned to a noticeboard. Before looking at the bus times, I asked if she knew who the little white and tabby cat with the blue eyes belonged to, that was frequently in the hotel gardens.

"Oh, that cat's just another stray that hangs around the grounds." She replied. So my worst fears were confirmed.

I felt so sad and instantly sorry for Misty. My own cats don't know how lucky they are, I thought. Pampered, and every whim pandered to morning till night, they're living the dream. With a slightly heavy heart I went back to the room with Lucy to get ready for the bus. It was only 11am and already the heat of the sun was strong, and starting to slow us down as we walked to the bus stop. Our bus was due at twenty past the hour, so we were in good time when we arrived at the bus stop in Messonghi. A queue had already formed and was growing longer as we waited. And waited. It was now midday and we were in full sun. More tourists had joined the queue but after an hour had passed there was still no sign of this elusive bus. Some people started to drift off as they gave up waiting and other tourists were walking to the taxi tank. In dribs and drabs people started to fan off in all directions.

By half past twelve, we too decided to give up on waiting. Sweat was dripping off us both and we were very thirsty. Lucy was disappointed but I told her not to worry. We would have a chance to see Corfu Town as part of our Highlights of Corfu bus tour that I had booked for Thursday. So we decided to have a leisurely walk around the local shops in Messonghi. It was a vibrant, busy little place. There were mini-markets, clothes shops, gift shops and cafés. Glorious aromas of coffee and sizzling food being cooked on open air griddles mingled with the tang of hot tarmac and petrol fumes. It felt very exotic and the heat, unrelenting.

Seeking relief from the sun we browsed through shops selling beach goods. Lucy picked up a large pink inflatable float which she thought would be ideal for the beach. I had already given her some spending money at the beginning of the holiday and so she pulled out her purse and treated herself. Enjoying the relief of the shade from the sun we hopped from one shop to the next. In a little gift shop tucked away a little off the beaten track I found a delightful little white furry cat ornament. It reminded me of Simon and Louie, who I was really beginning to miss. Lucy laughed at my purchase as I lovingly unwrapped it from the tissue paper to show her.

"Mum, that's really tacky!" She laughed.

Each to their own I thought to myself; my cat was far more tasteful than the monstrous and garish pink float. But I kept my opinion to myself of course. We found the supermarket that we had shopped at previously. I made a bee-line to the scant pet food section. I filled my basket with more cat food pouches for Misty, choosing the tuna and salmon varieties as carefully as if she was my own cat. I wondered if I was doing what other holiday makers had been doing, following in their steps and stocking up on food for that dear little cat who belonged to no one. It was funny though, as now we seemed to pass so many more cats on our way back to the hotel, unless it was just me being far more tuned-in and aware of them. One of these was a large white scruffy looking Tom cat. I wondered whether perhaps he and Misty were the parents of the little white kitten at the drain that the Germans had rescued.

Laden down with our booty, we slowly walked back to the hotel. There was no breeze to cool us on the way, only the fierce hot sun still beating down on us. We dumped our bags back in our room and went to the pool bar to buy some ice cream to cool us down, then spent a long and lazy afternoon by the pool. Sometimes we'd swim, sometimes we'd lie on the sun loungers, drying off in the sun until too hot, we'd jump back into the pool. This is the life

I thought to myself, temporarily being able to put Misty out of my mind for a while, and just living in the moment. The cicadas were making their usual racket in the trees and high up in the endless blue of the sky, small birds drifted on the thermals. No sign of any cats at all. The water sparkled in the sun as the light dappled the surface, glinting and bobbing about in the sultry afternoon.

* * *

Much later on, after we had had dinner, we wandered down to the beach again. It was by far the best time to come down here as it was still very warm but a lot quieter in the evenings. Lucy was happy just to splash about in the sea with her new inflatable float and I paddled, keeping an eye on her. No Elvis tonight luckily, I mused. No sad thoughts, just the sheer simplicity of being in the moment. I watched mesmerised as the waves gently lapped around my ankles. Rolling forwards then retreating, new waters mingling with the old, regenerated, then doing it all over again. Forwards and retreat, forwards and retreat. Constantly the same but ever changing. Like life itself. I pondered on this contradicting philosophy. It reminded me of an L.R. Knost quote which had stuck with me many years after first reading it. She wrote that; 'Life is amazing. And then it's awful. And then it's amazing again. And in between the amazing and the awful, it's ordinary and mundane and routine.'

I had always interpreted that as meaning life was both constantly the same but ever changing. Life is just like the sea. So lost in these profound and reflective thoughts was I, that I didn't notice Lucy until she just appeared at my side. Looking puzzled, she asked me what I'd been thinking about.

"Oh, just Life," I told her.

I could tell that she was thinking how boring a subject *that* was, as she rolled her eyes by way of a reply. I grinned, and called out that, 'the last one back to the hotel's a sissy', over my shoulder. I hot footed it over the sand. No way could I have run back to the hotel, the beach front was all I'd had in mind but it had the desired effect. It assured her that her Mum wasn't getting morose or going all inward, and that all was well with our world. Lucy was hot on my tail and caught me up as I'd stopped to get my breath. We stood together looking back at the glorious blue and orange horizon over the island, the colours of a Salvador Dali painting.

We turned and walked along the road back to the hotel in the balmy evening. The lovely peace of my earlier mood started to give way to unease and trepidation as we were about to pass by the drain where the white kitten had previously been. I felt scared. Scared of what Lucy and I might find. But there was nothing there. No evidence of a little kitten being in residence at the drain. Relief swept over me. Lucy asked what had happened to the kitten and I told her that the German tourists must have taken the kitten to one of the animal charities to be checked over and homed. The total quiet and complete emptiness of the drain was reassuring and I felt the earlier, philosophical calm descend on me once more. All was certainly well with our world. But Lucy was still questioning.

"What, like the Cats' Protection? Like where we got Simon and Louie from?" asked my ever hopeful daughter.

I replied yes, that's exactly it, and mentally crossed my fingers. I thought to myself that perhaps Misty was the white kitten's mother, and if so what a shame that they had been separated. Of course I didn't dare mention this to Lucy as I knew she'd become upset, but the emptiness of the drain was certainly a good sign that the kitten had been taken away to a place of safety.

Once back in our room, Lucy was in bed within minutes and was soon sound asleep. I marvelled at her ability to just switch off from the world like that, especially in a place far from home. Her gentle steady breathing reminded me of the earlier sounds of the sea, it's ebb and flow sounding like sighing. However, I was far too tired to start contemplating the meaning of life again. I helped myself to a diet coke from the fridge. No sooner had I shut the door than I heard that faint mewing sound that I was becoming so used to. Misty had arrived for her supper no less. I wondered whether she had also asked at all the other neighbouring balconies and, as I was on her supper run she thought she'd give me a call to see if I was around. Maybe.

I went through the usual evening ritual of cleaning food bowls, emptying food pouches and carrying them out quietly onto the balcony. It was really funny because this little chore was so dear and familiar. I had been doing this for my own cats longer than I cared to remember and now here I was on holiday in a foreign country doing exactly the same thing. I loved the continuity of it all. It felt strangely comforting and grounding to be carrying out this little domestic ceremony which would always be a part of my daily routine, irrespective of where I was in the world now it would seem. I felt very at one with the universe this evening.

I was able to get a very good view of 'my' Corfu cat this time as I'd moved the bowls nearer towards me. Misty didn't seem to mind this new dining arrangement either. As she bent down to eat her supper, I noticed a very large scratch on the back of her neck. Whether it had been there long I didn't know as this was the closest that I had gotten to her yet. It could have been made by another cat, or dog, but these were secrets that only Misty was privy to. Well, Misty and her opponent that is, if it had been caused by fighting. It was sad that this otherwise beautiful little creature had no proper home but I really didn't see what I could do about it. I thought that she'd be fine anyway; she'd got this far so obviously she can look after herself. Cats are renowned for it. I could imagine her being the apple of all the tourists' eyes, being spoiled with all sorts of delicacies, but always on her own terms. She knew where to go for food if she was hungry, and she knew where to go for privacy and secrecy for the one thing that cats love most: sleep. Now if that wasn't living the dream, I thought to my new, glass half full self, then I didn't know what was.

All that earlier philosophising about the sea as Life and Life as the sea, this sense of well-being and epiphany, had filled me with new optimism. I had spoken to a local shop-keeper earlier and he told me that this is just how cats live here in Corfu. They get by. And if anything is going to get by, then it is surely The Cat, and usually with great aplomb. Too much thinking and all this 'being at one with the universe' business had made me feel nicely tired, so I turned in for the night. Misty was still at her feeding bowl and finishing off the final few morsels of food as I gently pulled the patio doors too and locked them. I climbed in under the covers and sank luxuriously back in the cool cotton sheets. I imagined Misty having finished her supper by now and quietly carrying out her feline ablutions under the tree.

Well fed, warm, and feeling the love of a stranger she would slope off into the night to her secret space to sleep. Contented. Her simple needs being, once again, fulfilled for that day. Drifting off I thought how all must be well in her world.

Chapter 5

On Tuesday we went on a boat trip to Paxos and Antipaxos for the day. These are the smallest islands in the Ionian sea, full of natural beauty, they are the jewels in its crown. As we left Corfu harbour we were able to see Old Corfu from the perspective of the coastline and it looked very beautiful with it's two Venetian fortresses, the old and the new, like silent, sleeping sentinels.

On our way out to the islands we stopped at the famous Blue Caves. These massive naturally carved sea-caves were breathtaking; huge great vaults of rock rising up and out of the phosphorescent blue water that surrounded and filled them. As our boat entered one of the largest caves it was like stepping inside a cathedral. Cavernous, cold and solid. The rhythmic slap-plap of the water hitting the sides of the boat echoed eerily, and the 'oohs' and 'ahhs' from us passengers were ghostly and ethereal. The sheer majesty of it was humbling and made us feel very small and insignificant in this tiny craft by comparison. We were told to keep an eye out for the Mediterranean Monk seals as this was their natural habitat, but there didn't seem to be any about today.

Once we had completed our little tour here the boat left the cave and continued across the dazzling, crystal clear sea towards Antipaxos. A little way on the boat stopped again and here we were able to go snorkelling, climbing into the sea straight from the boat. With our snorkel masks on we lay flat on the surface of the sea moving as one on the gentle, undulating surface. Looking down at the busy underworld of sea-life happening below us was quite spectacular and the sandy bottom of the sea looked so near as if all we had to do was reach out to be able to touch it. The waters were deceptive though as we were actually meters deep; it was just the sheer clarity of the sea that made it look so shallow. Our bodies were making shadows on the bottom.

Soon it was time to be back on our way once more to Paxos. We climbed back on board again and the boat drifted peacefully on its journey to the larger of the two islands. Paxos doesn't have an airport and can only be reached by the sea so it hasn't fallen prey to mass tourism, and is quite unspoilt. It is home to some of the oldest olive groves in the whole of Greece and from our viewpoint on the boat it looked lush and green as we approached the harbour at Gaios, the island's capital.

We spent a very pleasant, leisurely hour here exploring the sleepy fishing village. There were some wonderful, quiet little coffee shops here and Lucy and I indulged in some of the specialty ice creams which they sold and tasted like Manna from heaven. Once we'd finished these delights, we walked around some more of the village just taking in the scenery and the little gift shops and clothing shops. We even found a pet shop, but as it was time to head back to the boat we didn't have time to go in and browse.

Despite the coffee and the splendid ice-cream earlier, Lucy and I were still hungry so we made our way to the bar on the boat. There was a simple menu on offer but that suited us as we ordered a Margherita pizza and a glass of lemonade each. The boat started to leave Paxos behind as we tucked into our very late lunch. A more blissful way to enjoy pizza I have still yet to find, as we glided back out to sea in the late afternoon sun, a gentle sea breeze ruffling our hair.

The trip back to Corfu took about an hour, passing again the paradisiacal, tiny Antipaxos and the sea caves. I had a sense of everything being in reverse now, all the delights and explorations of the day suddenly being on fast rewind as we seemed to hurry over the turquoise sea. It dawned on me then that we were over half-way through our holiday. I wanted time to stand still. I could really get used to this temporary way of life, I thought to myself. The sun, sea, the odd bit of culture here and there, withdrawing to poolside shade and the evening sandy beach whenever we felt like it. The little niggle about Misty's own domestic set-up was a worry, but on the whole I felt that I could easily spend the rest of my days like this, being a bit hermit-like one day then exploring the next.

Arriving back in the harbour at Corfu Town we found the bus was already there and waiting to take us back to the taxi rank at Messonghi. We were back at the hotel by seven o'clock and went straight to dinner, hungry after the journey, the sea air having whipped up our appetites again. We wolfed down our fish and chips and then Lucy told me she wanted to go to the beach again. I felt far too tired to even think about leaving the hotel but somehow she talked me into it, because I have the breaking strain of a soggy KitKat. So off we trundled, passing the luckily, very deserted looking drain, and the bars and the restaurants which were all by now so familiar on our route to the beach.

I didn't paddle this time, being content to just sit on the warm shoreline and watch Lucy swim to her heart's content. I felt I could easily have just laid back and drifted off to sleep but I resisted the urge, not wanting to seem like a party-pooper. Besides, after my earlier jolt of realisation about the stage we were at on our holiday, I wanted to savour as much time here as possible. And that would only be achievable if I stayed awake, I told myself. However, in the end Lucy didn't swim for long and she was soon at my side again, tired, happy and sun-kissed. Trudging back along the beach to the road we went over our day again, marvelling at the caves and the beauty of the islands we'd seen and the waters we'd snorkelled in.

Misty was waiting for us on the balcony by the time we got back to our room. I almost felt like she was our own little cat now. I looked at my watch. Half past nine; and on the dot of. Astonished by her impeccable time-keeping, I started the usual routine and set about preparing her supper as Lucy got ready for bed. I heard Lucy call out to me.

"It feels just like home Mum!" I popped my head round the door with raised eyebrows, questioningly.

"You, clattering about in the kitchen washing cat dishes!"

I laughed and told her I'd been thinking the very same thing not so long ago. She got into bed and as usual was out for the count within a few minutes. I think that the heat and the sea air really tired her out. I wished she would go to bed like that at home as usually it was quite a battle to get Lucy to go to bed. I carried Misty's supper bowls out onto the balcony, returned to grab a bottle of diet coke from the fridge and then sat and kept her company while she devoured tonight's offerings of salmon. When she'd finished, she surprised me by jumping up onto the other chair under the table and cosied herself up, no washing tonight.

"Oh Misty, I am *so* going to miss you when we go home", I whispered softly to her.

She ignored me. I was sorely tempted to try and stroke her but I knew that she'd probably flee and I'd regret it. She looked so thin compared to my great lumbering boys. Quite young too, and I doubted that she was fully grown yet. Perhaps she'd fill out as she got older I thought. All I could do was hope. I sighed as I watched Misty and thought about the day's outing. It had been a lot of fun and a lovely respite to our almost hermit-like stay here so far. But we both liked it this way, and so I didn't feel guilty. We were having the best of both worlds, I thought wearily as I wandered back indoors and got into bed. I could hear Lucy's gentle snoring but I stayed awake for quite a long time just puzzling over Misty and wondering how such a beautiful cat like her could ever end up as a stray.

Lucy and I were still exhausted from the previous day's boat trip when we awoke the following morning. After the usual early morning feed for Misty I showered and then we went down to breakfast. We popped to the local supermarket afterwards as I needed to stock up on more cat food, and snacks and drinks for us. We decided that today we would just have a lazy day and spend it by the pool. Lucy had her large pink rubber ring with white spots on it, so she was happy to just splash about in the pool while I read. It was another luxurious and languorous day where we did absolutely nothing at all. An uneventful sort of day that began and ended with my Misty routine.

Chapter 6

The following day we were glad that we'd been able to recharge our batteries. We had booked the 'Highlights of Corfu' bus tour around the island. This was an interesting and historical sightseeing journey which first took in the Old Fortress, which we learned had been one of the locations for the Bond movie, *For Your Eyes Only*. Our tour guide was great fun. She added plenty of humour and interesting anecdotes to her talk which really animated the whole experience and kept our attention at all times. After we had been shown the fort we were able to have a few minutes to ourselves to explore.

We then went on to Corfu Town where we visited the Church of St. Spyridon. We learned that Spyridon is one of the most important and revered saints in Corfu with apparently many men and boys being named after him. As we walked back down the street to the bus it was very warm, even though it was only 10.00am. We could hear the cicadas in the olive trees. Our friendly tour guide told us that the hotter it gets, the louder the cicadas get. Lucy was really beginning to feel the heat so on our way back to the bus she bought a baseball cap at one of the gift shops to keep the sun off her head. We also stopped for an ice-cream to cool us down.

The bus drove off passing some beautiful horse-drawn carriages that were waiting by the roadside. The next part of the journey took us past the one-time family home of the famous naturalist and author Gerald Durrell who had come to live here with his family when he was ten years old. We stopped a little further on at the Achilleon Palace, arriving at the same time as many other tour buses so at first it was very busy. The Palace had been built by the Empress Elisabeth of Austria at the end of the nineteenth century. Our guide described Elisabeth as one of the most beautiful women of her time, with her long dark hair and very slim, delicate frame, the latter due to anorexia as it was discovered later. Her life was not without tragedy it seemed. She lost her only son at sea while travelling to Corfu by boat and then in 1898, she was stabbed to death by an Italian anarchist in her home country of Austria. It was hard to imagine such sadness amongst this beautiful setting however. Lucy and I both thought that the Palace was incredibly grand, with its pillared colonnades and hanging gardens. This had also been a location for another Bond movie, *The Spy Who Loved Me*, we learned. There were some prettily decorated ceilings here and Lucy photographed a painting of angels in the main hall, which had special appeal to her.

We left the cool sanctuary of the Palace and were shown the beautiful formal gardens. There were statues and fountains here amongst the palm trees, and as I gazed at one statue in particular, of a boy with dolphins, I wondered if perhaps she'd built this in memory of the son that she had lost. It was all very thought provoking. After the Palace we went onto a beautiful bay where we found a small restaurant which overlooked the sea and had a light lunch. The gentle breeze coming off the sea was cooling as we sat under the sun parasols. Lucy and I were really beginning to develop nice tans now. We had been very careful to keep applying sun lotion, our pale Scottish skins not at all used to such intense heat, let alone the appearance of such ebullient sun. Now, all our fastidiousness was paying off and although there was no way we could have been mistaken for locals, we might not have been taken for Scottish!

After lunch, our next excursion was a short trip around the bay by boat. It was refreshing and exhilarating, and although not in the same league as Tuesday's island tour, it was wonderful to just be able to sit back and take in the landscape from our vantage point of the sea. Soon, our round trip would be over, so next on the list was a visit to the Monastery of Paleokastritsa. Situated at the very top of a hill it was a very small monastery but with the most incredible views over the lush green vegetation that surrounded it and cascaded down the hillside to the triple bays. On the inside, the monastery was impressive with its carved wooden ceiling and small museum of embroidered robes, ancient illuminated scripts and Byzantine icons.

The arched inner courtyard and surrounding paved gardens of trees and flowers was, surprisingly, home to lots and lots of cats and kittens. All were very well fed and cared for here as they sat around contentedly here and there. I noticed a very large ginger cat who was sitting on top of a wall. From his eyrie he was watching all the visitors come and go with a very wise expression on his face, us lesser mortals all meeting with his approval. He reminded me of James Bowen's Street-cat 'Bob' with his colour and markings, and also a little bit of the Cheshire Cat in *Alice in Wonderland,* with his inscrutable gaze. Lucy and I both agreed that it was very good to see that the monks obviously really cared for all these cats, as well as seeming to appreciate them being around.

It was now time for the tour guide to gather us all up again. We made our way down the hill and were told that our last stop would be at a local café for refreshments before returning to the hotel. We were both quite tired by this time so we welcomed the chance to relax and have an ice-cream and a cold drink. The bus dropped us off near the supermarket by the hotel so I quickly dashed in to stock up on more cat-food. Misty had a big appetite for such a small cat. By the time we reached the hotel it was already half past seven in the evening. We made our way straight to the restaurant and had our dinner. I felt truly exhausted after the busy day we had had and yet, once again, I allowed Lucy to drag me down to the beach.

We were just walking past the drain when we heard a very faint mewing sound. We walked right up to it but couldn't see anything, no sign of life there at all; and then Lucy pointed to something behind the wall next to it. Horror of horrors, it was the same little white kitten that we had seen the previous week and he was sitting down meowing quietly. He looked in a dreadful state and he certainly didn't resemble the kitten we had seen last week with the German tourists. His coat was matted and covered in dirt, his eyes were sticky and weeping and his mouth was sore and dry looking.

I was devastated. To think that he had been here all the time, despite my thinking that the German tourists had rescued him and been able to take him to a local animal shelter. That had obviously never been the case. I could not believe how such a tiny little scrap could have survived a further week here in this condition, and a million thoughts rushed through my head. Dreadful thoughts of all those times Lucy and I had walked past the drain since first seeing the kitten. We'd have always been either on our way to, or back from, a pleasant day out. We would have been full of good food, holiday-happy and without a care in the world. And how many times had the kitten just been a stone's throw away from us perhaps? Why hadn't I gone and searched for him? Why had I continued to hold on to that stupid, naive belief that he had been rescued? He hadn't been sitting in an animal shelter at all, being fed and looked after, kept safe whilst waiting to be found a home. He'd been here all the time, while we had just laughed, sunned ourselves and got browner and fatter by the day. The extreme guilt was exactly that. Extreme.

But all this wasn't helping the kitten, who needed our help right here, right now. I sprang into action, trying to be practical. There was a small plastic tub lying by the roadside. I quickly grabbed this and filled it up with the water from the bottle that I had in my bag. Lucy caught the urgency and, being brave, snapped into action.

"Lucy, I think we need to go back to the hotel quickly and grab Misty's food off the side", I said hurriedly, trying to keep any panic out of my voice, which wasn't easy.

Lucy started running along ahead of me and in no time at all were we back in our room, breathless and hot. The situation made me clumsy as we scooped up the cat food pouches and some bowls that then went clatter to the floor when the bottom of the cheap plastic carrier bag split. Lucy grabbed her back-pack and tipped it upside down on her bed. Now empty, she helped me retrieve the bowls and shoved them into the bag while I re-filled the bottle up with water. Then we were off again, out through Reception and, breaking into a jog once we got onto the pavements, were soon back at the drain again. The kitten hadn't moved and was just sitting where we had left him.

I took the backpack from Lucy and emptied a sachet of wet food into one of the bowls. The food was for adult cats not kittens but I didn't think that was going to matter in this case, any food being better than no food at all. Lucy was making soothing noises to the kitten as I placed the food down in front of him. He fell on the food immediately, not shy at all, eating as if he was ravenous. He didn't even seem to be aware of us being so close, our toes almost touching the side of the bowl. I bent down slowly and he let me stroke his back as he arched it and leaned into my hand in friendliness and acceptance. I realised suddenly that he was purring away at the same time as gulping huge mouthfuls of food. It was a strong, loud purr and I could feel his whole body vibrating with the ferocity of it.

Once he'd completely emptied the bowl and licked it clean he seemed to liven up and started to rub himself against my leg. Lucy asked me the dreaded question, which I could feel had been boiling up in her a bit.

"Why is he here still Mum?"

I could see she was really trying to fight back the tears now that the earlier frenetic and practical activity had calmed down and we were able to take proper stock of the situation. I didn't know what to say then. I was feeling quite helpless and so I just shrugged my shoulders, not taking my eyes off the little kitten. I told her that I had really believed that the Germans had taken him away to the safety of an animal shelter. But my voice sounded small and inconsequential. I needed to act fast now and put a plan into action. But what? I bent down slowly and tried to pick the kitten up, but he was too quick for me and he ran away under the cover of the drain. Now what do I do? I thought to myself.

"Please Mum, let's take him back to the hotel with us," begged Lucy.

I knew that was not an option, that taking the kitten back to our room we'd run the risk of being thrown out if they knew we had him in the room, and I told her so. All I could do was to reassure Lucy that I would think of something. As the kitten had run away back under cover of the drain, I wasn't able to get to him anyway. I knelt down and looked at his little nest he'd made there. He had curled up and gone to sleep, nose tucked tightly into his tail and completely motionless, apart from the odd flicker of his ear when a fly landed on it. I straightened up again and tried to think sensibly and rationally. Despite Lucy being with me, I did feel terribly alone with this new weight of responsibility, for now I was seemingly in charge of rescuing this kitten. I realised there was nothing that could be done immediately as the light was fading, and soon it would be dark. I made a decision.

"Look, let's go back now," I said to Lucy. "He's had a big supper and got some water too, and he's sleeping. We'll come back down here first thing in the morning to check on the kitten."

I didn't add 'and we'll take it from there' because I didn't know where or how we were going to take anything. What were we going to be able to do for this little soul in a country where we knew no one, and couldn't even speak the language? We walked back to the hotel in silence, both of us far too distracted about the kitten to talk. Lucy went straight to bed as usual and I cleared up some of the devastation we had left behind us, before we had hurried back out on our rescue mission. Lost in thought, I realised that Misty was meowing for my attention outside on the balcony. She wanted her supper. Luckily we still had plenty of cat food left so I deftly filled up both bowls of wet and dry food and carried them outside.

I didn't stay with Misty tonight as all of a sudden there seemed so much to think about and, to somehow, try to organise. My brain was addled and as I got into bed I thought that I would never sleep. However, within five minutes of being under the covers I started to relax and think more rationally, trying to formulate a plan. I decided that on the morrow I would get up early, well before Lucy woke, and go down to the drain. I would take some food and fresh water with me. Perhaps in the morning when it's light things won't seem quite so bad and a proper plan of action will come more easily, I thought to myself. This seemed to satisfy my nagging conscience and luckily, a few minutes later, I too was fast asleep.

Chapter 7

I woke early the following morning, not having slept at all well in the end. I had been woken up in the night sometime after 1am by the sounds of what I thought sounded like gunshots being fired. In the stilly watches of the night I lay there, eyes wide open and heart racing, beating so loud that I thought it might even wake Lucy, as it drummed a tattoo which seemed to echo off the walls it was so loud. I was thinking about the kitten at the drain.

My imagination was of course working overtime. I had visions of the kitten lying terrified under the cover of the drain; was he being hunted down by some unscrupulous local? Being used for target practice, for fun? In those dark and lonely hours, when the imagination can be at its most fertile and destructive as it twists and distorts all rational, logical thought and reasoning I lay there, wide awake. My spirits at their lowest ebb, I was picturing all sorts of terrible destinies for that lonely and frightened little kitten out there in the Corfu night.

The gunshots subsided and the silence that now ensued was almost just as eerie. Had I imagined them? I was sure I hadn't. I must have dozed off again but the little sleep that I did get after that was fitful and full of terrible nightmares. I was fully awake again by 6am so I decided to get up and go down to the drain immediately to put my mind at rest, and find out how the kitten had spent the night. Would he even be there still? I was sure that I had heard Lucy crying in her sleep too in the night; pitiful little mewing sounds, or had that also been my imagination? Could those sounds have been Misty at the patio window trying to alert me to some danger outside? Lucy had kept asking me the previous evening what was going to happen to the kitten and I just had to come up with some sort of a plan. But what?

I dressed as quickly and silently as I could without waking Lucy. I refilled some water bottles and then hastily scrawled a note to say where I'd gone and that I wouldn't be long. I shut the door behind me quietly and made my way through the reception, out through the main entrance and down the road to the drain. I didn't know what I would find, and although the dreadful visions I'd conjured up in the night were slipping away now as daylight brought its usual reassurance, I was still feeling nervous nonetheless.

Within minutes I was at the drain. Oh joy of joys! The kitten was still there, curled up in a tight ball and apparently fast asleep. I crouched down so that I was almost eye level with him. I didn't want to startle him so I made a gentle chirruping noise. He stirred in his sleep and then opened his eyes. He wasn't at all startled to see me peering at him at such close quarters, so that was a good sign; perhaps he had already decided that he and I were going to be friends. He gave a huge yawn, revealing a very pink mouth and very clean and white little teeth. Definitely those of a very young kitten.

He got up on his front legs and gave an almighty stretch and came to the entrance of the drain. I knelt down to stroke him. He seemed very pleased to see me as he rubbed his chin and then the rest of his little body against my leg. I was at an awkward angle crouched down like this but somehow I managed to open up a sachet of the cat food I'd brought with me in my pocket and empty it into the dish left from the night before. Pins and needles started to invade my lower extremities so I stood up slowly trying not to alarm the kitten as he tucked into his breakfast. He wasn't at all shy in my presence. I felt relief flooding through me as he appeared to be unharmed from his night there, despite those real, or imagined, gun shots. Once he'd finished his bowl of food he started to groom himself. His eyes were still very sticky and debris and dust from the drain clung to his coat in places.

Another huge yawn and then he crept back underneath the grating of the drain again. I knelt back down again so that I could get a better view of exactly where he had made his home. He was now lying on his back playing with a piece of barbed wire. I winced at the thought of him cutting himself on its razor sharp barbs. It could easily have taken his eyes out had it pinged back in his little face with one misplaced paw-pat. I looked around for something to try and hook it back out. I found a stick lying nearby and very carefully tried to prize the barbed wire through the grating. It was a delicate task as I was scared that the kitten would think this was all part of a game and try to grab it back between his paws.

Luckily he surrendered the wire, being more interested now in the stick itself. I was able to hook the wire and prize it back through the grating. I disposed of it in the bin nearby. I cut my finger very slightly in the process and not having anything to clean the tiny puncture wound with had to lick it clean. It wasn't a deep cut and I was up to date with my tetanus injections. As for being poisoned by licking the wound clean, well, I would just have to trust in luck and hope that if there *was* anyone looking down on my actions for this kitten, then they might have a little bit of mercy for me, too.

The kitten, having now had his toy removed, was settling back down to sleep again. It was still too early for many cars and tourists to be about, despite being one of the main roads into the town. The only witness to all this activity here at the drain was a very noisy little bird in a nearby tree, chirping his head off. The day promised to be another scorcher, but I had come to expect nothing less from this island. I was relieved in a way that no one else had passed me while I was ministering to this kitten's needs as I was still so unsure what to do about him or who I could approach for help.

My assumptions, days ago it seemed now, that the islanders seemed to really care about their cats, with food and water bowls dotted about everywhere, had been turned on its head. I was really at a terrible loss to know what to do. I bent down and looked in on the kitten in his little nest one more time. Confident that he had had enough to eat and that, for the time being, he was safe, I left him and darted back to the hotel. There were a few staff milling around by now, going about their early morning duties, but they didn't bat an eyelid at my early rising. I let myself into our room quietly. Thankfully Lucy was still fast asleep so I screwed up the note I'd left her and threw it in the bin. At least I'd have a little bit of good news for her when she awoke; the kitten survived the night and had had a hearty breakfast.

I had a shower, thoroughly cleansing the wound left by the barbed wire. By the time I was out again and dressed Lucy was awake. She looked very tired still, dark shadows under her eyes and I guessed that she too had had a troubled night's sleep. As far as I was aware though, her bad dreams had not woken her up in the same way mine had. Grateful for small mercies, I went over to sit at the end of her bed. She propped herself up on her pillow and looked sorrowfully at me.

"Mum, can we go and see the kitten soon please? I'm so worried about him," she whispered, her voice still husky from sleep and I wondered if she had been crying in it.

"It's alright, I've just come back from seeing him and he's fine. He's had a big breakfast and now he's fast asleep again where we left him last night." Lucy seemed cheered by my news, seemingly satisfied that I had everything under control. She didn't mention the kitten again until we were making our way down to breakfast. The dreaded, 64 million dollar question.

"What are we going to do about him then Mum?" In my sleepless hours earlier, in between the fretting about the gun fire and my heart threatening to explode out of my ribcage, I had come up with a few ideas. Funnily enough, they still seemed quite sane and do-able in the cold light of day – which is, as you will all know, not always the case.

"We won't talk about it now, but after breakfast let's go out to the pool and I'll tell you about some ideas I've had, that might just work." I said no more than that, and as Lucy didn't press me any further that's all I gave away.

I had nothing more to say than that anyway and hoped that over breakfast I would come up with some satisfying plans and possible solutions that we could both be optimistic about. My main hope revolved around Google and animal shelters, and I just hoped and prayed that would be a way in.

* * *

We finished our breakfast and went straight out to the pool. Lucy took the lead in what looked almost like a triumphant march. I realised to my horror that she obviously thought she was about to hear the solution to the problem: that Mum had got it all in hand and knew exactly what to do and all would be well again shortly. What a responsibility and how wrong she was, but I couldn't disappoint her now that I'd led her to believe that I could sort this terrible problem out. Perversely, this gave me the added shove I needed. That logical, head ruling heart type shove. Another searingly hot morning greeted us as we went outside to the pool. It was empty and as usual we had the pick of the best sun loungers under the parasols. Once we had settled ourselves down Lucy looked at me expectantly. So here goes, I thought. I told Lucy that the first sensible thing we should do is to find out if there were any local animal shelters that might take the kitten in.

"I'm sure that if we Google rescue centres then something will come up. If there's one nearby then we can take the kitten there ourselves." Lucy stayed silent, seemingly lost in thought for a moment. I could see her forming the words in her mind carefully before she finally replied

"But Mum, what happens if there aren't any?"

I couldn't answer that question of course, and didn't even dare contemplate that being the case. Failure was not an option and right now I had to try. I told her that I was sure there would be all sorts of animal shelters that would take him in. After all, I reminded her, he was only a kitten, maybe no more than only a few weeks old and I was positive that he wouldn't be turned away. I surprised *myself* with this speech. I sounded so confident, so utterly convincing and completely self-assured that I felt I had surpassed all Lucy's expectations too. She beamed at me and said she'd like to help too. I reached for my bag and took my phone out of it and also the slip of paper I'd had the presence of mind to include before going to breakfast, pre-empting it's necessity for the work ahead. Luckily I had a very good signal on my phone out here by the pool. For once even the hotel's Wi-fi seemed to be firing on all cylinders.

I tapped into my phone's web browser 'Corfu Animal Shelters' and waited for the information to filter through. I had been expecting to have to wade through scores of helpful names and numbers and useful links but I was very disappointed. Some of the helpful links weren't even on the island itself but mainland Greece. However there were three centres that were based in Corfu and this ignited a little hope in us both. I handed my phone to Lucy and asked her to read me out our only three avenues of help. With pen in hand I made a note of the Agni Animal Welfare Fund (A.A.W.F.), the Corfu Animal Rescue Establishment (C.A.R.E.) and The Ark as Lucy dictated each name and contact number.

A little surge of happiness at being proactive started to creep up inside me as I really thought we were getting somewhere now. I took the phone back from Lucy and giving her the pen and paper in return I called the first number of A.A.W.F. It seemed to take a long time to connect the call but at last I heard it ringing at the other end, sounding unfamiliar and shrill. I hadn't stopped to consider whether there might be a language barrier with this Greek organisation, let alone with my Scottish accent, but undeterred I just launched into my opening speech that I'd mentally composed as I waited for my call to connect. After a few more short rings my call was answered by a female voice. An anglicised one. Luck appeared to be on our side. I started by saying who I was and where I was staying. There was a brief silence and then the voice enquired;

"Yes. How can I help you?"

"I've found a stray kitten living in a drain and I wondered if you would be able to take him into your shelter please." I was sure that I heard the voice at the other end give a little intake of breath, but she was kind and sympathetic in her reply. She went on to ask me if the kitten had been injured or was ill and so I admitted that, no, he was just a stray who seemed a bit thin but was homeless. She must have been quite used to calls like mine and so her response was probably as I should have expected.

"I'm so sorry, but unfortunately we do not have a dog or a cat shelter and we don't take in dogs, cats or kittens from the street unless they are hurt and in obvious danger". She went on to explain very gently and regretfully, and to what I am sure was the hundredth call that day from a well-meaning animal loving tourist, that they were also very busy at the moment.

"I'm afraid that we get many calls like yours every day. We just cannot physically take in all the stray kittens, unless of course you wanted to adopt him yourself perhaps?" Kindly spoken but business-like, and final.

"Oh, I see," I replied, and then, "So you're not an actual animal sanctuary as such?" I knew she could sense the disappointment in my voice now. It was hollow and deflated compared to the one which had started out so confidently and with such optimism. The lady's voice at the other end had really softened now and I could tell that she desperately wanted to try and help me, and our kitten, but in our particular circumstances and location it was going to be nigh on impossible.

"You have to understand. Corfu has a huge stray cat problem. We just cannot take in every single one that is homeless, especially if they're not in any immediate danger or are healthy. We can help with rehoming but we don't have the sort of shelter here for them in the same way that I think you mean, like an animal sanctuary. I'm really ever so sorry." The conversation tailed off and I thanked her for her time. Just as I was about to hang up she said,

"Look, before you go, have you tried The Ark? It's much closer to where you are staying than we are, they might be able to help you."

I replied that she was the first person I'd contacted but that I would call The Ark now. We finally rang off. Lucy had been following the conversation and had got the gist of the way things were going. I tried to hide my despondency from her and briskly told her not to worry. I reassured her that I still had more numbers to call so not to give up hope just yet.

"Someone will take him in. I know they will," I ended, and then I picked up my phone again to repeat my spiel and plead our case.

I tapped in the number of The Ark. The line connected almost immediately this time, but instead of it being answered it just rang. And rang. And rang. I imagined an old and very dated telephone handset at The Ark's end, trilling tunelessly all to itself in an empty office, and to an audience of none. After a while it was clear that The Ark wasn't going to answer the phone and although I tried one more time without success it seemed pointless. There seemed to be no one there. Perhaps there never would be, perhaps they'd closed their doors, shut up shop and I was going up a blind alley. So I gave up on The Ark and Lucy looked at me with a 'what now?' expression on her face. Still having one more number to try I called C.A.R.E., our last hope. Again, the unfamiliar ring tone at the other end but this time the call was answered within a few seconds. My heart gave a little jolt as I realised this was it. The final enquiry.

As before with A.A.W.F., it was a female voice that answered the telephone. She sounded harassed, as if in a hurry to get this call over with so that she could go and deal with something else more important. It didn't bode well this impression that she gave me in that one 'Hallo'. However, undeterred I went into my speech. The lady at the other end appeared to have picked up some interest as every now and again she would say 'ahhh' and 'hmmm' and so I thought she sounded as if she might be able to help, such genuine interest she was apparently showing. That is up until it got to the point where I asked if she would be able to take the kitten in and a home found for him.

She almost repeated word for word what A.A.W.F. had said. They were too busy, too full, the massive stray animal problem in Corfu and lastly, had I tried calling The Ark? I told her that I had tried to call them twice but that they weren't answering the phone. I had the presence of mind to add that I was worried that The Ark no longer was in business, despite twice being recommended to them now. The lady assured me that as far as she was aware The Ark was still operating. Had I tried sending them an email? I told her no, I hadn't. Again she assured me that it was worth it to keep trying The Ark as they really were my best bet. I thanked her and rang off. So now what?

Lucy, having followed this conversation closely, looked utterly dejected. We sat in silence for a long while it seemed but it was probably only seconds, my mind working overtime now as to what we could possibly try to do next. Without speaking, I tapped in The Ark's number one more time and let it ring on speaker phone to it's heart's content. Still it rang and rang, and when I eventually shut the call down I could still hear that incessantly annoying and continuous ring in my head going unanswered and unloved. It seemed to just linger in the atmosphere. I made a decision there and then.

"Right then. We'll send The Ark an email." I said to Lucy, trying to sound undefeated.

She didn't look at all impressed, being (perhaps quite rightly) none too hopeful of any success by now. It was clear to me that that was the only option left. The Ark was apparently still operating and they were our nearest help point, and as I'd been told this twice now by the two other Shelters, it seemed silly not to try that simple way of communicating. Luckily the internet access on my phone was working well still. It wasn't difficult writing the email as all I had to do was put down in words my, by now, well familiar speech. I read the email back to myself and realised that being able to write down exactly our predicament, with no interruptions or the feeling that it was falling on deaf ears, was actually quite liberating. I felt I had been able to push the barriers a little too, as it was now more a begging letter to The Ark.

It was far easier to plead this little kitten's case in writing. In fact not just the kitten's, for I had included Misty into the equation now. I pressed **send**, and breathed out a long sigh as I'd been holding my breath writing the last few sentences. I closed my phone up and put it back in my bag. We had done our best and now it was in the hands of the Gods. Perhaps even the Greek Gods, and there were plenty of those from what I remembered from my history lessons at school.

I felt absolutely drained and exhausted beyond belief. The combination of very little sleep, fear for the kitten's safety and the soaring heat had taken its toll, and I just wanted to drift off and try to forget for a little while our troubles. I really had done all that I could do, for the time being anyway, and so I shouldn't have felt the little stab of guilt that niggled. Should I, *could* I, be doing more to save these two little creatures? And if so, what? Lucy leaned back on her sun lounger staring into space. I could tell she was thinking about what we could possibly do next. Through both tiredness and genuine helplessness, this time I just didn't have the answers.

Chapter 8

We dozed together under the shade of the parasols to the gentle hum of the cicadas for a couple of hours. When I properly woke again I was feeling much more refreshed, the earlier imagined terrors of the night having completely gone now. I stretched, got up off the sun lounger and had a swim in the pool. Lucy was already in it, languishing in the cool water as she laid on her lilo, just floating on the gentle, undulating blue surface, arms trailing lazily in the water.

After we both felt properly cooled down I suggested that we go to the pool bar and have a snack lunch, although by now it was early afternoon. We ordered a bowl of chips and some Coke and sat at one of the pool side tables. I heard my phone ping so I took it out of my bag to check it. I noticed that I had received an email from The Ark. My heart did a funny sort of little leap. Lucy leaned in close to me so that we could read it together. I couldn't really make a lot of sense out of it at first as the English wasn't that good but after reading it for a third time I understood it a little better.

The Ark had written to say that there were many stray cats and kittens in Corfu. However, the email went on to say that they could take the kitten in on a temporary basis on the proviso that I could find a permanent home for him. This would include stumping up a certain amount of money to get him treated by The Ark's vet first, and from there to his designated and assured home. It was signed; Louisa Van Vouude. My heart sank. That was a huge ask. We were due to be flying home in six days time and I really couldn't see how we were going to be able to organise a home in the UK for a kitten. And wasn't that what I'd been told by the other charities? It would be impossible to arrange all that. How on earth could I find a UK home let alone arrange to transport the kitten there?

It all seemed a hopeless and quite ridiculous request and I wondered whether I was being deliberately put off the idea.

I decided to telephone The Ark to get some more clarity on all these issues. Perhaps now that someone was replying to emails it meant that the office was open and someone would be there to answer my call this time. The Ark's telephone number was the last one I'd called so it was easy to find. I tapped the top of my call list and, for the third time that day, listened to the by now familiar drone of the call trying to connect at the other end. My heart was in my mouth as I waited for someone to answer. This time I was successful! My call was answered within a few rings. The voice at the other end sounded neither Greek or English, but spoke in a rather clipped way. I imagined that this was Louisa answering the call herself and from what I gathered, by the sound of her name and accent, I guessed she was Dutch.

I introduced myself and thanked her for her email. I then asked if she could explain to me exactly the terms on which she might be able to help home the kitten. From what she had written earlier I was still unclear as to what she meant. She appeared very kind and calm over the phone, and firstly, thanked me for caring about the kitten. She explained that at her own particular set-up of The Ark, she could not take kittens in unless they had a guaranteed, permanent home in the offing; she could only take a kitten on a temporary basis and it would be up to me entirely to organise a home and it was my full responsibility to ensure that these terms could be met. Otherwise the kitten would sadly have to be turned away.

Louisa asked me if I could tell her about the kitten's health, especially the state of his eyes. Were they clear and bright or were they sticky? I replied that no, they were not at all healthy looking and yes, they did appear to be quite gunked up. She also suggested that if I could not find a UK home for the kitten, then perhaps I could try asking around locally to where we were staying. I was determined to do all I could to help this kitten of course but the thought of going round door to door in this place, not knowing the language and trying to plead my case with complete strangers seemed to me an impossible task. But I had to start somewhere. I told Louisa that I would try my best then we said our goodbyes and I ended the call.Lucy had completely grasped the situation as I'd had Louisa on speaker phone. She looked miserable. All I could do was to keep reassuring her that there must be *someone* out there who wanted a kitten and it was up to us to find that person. Miracles do happen. We would do our utmost best and make sure that a home was found, some where, some way. And if it came to it we'd have to try and perform our own miracle.

We weren't terribly hungry by the time the restaurant was opened for the evening meal. Lucy just picked at her food, looking sad and saying very little. I think that we both felt a sense of guilt at having all this food placed in front of us whilst out there 'our' kitten was sheltering in a drain and wondering where his next meal might be coming from. It seemed so wrong somehow that here we were with the potential to stuff our faces. And out there....

* * *

After dinner we made our way back to our room to pick up some more cat food sachets. We filled a bottle with fresh water and then made our way down to the beach to feed the kitten at the drain. I prayed that he would still be there, and somewhat safe. A gentle breeze had sprung up from the sea and was just starting to stir the trees that lined our walk. The evening was still very warm, despite the breeze, which only served to fan us with more heat. A myriad of thoughts were running through my head. The hopelessness of it all. It was a seemingly impossible task that faced us in finding this kitten a home. I knew from my own experiences that the animal shelters back home, especially the Cats Protection, were usually full to bursting. It was hard enough for those charities themselves to find homes for their charges in an apparent nation of cat lovers.

With all their publicity and promotions and Open Days, the CP still had more cats than they could cope with. So what would be our chances over here then, where cats were looked upon as little more than vermin? Very slim I imagined. But even if I could have spoken a little Greek, I did not have the sophisticated vocabulary needed, in order for one to get across to the locals that I was a well-meaning cat-lover, with an urgent appeal for someone to give a hungry, tiny stray kitten a home. Please. Thank you.

Not a cat in hell's chance, and for this little cat along with many others, life could be just that. It certainly wasn't the proverbial peach, that's for sure. But all these misgivings and my laments on the stray cat situation in Corfu wasn't getting me any closer to finding a solution, and was in fact proving most unhelpful as it was really starting to bring me down. The idea was to think positively, and the universe will provide. Of course, I knew that.

I was trying to wrack my brains about something I had read recently about the power of positive thought, versus negative ones. It came to me in a blinding flash, and had our situation not been so critical and emotional I might have even laughed out loud. Instead I gave a wry inward smile when I remembered the term they call negative thinking. *Catastrophizing.* Cats again! This is when you imagine a disastrous outcome to whatever event you are thinking about. You are meant to take a moment to ask yourself, 'What evidence do I have that things will turn out as badly as I'm predicting?' It was true. I didn't have any evidence that we were going to fail. However, it was also true that, so far, all our options seemed to be null and void and so I felt bound for a disastrous outcome. I was not normally this gloomy and pessimistic over situations in life. Perhaps it was the feeling of being so utterly alone in our mission. We needed sympathisers and helpers. We needed an ally. As things stood at the moment it was just me, and it was lonely waging a one woman battle in a too-hot foreign country where I didn't speak the language, and was apparently the only cat lover on the island. Or so it seemed to me anyway in these desperate hours.

We could see the drain now as we drew nearer. Up until now I hadn't really noticed the little bungalow which stood just nearby. It was a drab, weather beaten looking building, its whitewashed exterior having long gone only to reveal great patches of cement and lichen. It had once upon a time, a pale blue painted balcony spanning the front of it, but now the wood looked rotten in places. It could have been such a cosy little snug; set back up a driveway, overlooking the sea and the unbroken blue of the sky. However, I was in no mood to romanticise. My disenchantment and frustration with the island was beginning to come to the surface I think. I could see on the balcony there sat an elderly Greek lady, dressed all in black and bare footed. She had a small dog who was sitting next to her, some sort of terrier it looked like.

As we approached the drain I could tell she was watching Lucy and I closely. I knelt down and peered under the concrete and iron barred roof of the drain. There was our kitten, tucked up into a tight ball and laying on his side, quite motionless. It melted my heart. I managed to dislodge a little gravel as I knelt further in and the noise of this stirred him from his slumbers. He opened his eyes a fraction, partly through being rudely awakened but mostly through the inability to open them any wider because of the sticky goo that encrusted the eyelids. He crawled out from under the drain and seemed very happy to see us though, as he rubbed around my ankles, making little chirruping sounds. Strangely, this action sent a little frisson of optimism through me as I thought to myself, how could anyone not want to give this little fellow a home? I was almost hopeful.

Lucy had already started emptying a food pouch into a clean bowl and she put it down in front of him. He just fell on the food. He ate ravenously. Whilst he ate I was able to study him minutely. He had an endearing little ginger blob between his shoulders. His tail was completely ginger and I thought perhaps his paws might have a sprinkling of colour too but that could have been just grime. His tiny little ears which flicked backwards and forwards while he ate were ginger. This constant movement was perhaps him being wary of possible threats while he ate: living the way he did, in potential danger, perhaps that had taught him to be constantly on his guard. He soon finished his bowl and started nosing around Lucy's haversack. He seemed to realise where his meals were coming from. Lucy looked at me.

"Can I give him another one Mum?"

I nodded, not taking my eyes off him. I have always loved watching cats eat. The absolute and total concentration they devote to the job in hand always gave me sheer pleasure to see cats enjoying their food. He was even purring, and quite loudly too. Lucy chuckled and told me it was his outboard motor. She bent down and gave him his second helpings and re-filled his water bowl as well. This time he was slower, more measured with his feeding, and I think that his eyes were probably bigger than his tummy. He did have a pot-bellied little tummy despite being thin all over. Oh, the poor wee mite. In between taking a few mouthfuls now he would stop and look up at Lucy and I every so often, as if to say 'thank you'. Or perhaps not being able to believe his luck that he was being loved and looked after and fed such tasty food. Any food at all in fact.

Eventually his bowl was once again empty. He gave the customary, languorous stretch and then settled down at our feet to start his washing regime. Now this is another little task I adore watching cats do. It is so peaceful. I had spent the majority of the nights so far watching Misty go through this identical ritual. Our kitten mirrored her technique, as did my precious boys Louie, Simon and Mimi nearly 2000 miles away in Glasgow. It is the same all over the world for all cats. The energy they devote to this serious business of feline toilette never changes as they try to keep themselves scrupulously clean.

Something made me look up. I could sense that we were being watched and I was right. I realised that it was the elderly lady that I'd spied earlier. She had obviously been taking quite an interest in our ministrations from her vantage point on her rickety old balcony.

I had a sudden brainwave. I lifted the kitten up as he had by now finished washing himself and was being tempted to play with a stick that Lucy had found. He didn't mind being picked up at all and seemed to be treating it all as one great adventure. Cradling him close to my chest, and with Lucy looking on after me in wide-eyed puzzlement, I made my way up the garden path of the tumbledown bungalow. As I walked towards the old lady I smiled to show that I meant no harm. She made an attempt to stand up and greet me but instead continued to stare at me, watching as I approached her.

Boldly, and not even stopping to consider whether she would be able to understand English, I asked her if she could give the kitten a home. She just shook her head and waved her arms about. Whether that was just to get rid of me, to warn me off, I just didn't know as she did not say a word, just gesticulated wildly. Her expression had a finality about it, tight lipped and not interested. She was making it perfectly clear that she didn't want to have our kitten, I was certain of that, so I turned around and made my way back down the garden path and back to Lucy.

"Mum! What were you thinking of? She could have been mad or something, she looked really angry!"

Lucy scolded me once I'd got back to the drain. I told her I had to try *something,* didn't I? I knew she understood my motives. It was just my sheer audacity that had shocked her I suppose as normally I wouldn't have been that bold at home. And so we were back to square one again. If we'd ever left it, that is.

Throughout all this I was still holding the kitten close to me. He had made no attempt to jump out of my arms. Not even a wriggle, while this crazy cat lady was going round door to door trying to get rid of him. I couldn't bear to part with him. I was enjoying the soft, snuggled little body that was so trustingly allowing me to hold him. Lucy tickled him under his chin and he began to purr rapturously. I could feel his whole body vibrate with sheer delight at being made such a fuss of and it was clear that he adored both of us.

"Can I go and have a swim before we go back please, Mum?" Lucy asked me.

I said of course she could. She ran off down the sand to the sea, her lovely long hair flailing out behind her. She looked just like a little girl again. My little girl at four years old, happy and free and blissfully unaware, as we all are at that tender age, of the future, of heartbreaks and the tragedies it was going to reveal for us both. Reveal for all of us at some point. But Oh! To be a little girl again. To have no worries. To take life minute by minute, too young to have regrets, the days filled with wonderment and the future always exciting. Life unfurling deliciously slowly. I still held the kitten, holding him so close as if he was a little baby human. My child.

Chapter 9

He seemed very content to stay in my arms, his little head nestling in the nape of my neck, his rattling purr so close to my ear. I just didn't want to ever let go of this bold little cat, but it was time to go back to the hotel. I crouched down next to the drain and still he snuggled up to me, not moving as I was trying to bend down on to my knees trying to keep my balance. I hated having to disturb his peace; as I tried to disentangle him from my hair now, as it had flopped forward having come loose from its scrunchy in all the activity from earlier. However, once he realised that he was again at ground level, and his food bowls were in sight, he released his grip on me and seemed to be quite content now to be gently placed back on the ground.

Although his bowl of biscuits had since been re-filled he wasn't interested in food now and crawled back to the safety of the drain, preferring to sleep. Perhaps his little adventure in my arms to meet the locals, although not not phasing him at the time, had now tired him out. I could feel my eyes stinging, hot tears threatening. All around us were hotels and holiday apartments. I was thinking hard. None of these would be much use in approaching kitten-homing possibilities.

I lingered for a few more minutes; that terrible gut-wrenching and heart-string pulling feeling of being torn between leaving him and having to press on with the rest of our evening was always an immense struggle. A little part of me anxious and worried that I might never see him again. Now that one plan of action, in offering him up to the lady at the bungalow, had failed, I was left feeling even more desperate. Not that I had had high hopes of instant success, I wasn't as naive as perhaps I had been just 24 hours ago, but it was still a massive blow. Would we *ever* succeed in finding him a proper home?

Lucy was swimming happily and the kitten was back in his little hole under the drain. He just lay there now and looked up at me, sleepily. I was running out of ideas, of hope and most importantly, time itself. It was slipping away like sand through my fingers, literally. The kitten decided that he'd had enough of my gloominess and moping, turned his head away from me and appeared to fall fast asleep. I was glad that he'd made his own choice to retreat, and that I hadn't had to put him there or leave him sitting watching me. Glad that he'd made his own mind up about going undercover again. I said my goodbyes to his sleeping form, made sure his water was still nearby and then wandered off down towards the sea.

I took my sandals off and let the warm, pale sand seep through my toes. It felt heavenly as it kissed the soles of my feet. With each step I'd sink just slightly as the grains engulfed each foot and made a lovely, scrunching sound. Although the sun was beginning to set now it was still warm. I kept going over everything in my mind; what we had done so far for the kitten and what we had achieved. One more hour of respite for him, that was all. He still had no home and because of that, any further contact with The Ark was pointless and hopeless at this moment. Think girl. *Think*.

Lucy waved at me from the shore line and started walking along the sand towards me. Her legs were getting so brown now, and the sand still clinging to them gave them a shimmering, sparkling effect. My beautiful girl, gradually turning into a woman. I stretched my arm out to her and taking my hand we slowly made our way back to the hotel. We didn't talk about the kitten again. Both of us were silent, each of us trying to come up with ideas, testing them out in our minds, realising they wouldn't work, discarding them only to go on to the next desperate idea. We went straight to our room when we got back to the hotel and Lucy quickly got ready for bed. It wasn't long before she was fast asleep, the gentle, rhythmic rise and fall of her sheets and the sound of her steady breathing giving a real peaceful calm to the room. I opened the patio doors for some air. It was a glorious evening, it never really seemed to get completely dark, the sky staying indigo.

I heard a rustle of leaves and then a 'mew', as Misty magically appeared at the corner of the balcony. She watched me from her safe vantage point and I whispered to her, telling her I'd go and get her supper now. I was still mindful not to wake Lucy. I was careful and quiet with the rustling of getting cat food pouches out of the shopping bag which was getting much use this holiday. I took the food still in its pouch outside with me, emptied it into the saucer on the table then placed the full to brimming dish down near the edge of the balcony. Misty and I both knew the routine now. I would quietly and reverently retire to the chairs.

Once Misty had decided that it was safe to do so, she would spring into action. She would then trot over to the dish and start devouring the treats on tonight's Menu at the ever reliable Chez Tourist! I pulled out one of the chairs at the table and sat down at it. Watching Misty made me think about her, and the kitten at the drain and their lot in life. Their only luck when it came to having proper food was down to us tourists. In the holiday season they could quite easily just rely on someone buying cat food for the strays.

I thought about our first night here when I'd heard a neighbouring holiday maker on her phone saying she'd been feeding Misty. I started thinking about the plight of humanity as a whole. How readily we might feed the strays and enjoy doing so, spreading a little happiness as we go along our holidays as standard. And yet we don't readily offer the same relief to humans. So many rough sleepers I'd seen in the last year in Glasgow and I couldn't help thinking that if they had been homeless animals, then actually they might also have regular food offered to them at least, if not someone pleading their case and going round saying 'Can you give this person a home please?' OK, so this might seem a bit extreme but everything that had happened lately just seemed to make no humanitarian sense to me any more and the world's problems had suddenly really started to get me down. It made me think of James Bowen and his Streetcat Bob.

I had read all the Streetcat Bob books, about a recovering heroin addict living rough on the streets. He meets a starving and injured cat and together they help each other in their recovery and become best friends, so much so that when James busks for a living his cat, who he names Bob, are inseparable. This partnership brings them fame and his books explore how this developed over the years. In all, a true and very real rags to riches tale of hope, struggle and triumph for one man and his cat. I found the books inspiring and 'un-put-downable' to say the very least. I was hooked, and as such, had joined a Facebook page for Streetcat Bob fans, called Bob The Big Issue Cat And Friends.

I suddenly had what felt like an electric shock run through my body. A blinding epiphany. All of a sudden I knew exactly where I could find some help, and where I could find the sympathisers, the allies that I had earlier longed for. The supporters, the cat lovers from all over the world! I grabbed the phone out of my bag and found the Streetcat Bob Facebook page, the WiFi connection still being as good as it had been earlier this afternoon. Serendipity perhaps?

This group was a good place to hear about other people's cats and their experiences, and the highs and lows of loving and living with these extraordinary creatures. It was also a very good place to get advice. What was more though, I had made a few friends through that site too, albeit I'd never met them in person. I already had a few photos of the kitten at the drain that I had taken with my phone so I gathered these together and posted them on Facebook. Along with those, I gave an account of the situation we were in, the dilemma of finding a home and our desperate need for help. I also stuck my neck out a bit and asked if anyone could offer the kitten a home, as mad as it sounded. I knew it was a long shot but faced with no other options at present I had a 'nothing ventured, nothing gained' mentality going on. Above all, we needed help to find a solution to the problem. So I put the call out.

> **It is breaking my heart being on holiday in Corfu. So many stray and abandoned cats. I found this abandoned kitten living under a drain by the road. I have contacted local animal welfare organisations to see if they can help but not much luck. What should I do? xx.**

In the past when I'd had problems or questions about my cats, a simple post to this page was usually worth its weight in gold. I had always been quite overwhelmed with all the help and advice that poured in. The members of the Bob page seemed very supportive of all things cat related and so reply posts were always plentiful. I didn't have to wait long. Within minutes, my post was being commented upon, varying from one end of the spectrum with 'it happens a lot, you can't do anything about it', to the other with 'bring the kitten home with you'.

There were all manner of different suggestions in between, and although kindly meant, some were just impracticable. However, there were a few people who suggested that I set up a Go Fund Me page. That way I might be able to raise enough money through donations to pay for the costs in getting the kitten home to the UK. It was certainly an idea, but I had literally no idea how to set such a fund up myself. I was aware that these new forms of Crowd Funding schemes were popular and proving very successful; but would complete strangers really contribute to someone they didn't know just to bring a stray kitten back to the UK? I started to see a glimmer of hope. I had underestimated the Power of the Paw.

The more people that agreed a Go Fund Me page might be the best solution, the more I thought, what have I got to lose? My only difficulty, and it was a significantly huge difficulty in my mind, was my not knowing *how* to. To make matters worse, the internet access at the hotel was scant enough most of the time; steam driven broadband might have been faster. Even if I did have the know-how, I might not have the necessary and reliable source of power. However, I was feeling quite charged now. I could feel a quickening of my pulse as more and more comments poured in to say that 'we could do it'. The sheer enthusiasm that members were filling me with was a terrific boost to my morale and confidence. If only I knew how to achieve what I was being urged to do.

One member, a lady called Sonia, commented that she was willing to offer the kitten a home herself in Jersey. She said that she had been really upset when she saw the photos of the kitten and read all about him living under a drain. She was quite serious about giving him a home, but I didn't have a clue how to go about it. Obviously we'd have to raise some funds to get the kitten transported to the UK. Just how? All these enquiries backwards and forwards drew the attention of another member, in a lady called Lisa. She very kindly offered to set up a Go Fund Me page for the kitten on my behalf, from her home back in the UK.

Reading all these posts was making me feel quite breathless at the rate of all this help coming in. All of a sudden this rescue mission was happening at warp speed. It was an incredible feeling; the optimism, the hope and, above all, just the sheer love that was pouring in from all four corners of the world was just incredible. I felt physically lifted by it all. These wonderfully kind and caring people, all strangers to each other, who all wanted to pull together and try and save this little kitten. Louisa had already advised me that with vet checks, passports and other necessary travel arrangements that would have to be put in place, it could cost up to £1000 to get a kitten back to the UK. Could we possibly raise that sort of money in such a short space of time I wondered?

Then smack-bang in the middle of this crucial and cliff-hanging point, my phone started to shut itself down as I realised with horror that it was running out of battery power. How frustrating! I let out an audible groan and out loud said 'Don't you dare!' But it was too late. All of a sudden I was staring at a black screen. I looked at my watch. It was 9pm, and right on cue, Misty suddenly entered (stage right), on the balcony. She was a welcome distraction to this feeling of annoyance and dismay at having to give up my phone to the charger for a few hours.

I greeted her with a whispered 'Hello sweetheart' and withdrew quietly back inside to get her supper ready. The room was stiflingly hot so I left the patio doors open wider than usual. Maybe subconsciously I was testing Misty, to see if she would follow me back inside. How lovely it might have been if she'd jumped up on one of the beds and settled herself there for the night. Even more lovely if we were to find her still there when we awoke. No chance of that happening I realised as I went back outside to find Misty sticking resolutely to her side of the balcony.

I put her food dish down for her and did the familiar, almost choreographed withdrawing backwards to my chair and watched her tuck into tonight's feast. It didn't take her long to finish up every scrap, and lick the bowl clean. The usual routine of washing herself from head to tail then followed, unchanged from all previous nights, and I sat on. I felt so tired now. Such a lot had been accomplished today and in such a short time too. Waking up this morning from that dreadful nightmare seemed like days ago, not mere hours. I let my mind meander. How strange it was that some days you seem to be able to fit in about three or four days worth of work, of achievements, and yet on other days we accomplish nothing; nothing noteworthy that is. I was also just dying to tell Lucy the news that help might at last be at hand. I looked over to where she lay, a tendril of sun bleached and almost hennaed hair just visible above the sheets, but she was fast asleep still. I hoped that she was having beautiful dreams, and although I wanted desperately, to wake her up so she could share in the exhilaration that I felt. I decided it best to let her wake up naturally. After all, the news could keep just for a little while longer. She'd know soon enough.

Misty had long gone by the time I'd come out of my contemplative mood. She had ventured back out into her secret world of the night; a world that I knew nothing about and was perhaps never likely to. I got up from the chair and took one last look at the bushy undergrowth that Misty always disappeared into. Mouthing a silent good night to her I turned in, plugging my phone into it's charger immediately before doing anything else. It was only half past nine at night, but with the prospect of an early start in the morning, I got under the covers. I still lay awake for a while thinking about tomorrow's boat trip to Albania that we were booked on. Then I went over the day's events all over again. My brain was acting like a video player that would insist on rewinding and fast-forwarding to everything that had happened. The excitement luckily was taken over by a tiredness that engulfed me at last, settling my heart rate and relaxing me in a way that I had not felt for a long time it seemed.

Chapter 10

I slept a dreamless sleep. When I woke up just before 6am, I felt as if a great burden had been lifted from my shoulders. At first I couldn't think why. Then the memories of the day before came flooding back. Of course! The 'Bob' page on Facebook and the realisation that help might at last be at hand for the kitten at the drain. Throwing the covers back and jumping out of bed I rushed over to the power point where my phone had been charging overnight. Having worn it out the day before with so many calls and internet use, I hoped it had now fully charged. It had definitely needed a long time to recover and charge its batteries from the onslaught of yesterday. I definitely felt re-charged this morning and was hoping that my phone (my salvation) was feeling the same. I'm not normally one to give inanimate objects feelings, but this morning I felt so light hearted and happy that I felt I could afford to lavish a little silliness on things. The green light showed that it was indeed fully charged and raring to go.

I quickly scanned further messages to my post about the kitten. It was much earlier in the UK than it was here so I hadn't expected any more news. However, the main consensus of opinion was all for setting up a crowdfunding page to get him back to the UK. Time was against me at present as I was in a hurry now to get going to see the kitten, take him his breakfast and be back in time to board the 7.20am bus. I had just under an hour to accomplish all this. I would be able to catch up on more news later on once I was back and we were ensconced on the bus. I quickly washed and dressed and left a note for Lucy telling her where I'd gone and that I'd be back soon. Stuffing a cat food pouch into my pocket I quietly let myself out of the room.

I decided to take a short cut round the side of the hotel to avoid the reception area in my self-conscious early foray into town. Within a few minutes I was at the drain having almost run the whole way. As it was so early, the morning was still relatively cool and the air fresh which made travelling at that speed quite comfortable. The little chap had heard my approach this time in the quiet of the morning and he jumped up to see me. I ran my hand along his little back by way of a hello and he broke into a loud purr as I started to fill his food bowl. I couldn't keep the excitement out of my voice as I told him he had what amounted to the beginning of a fan club that was trying to help him find a proper little home.

I knelt down on the hard ground next to him as he tucked into his breakfast. At first he couldn't decide what he wanted more of, attention or food. He would chin-butt my thigh in between mouthfuls as if by way of a thank you, and also perhaps seeking some sort of reassurance from me. However, I did have to leave soon so I stood up and allowed him to finish his food without any further distractions. He continued to lick his bowl clean with great fervour.

A dog started barking some way off and this made the kitten make a bolt for the safety of the drain. Quick as a flash, I watched his retreating little ginger tail disappear under the grating. I looked about but I couldn't see any sign of the dog and just had to console myself with the thought that at least the kitten was safe, for no dog would have been able to get into the drain. Nonetheless, it wasn't a very pleasant situation to have to leave the kitten in, but looking at my watch I realised that I had to get back to the hotel. It was already a quarter to seven. Time had literally flown.

I fairly sprinted back to the hotel, only to find Lucy outside the entrance. She had obviously been looking out for me. Luckily she looked ready to go as she had her bag with her and baseball cap on. All togged up and ready for the day's excursion; just minus a mother, and of course none the wiser as yet to the greatest news that I had still to tell her.

"Mum, the bus is picking us up in 20 minutes and I was getting worried about you!" she cried, relief spreading across her face at seeing me, at last.

"It's OK, I'm back. Let me just have a quick shower and I'll meet you back here in ten minutes."

I suggested she sit in the shade while she waited for me as the day was becoming hot now that the sun was truly out. My news would have to be put on hold for yet a little while longer. I hoofed it back to the room, quickly showered to cool me down from the earlier sprint and made it back to Lucy by five past seven. I even had time to take a detour via the restaurant to grab some croissants as we were going to miss breakfast this morning. Once back in the shade where Lucy had been sitting, I was able to catch my breath again.

"Was the kitten alright?" Lucy asked, standing up and brushing the dry, dead grass from her shorts.

I told her he was fine and he'd had a good breakfast. I didn't mention about the dog frightening him back into the drain directly afterwards however. I was acting on a need to know basis with my sensitive daughter. Always best, and in this case, a problem shared would have been a problem multiplied. However, at last the time had come for me to give her the momentous news. Part of me was just enjoying the build up to it all, in the knowledge that any second now she was going to hear news that would rock her world in the same way that mine had been rocked last night. It was just the glorious anticipation that I was enjoying, nothing more;

nothing selfish, just the sheer delight in the knowledge that you're about to give someone something special that you know they have always longed for. It was exciting because the time was now. It was time to give.

"Darling, listen. I've got some incredible news for you. Something brilliant has happened."

We had already started walking to the bus stop, but now Lucy stopped in her tracks and turned round sharply, eagerly anticipating what I had to say.

"What, about the kitten do you mean?" She said, in a sort of breathless rush of nervous excitement.

"Yes. All about the kitten", I beamed back at her and then I told her all that had happened after she had gone to bed last night.

She listened raptly, not asking any questions, nodding her head one minute and then shaking it the next in amazement and incredulity, the same way I had done last night when reading all the messages that had suddenly started to come pouring in. Wide-eyed with awe and amazement she listened as I gave her every detail of the events as they had unfolded last night whilst she'd slept. Not once did she ask me why I hadn't woken her to tell her the news as it had started breaking; I think she knew and also understood my reasons for leaving it all until now to tell her.

"Can I see what the people were saying about the kitten?" She asked me at last.

"Of course!" I exclaimed. "Honestly Lucy, you will not believe the amount of people that all want to help us."

I showed her some of the messages that I'd received on my phone and by the time I'd recounted and completed the whole wonderful tale of the night before, it started to sink in with me all over again in the telling. It felt good to be able to say all this out loud now as up until now, it was only the kitten himself who had been party to the tumultuous revelations.

By now we had arrived at where our bus was scheduled to meet us and luckily this was still in part-shade, the sun not yet having climbed too high in the sky. I looked at my watch. 07.15. Five minutes only to have to wait for the bus.. Not bad going. However, the five minutes wait soon turned into twenty-five minutes, but at last it arrived, swinging lazily into the lay-by, seemingly with not a care in the world, quite untroubled and unapologetic about its tardiness.

We boarded the bus and found seats at the very back where the windows were open at their fullest. This was the first time that I'd had a chance to sit down since waking up this morning and it felt good. I kicked off my sandals and just rested my feet on top of them, enjoying the feeling of freedom, and at the same time avoiding the rather unclean floor. Lucy rummaged in her bag for bottles of water and I added to this the croissants. They were still crisp and lovely and buttery, as there we sat munching our snack breakfast and watching Corfu through the windows of the bus as it was gradually waking up and coming to life.

The bus was making good time as by now it was speeding along and was able to catch up on it's lateness, arriving at the harbour within the hour. All on time then, I thought to myself, and running smoothly; a good start to the day. The bus pulled into the harbour, parked up and we alighted, making our way towards the Passport Control area.I had spoken too soon though it seemed, as we waited in an ever growing queue for over an hour to have our passports checked. It was hot, and a not particularly fragrant smelling place to wait. It was noisy too. People became impatient waiting and although the queue was always moving, it moved at a snail's pace.

At last it was our turn, as the very bored but stern looking officials scrutinised us against our passport photos. We joined the queue again to board the boat to Albania and at last we felt we were really on our way as the boat slowly chugged out of the harbour. I was eager to check my phone again for any kitten updates but now saw that I didn't have any internet access on the boat. I felt so frustrated as I'd been looking forward to properly catching up on all the comments and possible ways forward. Most of all though, I had no idea if the Go Fund Me page had been set up yet, let alone if it had accrued any funds. I sighed loudly, suddenly fed up with the heat, the chaos, and the abject disorganisation of this extraordinary country.

Lucy was far too absorbed in her music that she was plugged into with her earphones, to notice my loud, anguished sigh of despair, or notice me moodily shoving my phone back in my bag. I just hoped and prayed that the necessary funds would be raised in time to save the little kitten. I couldn't bear the thought of having to leave him behind. He'd never survive, I knew that much. All the angst of the previous few days threatened to quash my earlier light heartedness. Still, I just had to keep positive and remember all the helpful and constructive comments I'd received and focus on those. No reason to believe that, just because my phone couldn't connect to the ether, that things weren't falling into place already.

Little did I know in fact, that things were actually moving at a great pace…

Chapter 11

A few hours later we arrived in Albania. Compared to the relative peace of Corfu, this place was altogether a very different land. The journey by boat had been uneventful. I had reluctantly tried to put all thoughts about the kitten to the back of my mind as the boat had made its way across the Straits of Corfu. Things were quite out of my hands at this point so I had to be content to just try and be patient. The boat was very busy. Everyone jostled together, all speaking loudly in their respective native tongue within their family groups. As the boat rose and fell gently on the sea's surface, so did the volume of the crowd seem to swell with the movement. It all seemed to have its own natural crescendo.

At last the boat docked at Saranda. Lucy packed her earphones and music away and stayed close to me as we very slowly alighted the boat. It was a slow procession. We had previously been told that on arrival we were to make our way towards our appropriate coach depending on our nationality. We weaved our way in and out of what was just one big seething mass of hot and sticky humanity. Eventually we found our coach with the English speaking Tour Guide, having passed Russian, French, German and Italian-speaking buses, all just buzzing with people climbing excitedly aboard. We hauled ourselves up the very high steps onto the coach and settled in our seats. Now we were able to gather our wits but the temperature seemed to be climbing again, especially as the air conditioning wasn't very effective, if it even existed at all.

At last the driver turned the ignition on, the engine making a gruff sound as it roared into life and belched out black, sickly smelling diesel fumes. The bus ambled forward slowly out of it's parking space and away from the general melee of the crowds. We were on our way again, to explore Albania. I hoped it was going to be worth it. Our first stop was at the archaeological site of Butrint, some 20 kilometres from the modern city of Saranda. This place definitely proved to be a well-established tour-bus destination. The site itself, set in Butrint's National Park, is a UNESCO World Heritage site which these days, the Lord Rothschild's UK-based Butrint Foundation helps to maintain. We clambered out of the bus hotter and stickier than when we'd boarded it. The sun was shining as fiercely as it possibly could, as it blasted our faces as soon as we were out into the open. The coach had then seemed cool by comparison, and I momentarily vowed I would never complain about the Scottish climate ever again. I checked my phone for any internet connection. Nothing.

The tour around this site proved to be very intensive, during which our guide announced quite casually that Albania was experiencing a heat-wave at present. We all trooped behind our guide taking in our surroundings. We followed an uneven, dusty path to our right which led us to some very ancient ruins of a Greek theatre. Our guide started to hold forth, once the stragglers in our group had caught up at the back. We were informed that this theatre had been built in the third century BC. We were quite thankful of the relative cool it offered us as it stood partly secluded by the surrounding forest. It was an incredible sight to behold, the pale, sun-baked stone a stark contrast against the greenery around it. When it had been in use all those centuries ago, the theatre could seat some 2,500 people. Now we could only imagine what it had been like back then. Long curved tiers of stone were set in a semicircle, an occasional stone stairway still clearly visible linking each section of seating. These looked down on what would have once been a stage alive with entertainment, a classic Greek Tragedy perhaps or a festival of song and dance; I could picture it all quite vividly as our guide continued her story about it's history.

A few short steps further and we came to the Roman public baths, their still waters a greenish grey and laid in small pools that sat adjacent to each other. These were now home to colonies of turtles. It was a strange sight to see these creatures languishing in the murky waters or lying sunning themselves where once humans would have bathed. There were mosaics preserved here too, but buried under layers of mesh and sand, there to protect them from the elements.

We walked a little deeper into the forest. The tour guide pointed out to us a wall which was covered with Greek inscriptions, fresh and crisp as if they had only recently been scribed. A pale stone palaeolithic Christian baptistery stood nearby in all its sixth century splendour. It was still quite beautiful to this day I thought, with it's mosaic tiled flooring decorated with colourful illustrations of birds and other animals, and again under the sand for protection.

Our guide next directed our attention to the sixth century basilica, its impressive stone arches which had been built over the course of many years spanning it. There were earlier relics here too, with a Cyclopean wall that apparently was dated to the fourth century BC. On the wall was an image of a bull being killed by a lion which was set in relief over one of the gates. We were told that this was meant to be a symbol of a protective force from any vanquishing assailants. It was all such an unimaginably long time ago that these buildings and carvings had been constructed it was hard to comprehend. My head was feeling thoroughly dizzy with all these dates that our guide was reeling off so easily. Again, I checked my phone for any internet ether that might happen to be floating around, just in case a miracle had happened and the Gods of Cyber were feeling in a generous mood. Apparently they weren't, and so back into my bag, went my phone.

In spite of the dizziness, I was enjoying this historic tour; I had loved studying history at school and this excursion was bringing back memories of how visits like this had really fuelled my passion and curiosity for ancient history in particular. However, I could see that by now Lucy was less impressed, and getting rather bored and tired of all this culture. We were both hot, despite the on and off shelter and shade afforded by these massive structures and the trees. Unable to leave though, we traipsed on and then started to climb some steps up a very steep hill. The steps were those annoying sort that are too shallow for two steps per ledge, but too deep for one and which in the end make you feel as if you've developed a limp or got one leg shorter than the other as your weight is always on one particular leg. By the time we got to the summit, our calf muscles were aching and we were quite out of breath, the sweat literally dripping from every pore in our bodies. Lucy was by now getting quite irritable in the heat and was showing signs of wanting to get back on the bus. Nonetheless we couldn't just leave the group, and as our tour guide carried on quite unaware or maybe just unphased by the obvious discomfort of her charges, we were shown the site of where the acropolis had once stood. In its place now was a castle and we ventured inside and browsed the small but informative museum that it housed, glad of the cooler temperature but still rather uncomfortable.

Walking out through the other side, we were able to gaze at the surroundings below from the vantage point of the museum's courtyard. Looking down we could see the Vivari Channel which connected Lake Butrint to the Straits of Corfu. It really did look so peaceful, cool and serene down there. It took us both long to be able to just get back down the hill, and jump into those cool waters; but unfortunately that wasn't on the tour's agenda. Instead we were encouraged to browse the varied community run stalls that lined the castle's gates. These were an interesting little collection of stands, selling all sorts of souvenirs that had been produced locally, from necklaces to sweet treats. I thought perhaps that up here at least, at this great height, I might at last be lucky and have some sort of internet connection, just a little signal to reassure me that I was still in the land of the living, instead of what seemed to be the land of the forgotten. But there was nothing. Absolutely zilch all. The stalls did not hold any lure for Lucy, she wasn't interested. She had reached saturation point by now, literally, and her irritability was catching. We drained a couple of bottles of water each which were useful in that it made our backpacks a little lighter. I felt like tipping a bottle of water over my head although to tell the truth, the water was by no means cool by now. Having taken a beating from the sun on our backs throughout the tour it was lukewarm, but still refreshing.

At last we started our descent back down the steps, quicker than we'd climbed up them previously. Thankful for the coolness of the coach, of which the driver had had the great presence of mind to park in the shade, we made our way to the same seats that we'd sat in earlier. Although we hadn't been first in the queue to re-board the coach, people just naturally gravitated to where they'd sat previously; a peculiar human habit I mused, and perhaps just a British one. The tour guide made sure that we were all accounted for with a head count, then nodding to the driver, we reversed out of our parking slot. We journeyed through vast plains, passing lakes and rivers and had some stunning panoramic views of Albania. We were travelling in shade too and this was pleasant as we were able to sit back in relative comfort and just admire the views. Dotted about was the odd shack set amidst a backdrop of sometimes dry and dusty landscape on the one side, which would then suddenly give way to a more lush looking vegetation on the other. The road was fairly quiet too, hardly meeting much traffic as we pootled along, the vista extraordinarily unspoiled.

Eventually, and whilst still out in the countryside, the coach slowed to a halt outside a restaurant. It was a low, whitewashed little building, with a red pan-tiled roof and here we were to stop off for a light lunch. As we climbed down off the coach I could smell food cooking and it was all quite delicious and, rather like our hotel, all set out in the style of a buffet, with everything from cocktail sausages and cold cooked meats and fish, to olives, salads, cheeses and bread. There were also dishes of fruit cut up into quarters which looked tantalising. We chose a table outside as they all had large sun umbrellas over them and were set in part shade at the back of the building. Lucy had certainly cheered up by now and was happily tucking into the vegetarian aspects of the lunch. As we ate, several cats started to appear and make their way to all the tables where everyone was enjoying their meals. I gave them some broken off bits of cold meat and fish which they fell on eagerly. People at the other tables seemed to be doing the same, which was nice to see. All the cats looked in good condition and none of the restaurant staff seemed to mind them being there at all; they certainly weren't being chased off here, and so the humans and the cats had a quiet and harmonious lunch together. It was very reassuring to see, especially as I also noticed several bowls of water and dishes of dry cat food in the garden area put out especially for them. They really did seem quite happy and content here, these cats.

There was one beautiful little grey cat who kept brushing against my legs as I peeled off bite-size chunks of tasty meaty morsels. I wondered what her story was and whether she might have even been in-kitten, she was very hungry and a little pear-shaped too. My mind harked back to our kitten at the drain, and a new longing for the internet rose up in me, but still I had none. I had been checking my phone since we had left Butrint but there was nothing. I hoped that it wasn't a problem with my phone, although Lucy's was the same; same network, no signal. At last, our meal over with, we were summoned back to the bus. Without fail, people returned to the same seats, and we sat back once again and travelled off to our next and final stop, which was the beach at Saranda, winding our way through its streets on the way to our destination. Our immediate impressions as we watched this foreign world from the bus, was that Albania was a very poor country. We passed many buildings that just appeared to be half-built. Had the money run out or was this deliberate, I wondered to myself. There were piles of rubble and rubbish heaps lying about here and there and all in all it was just rather a sad and unloved place. All a bit of a mess.

Saranda's main beach, where we were headed for, was set in a horse-shoe shape, its town curving around it and sandwiched between the azure of the Ionian Sea and green of the plentiful olive groves that were set high on the hills above. Unofficially it is the capital of the Albanian Riviera, which sounds quite grand but it is in fact rather a misnomer. It was black with people. As we saw it that day, it looked like the world and not only his wife, but her closest relatives too, had all gathered at the very same spot. Apparently half of Tirana relocate here in the summer months to enjoy the beach and the night-life. It looked like it. In its youth, it had once been a sleepy fishing village. Now it was a bustling, thriving city which had lost much of its charm but apparently, none of its charisma. As it presented itself to us that day, I personally did not find it at all charismatic, and neither did Lucy.

When at last we were finally parked up and able to set foot on the beach, we were besieged by many small children begging for money, or trying to sell us tiny and pathetic little 'treasures' which they'd found from, I suppose, beach combing. It was very upsetting to witness, and Lucy drew closer to me as she was really affected by it all. Perhaps I should have read up more about Albania, I thought retrospectively, but we had been so caught up in the moment of wanting to do these little tours that I'd just glibly booked what we could. I felt embarrassed by my ignorance now, and more shocked than I care to mention. I could read on the faces of the others that travelled with us on our coach that they too were feeling the same. The guide beckoned to us and so we had to turn our backs on these little people, who went on to the outfall from the next coach that had arrived and had begun to spill out its unsuspecting tourists. I checked the phone. Nothing.

We made our way back towards the promenade and were able to have an hour or so to ourselves, to explore the shops, of which there were plenty. Some were garish selling the usual assortment of gaudy trinkets and souvenirs and other tourist paraphernalia; fridge magnets, shopping bags, postcards and lilos. Others were more authentically Albanian, selling locally produced honey and *shenditlie*. This proved to be a delicious dessert which I couldn't decide whether it was a cake or a biscuit; it was somewhere in the middle really. Made with honey and nuts it was definitely for those with a sweet tooth, of which I am one, but even then I could only manage a small portion of it.

Lucy bought herself a new pair of sunglasses, having left hers behind on the boat coming over here, and then we decided to make our way back towards the promenade. It was fringed with tall and lush palm trees that gave exotic shelter to the many ice cream carts here. We were spoiled for choice here in our quest for something icy cold. We downed a couple of ice creams under the expansive fronds of a palm tree and then went back for water ices, our thirst not quite having been quenched the first time around. All the time though, I kept wondering how our Go Fund Me page, if any, was getting on. I was itching to get back to the hotel now; to have internet access and all it might reveal. We still had a few more hours to go before that could happen, so I just had to content myself with living in the moment. Here I was, sitting in what really was glorious weather with my beautiful daughter, who was also my good friend. We were lucky enough to be on holiday. We were healthy. We were happy. Was I happy? Yes, if the plight of feline-kind was taken out of the equation for the moment. Sigh.

Chapter 12

By the time we were back on-board the coach (same seat, which goes without saying), we were all quite weary, and so the journey back was a quiet one. There was very limited chatter as heads started to nod off and I could hear some snorers. Lucy giggled at the man behind us who, being rather a large chap, had fallen fast asleep on his lady-friend's shoulder, she herself looked quite embarrassed about the noise he was making and every now and again nudged him to shhh him. It didn't seem to take long to get back to the harbour, and boarding the boat was hassle free this time. The boat seemed to move off within minutes as all of a sudden I realised we were in motion and on our way back to Corfu.

It was a pleasant trip compared to our outward bound journey this morning. It was now 6pm and it had cooled down quite a bit. We sat at the very top of the boat again and admired the views as we slowly sailed away from Albania. From the boat, Albania became smaller and smaller as we retreated further into the sea. The chinks in its armour, such as the rubbish and the sad spectacles on the beach, went unseen from this distance, as all we could see now was a green and golden coastline. Lucy and I waved goodbye to the mainland, both lost in thought but undoubtedly thinking along the same lines. Our particular experiences on the beach and the glimpses we'd had into the more troubled side to this part of the world has left a mark on us as the boat sailed on, gently bobbing up and down, slowly over the still glittering surface of the sea. It was good, and actually quite unusual, to feel so cool in the sea breeze, to have my hair ruffled by it, and yet still be in the brightest of sunshine. At this time of day, although the wind could speed up a tan, it's rays wouldn't have been half as harmful as earlier, and we still had plenty of sunscreen on so we were quite safe. Just for a laugh and some light entertainment I thought I'd check my phone again. In case. Just in case...

I closed my eyes against the glare of the sun and, enjoying the gentle sea-spray on my face, started to day dream a little. I wondered what to expect when I was eventually able to hook up to the hotel's internet. What sort of news would Facebook bring for us and the kitten at the drain? It could go either way, there would/ could be no middle ground, I knew that. Would I be pleasantly surprised or bitterly disappointed? Strangely enough, for the first time this holiday I started to think about Alan. I wished that he could have been with us to enjoy this holiday too. I could see him quite plainly now in my mind's eye. As if he was next to me. I could feel his shoulder against mine as I sat, head back, eyes tight shut against the sun. All those years ago, when I had wanted to recall him, when I had ached and wept to remember him as he had been, my mind had not cooperated. It had blotted out any but the dimmest of images as if to spare me the pain of such memories. And yet now I could see him so clearly. Those lovely blue eyes, kind and sensitive yet always with a twinkle in them. He was smiling, happy, as if knowing something that I didn't. I was suddenly jolted upright as the boat seemed to jerk unsteadily. I wondered what on earth was going on, then realised that we had docked, and the boat was mooring. I felt unsteady, slightly dizzy even as I got up out of my seat and went to the railing to look at the waters below. I realised that Lucy was studying me closely.

"Mum? Are you alright? You looked like you were going to faint or something, what's wrong?" I shook my head, reached out for her hand and replied, in as steady a voice that I could muster.

"I'm absolutely fine darling. I just fell asleep then woke up suddenly when the boat thumped, or whatever it was." I rubbed my eyes because I felt like I was seeing stars. But no, just the very concerned look on Lucy's face. I laughed and told her I'd been having such a nice dream and had been rudely awakened that was all. She studied my face for a few seconds to make sure I really was alright then shrugged her shoulders.

"You had me really worried there then Mum. You looked away with the fairies!" I didn't tell her that, to my mind, I *thought* I'd been away with Alan. And it was beautiful.

"Come on, everyone's getting off the boat, we'll be left behind at this rate", I laughed. Picking up my bag, and with Lucy walking close to me – really close, as if she was scared I was going to faint still I presume, we made our way through the exit and onto terra firma.

* * *

We made our way to the coach and climbed aboard for the last time that day. It wasn't long before the engine started up and slowly we pulled out of the harbour's coach park. We were at last bound for Messonghi and Moraitika. As we ambled along at rather a snail's pace dodging the tourist traffic, I could feel Lucy's head lolling and come to rest on my shoulder as she nodded off. It had been a very tiring day. I felt as if I'd gone through every emotion known to man in the space of this one little day. Elation, excitement, frustration, disappointment, awe and shock. Then that strange feeling of bliss and oneness at the end of it all, dreaming about Alan. It had taken its toll. I felt absolutely drained; and yet there was still this feeling of nervous anticipation bubbling away inside me. What news and developments might our Facebook supporters, our friends and allies, have in store for us once we were able to connect with them again I wondered. Salvation? I was aching to get back to the hotel to find out. However, we still had to get to some shops first for some food as it was nearly nine pm already and we'd missed our evening meal in the restaurant.

The coach conveniently pulled up outside the mini-supermarket on the way back to the hotel. Lucy was already waking as she'd realised that we were slowing down. Her nap seemed to have refreshed her and she was bright eyed and raring to go it seemed. We jumped down off the bus and headed straight for the cool of the shop. Stocking up on sandwiches and drinks, and more cat food sachets, I paid for our purchases and then as it was getting late, we both went to check on the kitten straight away. As usual, he was lying inside the safety of his drain, curled up, eyes tight shut with his tail wrapped around his little body. Lucy chirruped gently to let him know that we had arrived with his supper. He stirred in his sleep but didn't wake up immediately, so Lucy called to him softly.

"Puss-puss, come on, it's us! Tea-time!" He appeared to hear us this time and opened both eyes with difficulty because they were extra-sticky tonight it seemed, he yawned, stretched and clambered out from his nest.

I undid a pouch of food and no sooner had I finished filling his bowl he had his little nose in it, purring away in the usual rattly manner. I stroked him and told him that tonight we were in a little bit of a hurry because of all the internet issues, whether he understood, who knows. I explained to him that it was actually for his own good, and his salvation, that we had to leave him as soon as he'd eaten. He didn't mind. As soon as he'd finished his wet food, he ignored his biscuits, and his water, and went back to bed. He didn't even have the usual wash as if preferring sleep over ablutions tonight. Very well. I just hoped that in sleep that his little body was saving as much energy as it could and perhaps getting stronger with his frequent feeding routines. We said goodbye to him and then at last we were walking up the main driveway to the hotel. I grabbed my phone out of my bag and it started to ping into life at last. I could see that I had dozens of notifications from the Bob group on Facebook. However, the one I was really looking for was news about the Go Fund Me progress. And there it was; but not *quite* in the manner I'd expected. I stopped short in my tracks, Lucy almost cannoning into me.

"Lucy! Look at this!" I cried, hardly able to breath now. I felt so choked, knocked out completely. She took the phone from me.

"Read it out to me!"' My voice was shaky and not one that I recognised now.

"Mum...I c-c-can't..." Lucy gave a sort of strange hiccup and a gulp and then dissolved into tears.

They literally streamed down her face. Seeing my daughter like this, this kind, sensitive and compassionate young woman there in front me was too much to bear now. I felt my eyes hot and they started to prickle with tears, and my smile, although still there, probably turned into some sort of grimace as I too caved in. I let the tears fall unashamedly. They were the tears of weeks I guess. Perhaps months. Years? At this very moment I cried for everything. Most of all though I cried for the amount of love and compassion that still seemed to be there in the world. Overwhelmed with the sense of, I don't know; spirituality? The sense of an absolute miracle of faith that our story about the kitten at the drain had touched the hearts of so many. That there were those oh, so many people out there that felt exactly the same way as Lucy and I did. Faith restoring was an understatement.

I haven't told you precisely what I'd seen yet have I? I still find it hard to put it all into words, but this is what I am talking about. In the form of an artwork, the all important post:

It was from Lisa, and she had written:

'It's great to get notification from Go Fund Me whilst I'm at work that we have exceeded the target for the Corfu kitty which is just brilliant. Thank you sooooo much to everyone that has donated in the last 18 hours. I think we might have just saved a kitty's life between us…'

Lucy and I were both reeling from the news. I kept reading over and over again the last few lines Lisa had written.

Saved a kitty's life between us.

It just seemed all too good to be true, and yet it *was* true. The fact that we had even exceeded our original target of £1,000 was beyond my wildest dreams. All those kind and wonderful people who had contributed I just wanted to thank each and every one personally but at this very moment it was impossible. My hands were still shaking. Lucy's tears had stopped flowing but they had left dusty smudges on her tired face. I put my arms around her and kissed her cheek, still hot and salty. I rested my head on hers and felt my breathing become steadier now. We stood there, not moving, neither one of us knowing what to say. Dumbfounded and awestruck, no words could ever express our feelings at that very moment; there just *were* no words that would ever do justice to how we felt.

Time seemed to stand still just then. I sensed the occasional passer by either on their way to or from the hotel having to sidestep Lucy and I as we clung together so tightly. We didn't move out of the way. We were locked together in time suspended. The spell was at last broken however. I heard a meow nearby and, after a double-take, realised it was Misty of all things. It was akin to someone clearing their throat to try and make their presence known during someone else's private moment. I couldn't believe that this hitherto somewhat shy and aloof cat would do such a thing. Yet here she was at the front of the hotel. Perhaps she'd been waiting at our balcony for me to appear, and when I didn't, had taken it upon herself to come and find me. All very surprising and yet in light of the circumstances, all part of the weird magic that seemed to be happening all around us. Surreal to say the least.

Lucy was also speechless at Misty's bold behaviour, that she seemed to be 'claiming' us. However, now that she'd snapped us back to the present again Misty sensed this. She darted back into the undergrowth. I could just make out a white streak as she bolted round to the back of the hotel through the dense and tangled weave of bushes. She was fast and seemed to be able to negotiate the dark tunnel with apparent ease, this probably being a well-known passage of entry and exit for her. Lucy picked up both mine and her bags as I lagged behind slightly, amazed at Misty's speed and sudden return to being the illusive silver shadow that we knew and loved. I was still clutching my phone reading and re-reading Lisa's post as I walked back through the cool of the reception.

Back at our room, Lucy had left the door open for me, wedged by her sandal. I could already hear the taps running in the shower. I closed the door behind me and then a thought struck me. Would it be too much to ask to find Misty outside on the balcony, now that she knew we were back? In the last twenty or so minutes I'd had so many beautiful, dreamlike shocks (if you could call them those), of things suddenly starting to come together, that to find Misty on the balcony would be the icing on the cake - or the kibble on the cat food at any rate. I went over to the patio doors and opened them wide, and there sat Misty. Not in her usual quiet corner either, but she was sitting on the picnic table. What's more, when she saw me, instead of retreating to a safe distance at the other end of the balcony, she just sat and gazed at me with the bluest of blue eyed stares and started meowing.

I stood stock still. I wanted to savour this moment of dreams coming true. I also wanted to call out to Lucy so that she could share the wonderment but I knew that would probably break the spell and Misty would flee. I held these glowing little seconds to myself as I gazed back at the beautiful little white and grey cat sitting on the table looking back at me; communicating with me even. It couldn't last forever though and Misty did want her supper, albeit a late one. I went back indoors and selected a juicy sachet of tuna. I had the weird sensation of walking on air really. An air of inner peace and togetherness had set in. Performing the familiar and age-old task of cat-feeding, I could just as well have been at home and yet here I was in Corfu, basking in the glorious feeling that now perhaps the wheel of fortune had started to change for the kitten at the drain. Life was on the up.

Carrying Misty's full to brimming dish of food through to the balcony, I realised that my true inner hippiness was surfacing. I just felt very at one with the world. Restored of faith, Karma, Spirit, call it what you will. It wouldn't have surprised me if suddenly I could start talking to the animals like Doctor Doolittle, so electrically charged did I feel. Colours just seemed brighter, sounds clearer; touch more sensitive, scents more sensuous. Yes. A definite feeling of oneness with the natural world around me. I dare say that if I'd had a joss stick to hand, I would have lit it!

Coming out of this reverie and Misty watched me approach but this time wasn't brave enough to see my magical moments through to their conclusion. She sprang off the table like the proverbial cat on a hot tin roof and jumped down into the bushes below the balcony. I continued over to the edge and placed her food down in the usual place, then made my way back to one of the chairs and just sat quietly waiting for her to appear again. A rustle of leaves and up she sprang, her movement swift and balletic as Nureyev and as silent as an owl. She tucked into her meal greedily. It amazed me really, when I came to think about it, that she hadn't gone elsewhere for her supper when we hadn't arrived on time. Other guests at the hotel had been putting out dishes for her, I knew that much; were we special to her, I wondered fancifully. I was positive that she'd come to find us earlier, as there had been something quite deliberate about her manner.

I sat back in my chair content and suddenly realised that in all the excitement, I hadn't actually sent any response back to the Go Fund Me news yet. I retrieved my phone from my bag and sitting once again started to write my message. All I could think of to say though was Thank You, but that didn't sound enough. Words could never express the gratitude I felt for all those people who were supporting us, and so in the end my reply was just that; an explanation that I couldn't find the right words but just 'Thank You from the bottom of my heart and also the kitten's, and that I never thought that twenty-four hours ago I'd be writing this'. It looked a garbled mess really but it was all I could manage. It was all just too exciting for words now. I did have the presence of mind though to realise that the hard work, the practical side of things, was now about to begin. The reality of the kitten's funds raised meant that the next phase of the rescue mission would soon be under way; the physical aspect of bringing him out of one life and taking him to another. The thought was daunting but exciting too. Taking him to the safety of The Ark, who were still as yet unaware of our success with funds to transport him to a forever home in Jersey. I yawned. I was so tired now, too tired to speculate about the next stage of this adventure so I turned in for the night but checked my phone one last time. I still couldn't believe all that money had been raised.

Emma, one of the Bob page members, had messaged me to say that I should call The Ark immediately to let them know we'd reached our target and to get the Corfu Kitten (as he'd now been dubbed), picked up as soon as possible. Of course, it was later here in Corfu than it was back at home, but I did wonder what time I could feasibly call The Ark in the morning. I decided that as the news I was going to give them was so great that surely they wouldn't mind an early morning call.

It was difficult to sleep now as I watched the seconds on the clock tick silently away. Every minute brought the morning's work and the imparting of happy news closer. I sprang out of bed as I realised I should have plugged my phone back into its charger. The sudden jolt of thinking that I might wear the battery flat overnight alarmed me, and set my heart rate faster. This of course didn't help my chasing sleep once I'd got back under the covers, especially as no sooner had I got back into bed I realised I should have also set my alarm. Out I got again to set my phone to wake me for 5.30am. This would give me little over six hours of sleep. At last, getting back into bed for the third time that night, sleep did start to come. My last thoughts were about our kitten at the drain and how he must be one of the luckiest cats in the whole of Corfu, if not the most talked about on Facebook. Apart from Streetcat Bob that is.

Chapter 13

It felt like mere minutes, not hours, when my alarm went off the next morning. I didn't have the sensation of all the good news of yesterday suddenly coming flooding back as I woke, for I'd been dreaming about it all whilst I slept. Being awake now just felt like an extension of the night, a continuation of that lovely strange high. In my dream state, I'd planned to ring The Ark as soon as I woke up. Now, at this early hour I realised that it would be foolish and my words would be a tumbled mess, much like last night's 'Thank You's' on Facebook. I needed to collect my wits first and I wanted to go down to the drain to feed the kitten. After all, I had some important news for him. Lucy stirred just as I was leaving the room and she smiled sleepily. We didn't speak as she turned over and went back to sleep again.

How many times have I made this journey every morning, I thought to myself as I made my way through the quiet reception area. Would this be one of the last ones I thought? Surely I could start doing the countdown now, not that I was feeling sentimental in any way. Funny, but just at that moment I heard the distant strains of a transistor radio from way off down one of the corridors. It was playing Europe's song, *Final Countdown*. How appropriate I thought, and I knew then that it would be the ear-worm of the day now. I started humming along to it, the drum rhythm beating in time with my own footsteps.

It was 6am. The kitten, I was relieved to see, was curled up in his usual tight ball amidst the leaves and litter under the drain cover. He woke up when he heard me crouch down to open my bag and rip open the food sachet. He stretched and yawned to reveal almost blue-white perfect little teeth. This morning I saw him in a different light; I wished that I could speak cat, or 'felinese' perhaps it was called. I wanted to be able to tell him in no uncertain terms and in a way that he'd understand that he would soon be out of this hell-hole (literally). That a loving home now awaited him in a cooler, kinder climate; that he was fast becoming a famous Facebook kitten. I did tell him all this as I ran my hand along his spine as he ate his breakfast. He answered me in between mouthfuls by arching his back into the palm of my hand and, I think, looking grateful. Other than that, the conversation was very one-sided, which we were used to. I do the talking, he does the eat/listen/purr in response, that was our arrangement.

I still felt very happy and excited of course, but a new niggle had crept into my mind now. The logistics and the strategic planning of his transfer to The Ark and all the in-between bits worried me a little. Of course, I still had yet to call Louisa, and I felt sure she'd put my mind at rest about what we needed to do next so I resisted the temptation to over-think things. I was just truly thankful that we had gotten this far with everyone's help. I couldn't hang around any longer though as I did have the all important call to make. While I'd been idly day dreaming, the kitten had settled at my feet now and looked as if he'd fallen asleep again. Perhaps the early morning visits interrupted a normally late riser? All his personal likes and dislikes, his habits and foibles would soon become familiar to his new owner, I mused.

I felt a sudden, and very unexpected stab of jealousy; perhaps that's too strong a word. Envy. Completely irrational I know, but I couldn't help wishing it was Lucy and I that he was coming back to live with. I had to put that thought out of my mind at once though. It would have been impossible with my other three cats. No. The kitten was Jersey-bound to the wonderful Sonia and he would have the happiest of homes there. His little life was soon to become complete. At such a young age, only a baby, he had his whole life ahead of him. He'd be re-born.

I felt the familiar prickle of hot tears. Why cry now, for

goodness sake? I scolded myself. Pull yourself together and get on with it. This good talking to, by my better self, stirred me into action. I lifted the kitten, still curled up, put my face into his fur, which was brave I know as he was so dirty, and kissed him. Then I placed him back under the iron grate of the drain where he sleepily staggered back to his nest. Plonking himself down and with no backward glance he fell fast asleep again. I stood up, brushed the dust off my knees and seat and made my way back to the hotel, in haste now as I was hungry. My stomach was rumbling by the time I'd gathered Lucy from our room. We headed into breakfast. Lucy asked me when I was going to ring The Ark.

"Straight after we've finished our breakfast," I replied through a mouthful of croissant. I swigged down the rest of my coffee and could feel butterflies in the pit of my stomach, I don't know why. Perhaps because I wondered what sort of response I'd receive from Louisa. Surprise? Disbelief or relief? I was about to find out. We found our usual poolside seats and I took my phone out of my bag.

"Here we go then", I murmured out loud.

"You are excited aren't you, Mum?" Lucy asked, looking quizzical.

"Of course I am. I'm just, I don't know, nervous and happy all mixed together." Actually I felt a little sick with anticipation but I wasn't going to tell Lucy that. Quaffing down croissants and coffee too quickly probably hadn't helped, either. My call connected after a few seconds. I took a deep breath as Louisa herself answered.

"Hello Louisa? It's Beverley here, we spoke the other day about the kitten we've found in the drain near our hotel?"

After a few moments, during which I could almost hear the cogs going round in Louisa's head, she replied.

"Ah yes, now I remember. How are you?"

I then recounted the last few days to her in the minutest detail. She listened, with no interruptions, and sometimes I thought that the line might have gone dead as she remained so silent. However, by the time I'd finished up with the news that we had the funds to bring the kitten back to the UK, I heard her take a breath to speak. She couldn't quite believe that we had found the kitten a home and raised so much money in such a short space of time. However, our wires must have crossed at some point during my conversation because she thought that I had found a home for the kitten in Corfu. I had to explain again that no, it was back in the Channel Islands that a home had been offered.

"Ah, I see, but what experience of cats does this lady have?" she asked me.

I explained that Sonia already had two cats of her own and both were very much loved and well cared for. Secretly I felt as if I was being made to jump through certain hoops now. I assured Louisa that the kitten would have a safe and happy home with Sonia in Jersey.

"She lives out in the country and away from busy roads", I finished up with. To be honest, I thought that any home would have been better than the one he was living in at the moment.

Eventually however, Louisa seemed satisfied with the situation. One final thing she did insist upon was that I myself should be a guarantor. In the event that the home fell through, then I would have to assume all responsibility for the kitten and it would be down to me to take him home. She was strict about this and told me in no uncertain terms that these would be the arrangements. Otherwise there would be no deal. Although she didn't actually use these specific words, that's what it amounted to. It all sounded very harsh at the time, and some definite hoop jumping was in place.

On reflection though I did see her point. It was much later on that she explained in greater detail why she had to ask these things. She'd had dealings with many tourists who, just like me, had found a stray little animal and promised to find a loving home for it, if The Ark would just look after it in the meantime while plans were being finalised. In the heat of the moment promises had been made. Once the realisation had set in and the whole lengthy process of vet checks, overseas travel, passports, etc had been taken into account, not least the expense. Often the tourists thought better of it all and lost interest. They just didn't come up with the goods in the end.

Louisa did have the poor animals' best interests at heart. Out of the two evils, it would have been far more cruel to temporarily give shelter, food and some sort of socialisation to a stray, only to have to turn it back out into the streets again when the forever home didn't materialise. Too awful a scenario to contemplate; but this was all part of future conversations we would eventually have, and I'm racing ahead. Back to the present, and there I was now making arrangements for our kitten to start the first lap of his journey to his forever home. It felt quite unreal. It was also becoming quite business-like now; honeymoon period over and now for the serious business of putting all that love and hope into practice.

Louisa suggested that I call her back the following day as by then she would have a better idea of when she could pick the kitten up. As she was unable to drive, she had to rely on volunteers at The Ark to give her lifts. She couldn't arrange anything on the spot but by tomorrow she assured me she would have transport arranged. I explained to her that we were actually going home in three days time, in the early morning on Thursday. I could hear her making a few calculations to herself then she said:

"OK. I think it best then, that I come out to pick the kitten up some time on Wednesday."

It was already Sunday and so Wednesday wasn't that far away; it would actually be our full and final day here in Corfu. We agreed that I'd call her back tomorrow and the conversation ended. 'Phew!' I exclaimed, shoving my phone back in my bag. Lucy had been following our conversation and was equally in a state of relief herself at the way it had gone. I sighed heavily, loudly, feeling that we had really accomplished something. Well, of course we *all* had. As Lisa had so accurately and eloquently put it: 'I think that we might have just saved a kitty's life between us.'

We spent the rest of that Sunday doing absolutely nothing. Completely worn out from the day before, where so much had been crammed into eighteen hours, we did the opposite. We crammed as many hours as we could into doing absolutely nothing. The relief, the feeling of that great burden of worry having been lifted was immense. No longer did I have the constant niggle of guilt that I should be or could be doing something more for the kitten. I felt light and lazy. This new feeling of guilt-free slothdom was something I could really get used to! As I dozed under the parasols I thought to myself, this is how holidays *should* be spent. The song *Final Countdown* started to play quietly in my head.

The evening too was still spent in this relaxed state. Early evening saw us both back at the drain with fresh water and food for the kitten. He didn't seem to have moved from his bed since this morning. True, cats do just appear to eat and sleep, and in this heat and with no socialisation, I guessed that's all he knew, for one so young. Once again I had that feeling of our ministering duties being on their final lap. That old saying about being better to enjoy the journey than to arrive must in this particular case be quite wrong. Yes, I'd miss tending him but oh! How I was impatient for his journey to be over; for him to arrive in Jersey and start his life properly. I suppose that this in itself could be called the real journey but for now, I wouldn't miss this present one we'd embarked upon. Well, not that much anyway. It seemed like weeks ago, not mere days when I'd scooped him up in my arms in a desperate attempt to find him a local home, starting (and ending) with the lady on the verandah nearby. To that end, I hadn't seen her since that fateful day. Perhaps she hid every time she saw me now.

Lucy played with the kitten whilst I picked up the litter around his nest, then placed him back in his tidier lodgings and we said goodnight to him. Perhaps only two more night-time partings to go then Wednesday would come and the final goodbye. No tears now, I reminded myself, the happy ending I'd wanted was in sight so why did my eyes start to sting? It was always easier to be strong when Lucy was with me so I mentally shook myself and smiled.

"Well then. Three more sleeps for this little fella."

Lucy grinned and by reply just took my hand and we walked back to the hotel slowly together. We had dinner in the restaurant then Lucy decided she wanted an early night. I kissed her on her forehead and watched her retreating back as she closed the bathroom door behind her. I wasn't tired, which was hardly surprising after such a lethargic day. I decided to quietly read on the balcony and wait for Misty to arrive for her supper. An unremarkable, uneventful evening. When I'd spoken to Louisa this morning, I had also mentioned Misty. I told her that I thought she might be the kitten's mother, their markings being so similar. However, she had steered the conversation back round to our kitten. I wondered what could be done about Misty and whether she might also be able to be re-homed abroad. How fantastic would that be, saving two cats' lives.

Misty suddenly appeared, almost as if I'd conjured her up by just thinking about her. She was sitting ramrod straight at the corner of the balcony. Of course I did her bidding and moments later had laid out biscuits, wet food and fresh water for her. I hadn't even had time to retreat to the polite distance before she was tucking into her evening meal. Grabbing biscuits from one dish and then trying the wet food she to and fro-d between dishes until there was not a scrap left. She ignored the water and jumped back down off the balcony into the bushes below. With a little tail flick she was gone, with not as much as a by your leave.

I took the empty dishes away and went back inside to wash them up quietly, as Lucy was now in bed fast asleep. A minute later I too was under the covers and as I lay there just gazing at the ceiling I thought about Louisa and all that she was about to do for us. I wondered what her life must be like, and her volunteers. The distressing cases she must come across and the sheer hard work of it all. Rewarding when the animals were finally on their way to loving homes, otherwise a very busy and quite stressful life. I wondered how the kitten would adapt to suddenly having his freedom taken away and taken into captivity. Better than where he was now though of course; I hoped he'd feel the same way. Gradually I drifted off to sleep. Dreams tumbled through my head, the kitten and Misty always taking the lead role in one way or another in the stage plays of my sleep-ridden imagination.

Chapter 14

It was Monday morning and the start of the countdown proper. Lucy was up early too, having slept for almost ten hours, so we both went down to feed the kitten together which made a nice change. The sun wasn't fully up yet so we had plenty of shade to walk in. The odd cyclist or moped past us but other than that we were quite alone in the early morning quiet.

I'll miss this, I thought to myself. Feeling like Lucy and I had the world all to ourselves. Back at home at this time, Lucy would just be waking up; late and then madly rushing around getting her school kit together, trying to find her homework from the night before and generally rushing around like a headless chicken. I'd be multi-tasking, tripping over the cats in their attitude of 'me first' to be fed, and making our own breakfasts, packed lunches and searching for car keys all at the same time. The usual panic. I thought to myself, why don't we always get up early like this, and enjoy some time together. But I knew it wouldn't happen, it would never be like this; best laid plans and all that.

Fast asleep in his little nest, the kitten slept on as we crouched down beside the drain, organising his breakfast. He didn't stir as we scraped and shuffled about on bended knees filling his feed dishes. It was most odd. I gently called to him and for a split second a panic set in at his stillness. Then he sleepily opened one very sticky eye and yawned. He got up slowly and stretched and came crawling out to see us. I had a sickening feeling of dread. He didn't look at all well this morning. His reactions to us and his breakfast seemed so slow. I was sure I wasn't imagining things but my gut instincts told me that he just didn't seem right this morning. Unimaginable that at the eleventh hour he might suddenly go down hill and never survive the next couple of days, just when his luck was about to change.

That would be monstrous, and no way could fate twist so cruelly like that surely?

His appetite luckily seemed healthy enough, as he cleared his plate, but not with his usual great gusto. I didn't let on to Lucy that I was worried. For all she was aware, he might always be like this so early in the morning. As she didn't usually come with me on the morning feeds then I let her think that he was always sleepy at this early hour. I kept my voice light and cheery so as not to worry her, but it was a struggle. Once the kitten had finished his breakfast, she picked him up and cuddled him under her chin. He seemed to perk up then as he broke into rapturous purrs, his whole little body quivering and rattling with delight as they exchanged chin rubs. I was relieved to see that he was much more active now. Perhaps he really was just a late riser and we'd disturbed a long and peaceful sleep that he hadn't quite finished when we arrived on the scene.

On the other hand, conversely, he might have been up all night sheltering in fear from passing predators, man or beast, and come the dawn had at last been able to sleep as the night's terrors slunk away. Fanciful, my over active imagination always seemed to put a dampener on any given situation where the kitten was concerned. Living as he did in the drain didn't mean to say that he was necessarily out of harm's way. Although larger dogs wouldn't have been able to get to him through the grating, if he ventured out in the middle of the night then that was an entirely different matter, and one which I refused to think about on this glorious morning, with only two more days to go until he was safely ensconced at The Ark. It couldn't come soon enough. Talk about a ticking time-bomb.

Anyway, I consoled myself with the fact that he could at least start the day off on a full tummy now and that hopefully he'd just go back to sleep. Lucy placed him gently back on the ground again. He rolled over onto his back and gave an enormous stretch so that he looked twice as long and sinewy. He yawned and then collected himself to start watching. We both watched him as he furiously cleaned as much of his grubby fur as he could. Both his eyes were now fully open but still looking crusty around the eyelids. Once he'd finished his ablutions he sat gazing at us, expectantly.

We had to go back to the hotel as it would soon be breakfast time. I hated having to leave him behind when he was outside of his bolt-hole. I much preferred it when he was back in his nest, safely tucked away out of relative harm. He sat on, glancing around him and although I tried to coax him back under the grate, he didn't want to go. With a little tail flick he stalked off to just beyond the drain and sat back down again. He turned his head and looked round at us. Was it a mournful look or one of annoyance I wondered. Had we interfered too much now and overstepped the mark? Easily done with cats, but not usually with this little chap. Hmmm. I was puzzled by his unusual behaviour. It had to be said though, he was showing that independence of spirit that was so characteristic of cats, and so on the other hand not unusual at all.

By his body language perhaps he was saying: "Well now that you've woken me up, I may as well stay up!"

It really was time for us to leave so we turned around to walk back to the hotel. Lucy and I would every now and then glance over our shoulders, but he hadn't moved. He just gazed ahead of him ignoring us now. Gradually he was becoming just a tiny little white dot on the horizon behind us until we turned the corner and he was out of sight. The Parting didn't sit easily this morning.

"Maybe he'll just go back to sleep once he realises we've really gone and he's not distracted by us any more" I told Lucy, trying to sound nonchalant.

"Yeah, maybe," she replied, shrugging. I think that by now she'd caught on that I was anxious. So much for trying to conceal my real feelings. It wasn't a nice feeling having to leave him so exposed but who knows, he'd probably done this many times in our absence and always returned safely. I hoped that he'd been able to cram as much streetwise-ness as possible into his short life so far.

We went straight into breakfast not bothering to dump our bags back in our room. It was a bit of a gloomy affair as I kept thinking about how quiet the kitten had been when we'd first arrived. Now we'd had to leave him, and I kept seeing his tiny little profile receding into the distance against the backdrop of the dusty road in the shimmering heat haze. Anything could happen to him when he was out of the drain he looked so vulnerable. However, I had to put things into perspective now. If he could survive the first few weeks of his life so far unattended then he only had a couple more days to go until the safety of The Ark. I just hoped he'd make it in time. Every second counted now.

After breakfast, we found our usual quiet corner by the pool and I called Louisa, as pre-arranged. I couldn't help feeling a little frisson of excitement now though, which were luckily starting to replace the earlier black dogs. Louisa answered within a few seconds and recognised my voice straight away.

"Ah Beverley, yes hello. I have some good news for you and your kitten," she began.

Relief flooded through me and I held my breath wondering what this good news might be, but before I had a chance to ask her, she continued to say that she had arranged for one of her volunteers at The Ark called Anna to give her a lift to collect the kitten on Wednesday. She told us that she would meet us at the taxi rank at Messonghi in the morning. It would be then that she would talk us through the procedure for the forthcoming weeks while the kitten was in her care. I thanked her profusely.

"Oh that's fantastic, thank you so much!" I couldn't keep the excitement out of my voice and I could see Lucy's face breaking into a huge grin as she gave me the thumbs up. Louisa had given me the news that we had been longing to hear and now I felt much more positive than I had earlier. After that, there wasn't much more to say, so we rang off shortly afterwards and I snapped my phone shut.

"All sorted. Louisa is going to pick the kitten up on Wednesday," I told Lucy.

Ever practical, she asked me how we were going to get the kitten to the taxi rank from the drain, quite rightly pointing out that we didn't have a cat carrier. I thought for a moment and told her that, somehow, we'd just have to try and find one from somewhere. Lucy seemed excited at the prospect of going shopping for such necessities and her enthusiasm was infectious. We decided to go into Corfu town for a few hours. Lucy was dying to go to the McDonalds there. I thought it was a crazy idea seeing as we could go to one back home at any time but she was adamant and I gave in.

An hour later saw us walking slowly along the high street idly window-shopping, stopping every now and then to have a browse in shops that took our fancy. All the time I had the pleasant feeling that our kitten only had about 48 hoursish left to go in his present vulnerable state. I was filled with confidence that our mission was soon to be completed and oh, what a glorious feeling that was. I wondered how he would react to us capturing him and taking him to the taxi rank; how easy would that be? I also hoped that at that very moment he was fast asleep curled up in a ball in his drain. Maybe after he'd realised that we'd really gone and weren't stopping to play with him as we normally did this morning, he'd got bored and just retired to his boudoir. Some boudoir!

We passed an Asian Art Gallery on our meanders which I quite fancied having a look around. It was good to be able to step out of the, by now blistering glare of the sun, although the gallery didn't feel much cooler inside. Our eyes took a while to get used to the relative gloom of its interior but they gradually became accustomed to its velvety dimness. There were paintings hanging on the walls and placed on easels and exotic dyed and woven fabrics on display as well as sculptures, and other objets d'art. Lucy particularly liked the animal prints but after a while I could feel her itching to get away and sample the delights of Corfu's McDonalds.

It didn't take long for us to complete walking around the gallery. I too was getting hungry now and the thought of a nice fat burger and fries did have a certain appeal. I wouldn't have said no to the local cuisine either but this was a holiday and I wanted to treat Lucy to whatever she wanted. And if that meant dining out at a generic fast food outlet run by a global chain, then that's what we'd do. We didn't have to walk far and even with our eyes closed we could have found our way there just by the familiar smells emanating from the place. Lucy and I joined the small queue to be served and then placed our order at the counter. Had it not been for the heat and everyone being dressed for the beach, we could quite easily have been back in Glasgow with the customary menu-boards and the branding stamped everywhere in its décor.

We collected our meal from the other end of the till point, wound our way back through the queuing people and found a window seat. We started tucking into our meal. It was quite pleasant to just munch our burgers and people watch, the latter being one of my favourite pastimes, and the former coming a close second. Although it was noisy, the constant chatter was quite soothing really and it felt that we could have been anywhere, home or abroad.

We drained the last dregs of our milkshakes then headed for the loo to wash our hands of the sticky, syrupy, strawberry scented goo that had seeped through the paper cups. Once clean again and feeling replete, we stepped out into the glare of the sun and continued to explore the town. It was a pleasant little afternoon as we explored, turning down roads rammed with locals going about their day as island life seemed to be in full swing. Walking back up to the main street again we even spotted a Marks and Spencer store and, as I was curious to see what a Corfu version looked like inside, I had a wander round, more out of curiosity than anything else. I have always found something rather reassuring about good old Marks and Sparks and I was enjoying mooching around the Food Hall when I felt a little tug on my arm. It was Lucy with a pleading expression on her face.

"Alright, I've finished!" I laughed, and we turned around and made our way back through the shop and out into the busy thoroughfare.

After the air conditioned store the heat outside now seemed intense and so we decided to fill up on ice creams at a nearby kiosk. The day was passing quickly as it was already 5pm. We hadn't been able to find a cat carrier on our travels but I was sure that as we still hadn't explored every nook and cranny of the town there was still hope in getting one before Wednesday. A quarter of an hour later we got our bus back to the hotel which was easy enough, as by now I was quite confident at navigating around the town and had got used to travelling locally. The feeling of being full from the burgers, fries and milkshakes had long worn off and we were pleased to be one of the first to arrive in the hotel's restaurant for dinner that evening, though it was still early. The food was good, the buffet catering for all. Despite my guilty fast food feast at lunchtime I more than made up for it as I heaped plenty of green salad, tomatoes and olives onto a plate. Finishing off with a very healthy fruit salad my conscience was eased. The pre-holiday diet was long gone of course, and although I did try and eat healthily as a rule, to err is human.

I had booked us on another boat trip the following day. We were going to explore the small and luxurious islands of the Ionian sea once again as Lucy had really enjoyed the snorkelling she'd done there at the beginning of the holiday. I thought to myself how far we'd all come since then, and the twists and turns, and the shocks and pleasant surprises that fate had dished out to us since the discovery of the kitten. I was especially looking forward to seeing Paxos and Anti Paxos again now that I had a relaxed and happy conscience.

Chapter 15

That evening we went to the beach again, just for a little while. We found the kitten safe and well at the drain and gave him his supper. I thought to myself a few more hours have elapsed now, bringing us all closer to his day of rescue. He wouldn't have to live on the streets much longer. Lucy wanted to take the kitten back to our hotel room with her there and then. I must admit it was something that had crossed my mind, but no, we had to be sensible now. I had to tell her that I didn't want to run the risk of us both being thrown out of the hotel for breaking the rules. Under no circumstances were pets allowed in the hotel. For the time being the kitten seemed safe enough under the drain. He also seemed much perkier than he had this morning which was a relief to see.

Lucy then wanted to have a quick paddle in the sea. Taking our sandals off we walked down to the water's edge together. The water did look inviting and so I paddled with her. The sun's reflections dazzled me as they sparkled on the sea as it was still quite high in the sky and not yet dusk. The gentle waves that lapped backwards and forwards on the beach sounded like breaths being taken in and out. It was such a lovely sound. Very grounding. A constant. I sighed happily as I watched Lucy, head bent down low looking for gems under the surface, the odd pretty pebble or piece of smoothed glass. I used to love collecting these as a child, and would pretend they were precious jewels. The green and brown glass smoothed as wave after wave had pummelled it against the beach and with no sharp edges at all to leave a beautiful opaque, pastel shade of emerald and amber. It was like magic. I remembered the stone polisher I'd had as a child too. The constant tumble as it went round and round seemed to last for months, before producing the most amazing precious stones. Sometimes Jet or Tiger Eye would be revealed amongst the lesser stones, and that was always exciting.

Lost in thought over these childhood memories I realised that Lucy had suddenly joined me. We walked back up the beach together then stopped to put our sandals back on once we'd reached the road again. When we got back to the hotel Misty was already waiting for us. She was early tonight I thought, looking at my watch which told me it was only eight o'clock. She sat in front of our balcony staring at us with her baby blue eyes. I quickly fed her, told her that I couldn't linger tonight and then went back indoors.

I took a shower and watched as the last few remaining sand grains on my toes swirled and then disappeared down the plug hole. It really did feel like the holiday was slipping away so fast now as it was coming to a close. Today had really seemed to pass so quickly, and although I did feel that I was about ready to go home now, I would miss parts of the holiday. I was going to miss the constant good weather, the sea not far away and the freedom of being able to do what we liked and when we liked, not governed by the clock at all. Just governed by the feeding regimes of two hungry little certain felines.

I started to prepare for bed myself, setting my alarm first then clambering under the cool sheet. Lying under a high tog quilt would seem strange and heavy after the paper thin bedding here I decided, as I felt my eyes close. My thoughts then turned to Misty; why had she been early tonight I wondered? And she had the most beautiful eyes, and thinking about them they just seemed to appear out of the darkness of my closed eyelids. My last thought before falling asleep was that Misty just *had* to come with the kitten when he left Corfu.

* * *

Tuesday morning and I was awake early. I was still tired as I'd slept fitfully. I had been woken up in the night by what sounded like gun-shots, exactly like the ones I thought I had heard when we'd first arrived. I'd been too sleepy to check what time it was but I was certain that it was well past midnight. I had lain there in the gloom listening to the bang and the thumps that rang in the air some way off, feeling my anxious heart start to beat it's familiar tattoo. I had turned over to see if Lucy had woken but no, she was sleeping soundly, her face turned towards the wall away from me, Her bed clothes had risen and fallen gently as she slumbered, and wistfully I wished I could do the same. The night had then gone quiet again but the silence had then been eerie, portentous, as if a precursor for something else to happen and I had had a feeling of dread which I just couldn't shake off.

I thought perhaps it was my over-active imagination but no, something had definitely woken me and they *were* bangs. Fireworks? I had felt hot and clammy so I kicked off the sheets and turned my pillow over to the cooler, un-slept side and tried to settle back down to sleep again. It just didn't come though. It was difficult now as normally if that happened at home, I'd have been able to creep downstairs and make myself a cup of tea. Impossible to do that here, and so instead I just had to lie there and literally sweat it out and wait for sleep to come. Eventually I must have dozed off again, for when I awoke properly it was just beginning to get light outside. This time I did get out of bed and looked at my watch, which told me it was only 4am, I despaired at how early it still was.

There had been no further disturbances in the night, or none that I'd been aware of anyway. I crept out onto the balcony sliding the doors back very slowly and trying to be as quiet as I could. I eased my way through the small gap that I'd made, opening them any wider would have been too noisy as they made a certain squeak as it was and I didn't want to wake Lucy up. I stood on the cold concrete barefooted, letting my nightgown flap around my legs to try and cool myself down. The sky was definitely lightening up but the quiet was almost palpable. Even the cicadas appeared to be fast asleep still, and like in the poem about the Night Before Christmas, nothing stirred, not even a mouse, or perhaps in this case, a lizard.

I took down a great lungful of air and exhaled slowly. It was peaceful out here and very tempting to put the two chairs together and try and doze outside but I knew that I wouldn't be comfy. I crept back into the room leaving the patio doors open just ever so slightly for a little fresh air to filter in and got back into bed. The sheets were cooler now and that, coupled with the fact that the outside air had also cooled me down considerably, I was able to get another hour of sleep. But by 5am my eyes were wide open again and this time I was determined to get up and stay up now. We had an early start this morning as we were off on the boat trip around the islands so I thought I may as well go down to the drain and see the kitten. It was so early that it would be nice to be able to spend a bit more time than usual with him. I quickly put some clothes on and then let myself quietly out of the room. I made my way through the empty hush of the reception and then out through the double doors to the morning that was waiting outside for me. It was cool and fresh, the sap from the surrounding trees smelling extra fragrant this morning.

I walked on, enjoying having the world to myself and thinking about the day that we had ahead of us on the boat and the luxurious cobalt blue waters we'd soon be snorkelling in together. Life seemed good. I got to the drain moments later. It looked exactly how I'd left it the night before. The kitten's food bowls, one empty and the other half full of water still outside the grating; good, no one had taken them away. I knelt down so that I was eye level with the grating, making cooing sounds so that I wouldn't alarm the kitten by this very early visit as he slept curled up in his little nest. I was not expecting to see what I found there.

I found nothing. It was empty. Absolutely no sign of the kitten. My eyes couldn't quite take in what I was seeing and I had to blink several times; then my brain told me that it was no good, there's nothing wrong with your eyes, there really is no kitten there. I was aghast at this realisation. It had never ever, not once, been empty whenever I'd visited the kitten. Horror-struck I just stared at the empty nest of twigs, dust and gravel, almost willing my eyes to have deceived me and my addled brain to be playing tricks. But no, it was all terribly real and with my heart in my mouth I now just didn't know what I should do. Where on earth had he gone, and what had happened to him? The latter probably being more crucial than the former question my mind was asking me.

'No! Not now!' I cried out in anguish and despair. I was getting pins and needles crouched so low so I had to stand up and then staggered about as getting up too quickly had made me dizzy, plus I couldn't feel my feet now. I tried to steady myself and take proper stock of the situation, trying to gain some sort of semblance of ordered thoughts. I scanned the immediate surroundings but I already knew he wouldn't be anywhere to be seen. Are you really going to give up hope that easily? I asked myself. I tried calling out for him, but him not having a name wasn't helpful so all I could do was call out pitifully:

"Puss! Puss-puss, where are you? Puss-puss come on!"

My voice sounded hollow and bleak as it was obvious that he was nowhere close enough to hear me in the immediate vicinity. It all looked pretty hopeless then. Oh my God, I thought to myself. He can't possibly have run away, not now of all times. It was too much to take on board and I felt physically sick. My eyes were welling up at the thought of never seeing him again and the sheer cruel bad luck that we'd been nearly there with taking him away from this God-forsaken place. And now he'd just vanished. This was a hopeless situation to be in, and Sod's Law it would have to be now, of all times. I suddenly remembered the noises that I'd heard in the night and my unease I'd felt but hadn't been able to put my finger on exactly why. Could he have been hounded out of his nest, hunted down and been killed? It was all too awful to contemplate so I gathered myself up and tried to work out what I should do next.

If those bangs and thumps in the night hadn't been responsible for his disappearance, then perhaps a dog had eventually been able to get at the kitten. No, I couldn't go down either of those two paths yet, I just had to stay positive. Difficult. I had to start looking for him slightly further afield as he obviously wasn't anywhere near as he would have come to me when I'd called him, surely? I started a local search; part of me dreaded finding any scraps of white fur or anything else that might have remained to prove his once existence, the other part was ever hopeful that he'd suddenly turn up looking quite cool and unabashed.

However, I couldn't stop the feeling of fear and panic rising up in me and threatening to literally knock me back down onto my knees. I wanted to howl like a small child just then, at the unfairness and callousness of life. This was no good, I had to keep optimistic and proactive. In the drain itself there seemed to be no evidence of any sort of struggle or encounter with another animal – man or beast. No scraps of fur or anything to say that there had been any violence here, God forbid. There was nothing here to suggest that he'd been attacked so that was all good; so far anyway.

I kept walking further and further afield, going round in an arc. I must have covered at least half a mile around where he might have gone off adventuring. Nothing, I drew a complete blank. Feeling now that the situation was hopeless and that I was helpless I walked slowly back to the drain, heavy hearted knowing that it would still be empty. Too much to hope for that he'd slunk back inside the grate, while my back had been turned looking for him. Nonetheless, I still knelt back down again just in case a miracle had happened in my absence, but it was exactly the same as when I'd left it not half an hour ago. It was still empty, and despite the heat starting to warm the day up, it looked cold and deathly devoid of that little scrap of a kitten. A little ginger and white kitten whose life we had nearly saved.

As if my brain had decided to shield out this misery, it went into autopilot as I found myself putting down fresh food and water for him. This was my vain attempt of (1) not willing to accept the situation and (2) thinking that perhaps he might somehow scent the cat food and come back to the drain. A desperate measure I know, but I had to try something. Anything.

I wondered whether the kitten might just have got tired of his drain and naturally wandered off to find another place to bed down. At such a loss of what more I could do I looked at my watch and realised that I had to leave now. I didn't want to, and had we not had that blasted day trip planned I would have quite happily (or unhappily as the case maybe), stayed around until I'd found the little mite. But now I did have to go back and get Lucy up in order to be ready for the boat trip.

"Damn it all!" I thought as I hurried back at a run to the hotel, trying to fight back the tears.

If only I'd done what Lucy had suggested last night and taken the kitten back to our room then and there, we might not be in this sorry mess. I was convinced that was exactly what we should have done, it made sense now. In hind-sight I was sure that we would have been able to conceal him but we all know what hindsight is. 'If only' and 'too late' really are the saddest words, and this morning they weighed even more heavily.

Back at the room Lucy was already up and showered and ready for breakfast. I had to remain calm about the mysterious disappearance and try not to alarm her. My appetite had completely disappeared by the time we got into the restaurant and all I could manage now was a cup of strong coffee. I told Lucy that I hadn't been able to find the kitten this morning, pretending that I thought he'd probably got up earlier than us and found a tasty morsel somewhere else. Some of the story might have been plausible, in that I'd appeared at the drain this morning way earlier than I had ever been and who knows, maybe he'd always gone walkabouts at that time of morning only to return later already knowing by now when I would normally appear on the scene. But if that was the case, I *had* stayed on well into our usual 'time slot' in the end, and he still hadn't returned.

My story sounded unconvincing and highly unlikely of course, as I couldn't keep the tremor out of my voice this time. Of all the mornings to go AWOL. I think if I'd been on my own then I would have had no qualms in cancelling the boat trip only to spend all day searching the area for the kitten until I'd found him; or at least understood where and what had happened to him. I couldn't do that to Lucy though. She would have been really upset to miss the trip, despite the fact that she was also just as concerned that there had been no sign of the kitten.

Chapter 16

We finished the gloomy affair that breakfast had turned into (which was my fault because I just couldn't conceal my feelings, even for Lucy's sake, which in turn made me feel even worse). The bus was due to pick us up at the bus stop at 8am. We still had half an hour still on our hands, so we decided to have one more search for the kitten. We made our way back to the drain which was luckily on our way to the bus stop. Again, that empty feeling as I spied the even emptier drain, bereft of the tiny little white and ginger kitten who had, up until last night, always lived there.

The thoroughfare was busier now as it truly was the beginning of just another day to the rest of the world. Mopeds passed us and early beach-goers with towels slung over their shoulders and lilos under their arms making their way to the beach. If only I could have been that carefree at that moment. Lost in my sorry mood and deep, sad thoughts, I was jolted back to the present as Lucy suddenly grabbed my arm and said:

"Mum look! Over by that hotel!" I turned to where Lucy was staring and pointing excitingly at.

It was at the frontage of the Sea Bird Hotel. I looked closer and then there in the bushes I spied the kitten. He was sitting crouched low and quite still, the sun dappling his coat through the leaves of the bush and thus exceedingly well camouflaged against the shrubbery. In fact, Lucy did well to spot him at all. My heart leapt, and I shrieked out loud. The kitten heard me then and got up and ran over to greet us, rubbing his ears against my legs by way of a welcome. It was the warmest of welcomes, as if he was being reunited with people he knew and loved too I think.

The relief that he was safe and well was overwhelming and, as I scooped him up in my arms, laughing and crying at the same time, I gave him a friendly telling-off for scaring us both. Luckily I had got used to travelling around with a spare cat food sachet in my bag so I took the kitten, still in my arms, over to the drain. I handed him over to Lucy who took over the cuddles and friendly, loving scoldings whilst I tore open the wet food sachet and filled another food dish. The previous dish that I had put down I noticed had already been emptied, by whom or by what I would never know. We couldn't stay long enough to watch the kitten completely finish his breakfast but as we left him to continue our walk to the bus stop he was still busy eating away.

Boarding the bus, which arrived just before 8am, I started to feel a sense of elation and a calm had started to settle in all of me; my stomach, my heart and my head. The initial shock of finding him missing this morning however would take a long time to process in my mind, I knew that much, but knowing he was safe and well was enough to send us away happily on the bus to the harbour. More than enough. The bus pulled out into the increasing traffic that was building up in the road and with one glance back towards the drain, which was well out of sight, we went on our way. Thankful to the gods, the angels, literally everyone and anyone above that was looking out for us and the kitten. I was once again finding equilibrium. Only one more day to go, and then off to the safety of The Ark.

* * *

An hour or so later saw us boarding the boat for the second time this holiday, sea-bound to Paxos and Antipaxos. The boat wasn't nearly as busy as it had been on our first voyage. Also, with us being quite experienced Glaswegian/Corfu sea-faring folk by now, we knew exactly where the best seats were in order to get the best views.

On our outward journey we had the best vantage point to take in Old Corfu Town, with its forts and the bays as we gently drifted out to sea. The sea pennies danced on the surface of the blue water making us squint against the dazzling spectacle, despite wearing sunglasses. It made the sea look as if it was literally boiling like water in a pan on the hob as it bubbled and glistened all around us against the heat haze. The breeze was cooling but I was wary of the sun's power to really speed up sun-burn. We were both plastered in factor 50 sun cream and wearing hats too so I felt pretty safe under the sun's glare.

Such peace did I feel as the boat rose and fell gently, giving me the feeling of butterflies in the very pit of my stomach. I regretted now, not having eaten at breakfast, but looking back, things had been so different then. I had been a completely different person, or so it felt like. I kept thinking over and over again: 'He came back. He's safe', and in my mind's eye I could see him again when he'd suddenly recognised Lucy and I from across the way and came running towards us. Unscathed, unhurt, and also quite unaware that he had caused us both such angst, as well as being ravenously hungry for breakfast. I still wondered what had made him leave the safety of his drain so early but there, no one would ever fathom these creatures. No one would ever know what these felines got up to, or thought. That's why we love them so, and all the more for it. The mysterious and enigmatic Cat. Cause of worry, stress, real fear sometimes, and yet when they suddenly turn up as if nothing had happened, we always forgive. Of course we'd forgive a cat anything. We might secretly or mildly admonish but that's all. Then it will happen all over again and us humans, us 'Slaves to The Paw' will repeat the whole damn cycle of anxiety, whilst The Cat will just continue to be The Cat.

And so we drifted languidly on. When we reached the Blue Caves the boat came to a slow gentle halt. The engine was switched off and all was deliciously silent as we bobbed up and down, taking in the momentous view. I could never get tired of this splendour and natural beauty I realised. Because there were only a handful of tourists on the boat this time, voices were quieter, as tends to happen when humans are not en masse, as if they were too shy to speak in front of so few, conspicuous by their limited number. There was just a hushed, almost reverential silence as everyone gazed in awe at these quite magical caves. Lucy and I and a handful of others, started to take our outer layers off so that we could take advantage of one of the best snorkelling waters for many miles. Down the little boat ladder we all climbed and swam a little way from the craft and the shadow it cast. Once again, lying on the surface with our faces submerged we were plunged into a nether-world, the myriad colourful creatures astonishing us as we entered, quite uninvited but seemingly welcome, their kingdom under the sea. Floating there in those crystal clear waters the minutes must have passed like seconds and so subsequently we lost all track of time.

Suddenly I realised that it was only Lucy and I left in the sea; everyone else had clambered back on board the boat. The driver of the boat was looking down at us, half amused, half impatient I think, but laughed as we hastily swam back to the boat a little embarrassed. We hoisted ourselves back up the ladder, quite breathless, and the driver patted me quite jovially on the shoulder; we had been completely forgiven, I realised that at once, so it was no matter. He started up the engine and as it roared into life we could see some of the little fishes in the clear sea just dart and vanish for cover as we started to move.

It wasn't at all long until the familiar little docking bay of Paxos was in sight. The boat rocked gently as it pulled into the harbour and as we gathered our bags and moved into the queue to disembark, it suddenly hit me how time was flying by now. This would be our final visit to this pretty little island, and when we re-boarded the boat later on it really would be a homeward journey, in all senses of the word from now on.

Already there were people sat at tables outside the numerous bars and cafés that lined the route up into the small town. People were drinking coffees, frappés and cold drinks, and the glorious smell of food being cooked over charcoal was tantalising. Everywhere had the feeling of relaxation, of troubles left behind and I for one felt a part of all this joie de vivre, at last. A great sensation of joy was settling inside me; of optimism, achievement; that everything was going to be alright. I also had the strangest feeling of having actually just *arrived* on our holidays all over again, as if this was truly our first day, so light-hearted I felt. All that had gone before, the problems, the worries, they were all bound up in the past now and put to bed at last. Neatly, ordered and, just for now, compartmentalised. Today our holiday would really begin, albeit what was left of it, which was only two days. And so now to enjoy ourselves.

We walked on. Every now and then we would slow to look at the colourful displays of postcards and souvenirs on show outside the higgledy-piggledy assortment of shops. The sun was doing it's best to dazzle us, even with sunglasses on, but today it did not become a nuisance or a chore to have to keep stepping into the shade. All of a sudden I realised that we were at the pet shop that we had seen on our previous visit, and as we gazed through the window, I could feel a mounting excitement. At last we had a legitimate reason to purchase something very precious, and very special. A cat carrier. I smiled at Lucy and she, returning the smile, which really was ear to ear as we were both thinking the very same thing, we pushed open the door of the pet shop.

There was a certain feeling of both purpose and closure as we entered the dark and musky smelling building. The shop's owner, who was sitting perched on a stool behind a very cluttered counter, looked up as we approached her, and greeted us with an expectant smile. I pointed at a small cat carrier which was wedged on a shelf behind us and said we'd like to buy it. The lady behind the counter, small, dark and in her late sixties I imagined, continued to hold her smile as she came round to our side of the counter. Did I detect slightly quizzical eyebrows, or amusement, I wonder; I couldn't be completely sure that I hadn't. She politely waved us out of the way with her hand and clambered up on another stool which was there for the purpose, and reached for the cat carrier in question. She examined the carrier and in broken English told me the price, at the same time showing me the card with the price hand-written on it.

I nodded and said yes, I would like to buy it. Down she climbed from the high stool and then handed me the carrier once her feet touched the ground again. We followed her back to the counter where she rang in the price into what looked like an almost antique cash register. Taking my purse out of my bag I could feel the butterflies start dancing in my stomach, as who would have thought we would have ever reached this moment? I gave her the exact amount in euros, thanked her and trooped out of the shop with Lucy following. I wondered what the shopkeeper was thinking behind those still smiling eyes as she went back to her station perched on a stool behind the counter, without even looking up as we left the shop. Was she used to tourists coming in to purchase cat carriers I mused; having asked us no questions perhaps it was the case that nothing would surprise her about 'the crazy British'!

So, now we had a cat carrier to drag around with us for the next few hours in the merciless heat. Constantly banging against my legs every time we had to dodge on-coming pedestrians and the inconvenience of my rucksack strap continually slipping off one shoulder as I was walking lopsidedly trying to keep the cat carrier from scraping the ground. Yet I couldn't have been happier! No doubt I cut a strange figure, as I lugged the carrier around with us looking as pleased as punch, and as proud and excited with our purchase, as if it was the crown jewels themselves, so careful was I with our new buy.

By now, Lucy and I were literally gasping for a cold drink and I was ravenously hungry. This wasn't surprising seeing as I hadn't had anything to eat since the evening before, all appetite suddenly leaving me earlier when I found the drain empty. We decided to make our way back to the bay and soon found exactly what we were looking for; a café which offered tables under the shade of pine trees.

I sat down thankfully, placing the cat carrier reverently down at my feet. A carrier that was soon to have a precious cargo in. A waiter (and a very good looking one at that who could have been George Michael's double) descended on us almost immediately and took our order. I had already had a quick scan of the menu board while we were taking our seats and so rattled off our order without any hesitation: coke cola, chips, salad and bougatsa. This last was a delicious sweet, which is a kind of Greek custard tart and very moreish indeed. My sugar levels needed boosting! Our gorgeous waiter nodded, gave us a dazzling smile and then walked off to another table to greet some customers he seemed to know and took their order. I couldn't take my eyes off him and Lucy just rolled her eyes and tutted, giving me one of her despairing looks as she plugged her ear phones into her phone to listen to music.

I sat back in my chair and idly people-watched in these very pleasant surroundings until our waiter appeared again with a tray laden with our savoury and sweet lunch. It smelled so good and, as I tucked into the chips two or three at a time, all good table manners went out of the window as I believe eating chips with your fingers is the only way to enjoy them. Lucy also delved into her bowl of salad and chips with great gusto, taking alternate mouthfuls of each and it was a very happy affair indeed. We ate in silence just letting the background chatter and bonhomie wash over us, each in our own little world and lost in thought. I knew we were both thinking and feeling the same things though, the feeling of how far we had come mingled with a certain peace and accomplishment.

Every now and then I could feel the eyes of those at neighbouring tables glance in our direction and then lower their gazes to the cat carrier firmly planted at my feet under the table. As it was so shaded there, it would have been impossible for anyone to see inside it and so no one would have been able to see whether it was inhabited or not. It soon would be though and I felt a tingle of excitement and pride at the very thought. And so we just left everyone guessing as we carried on nonchalantly with our meal, as though it was the most natural thing in the world to take a cat carrier out to lunch with one.

I was so lost in thought as I ate, just taking mouthful after mouthful of those wonderfully crispy on the outside and soft on the inside deep fried chips that Lucy and I might have been the only ones there, so little did we notice anyone and anything around us. Every now and then I'd take a forkful of salad, and just daydreamed. For once, I wasn't pondering on all the frantically troubled past that had gone before; instead my mind was picturing the evening ahead, when I finally used the cat carrier for its intended purpose. How would I be feeling then, as I undid the little door of the carrier and finally placed the kitten inside it. I thought of how I'd then lift the carrier up very gently and be able to feel a tiny little animal inside it at last. How would he react, scared? Would he panic and be stressed? We would of course be taking away his freedom, but only temporarily. Would he work against us, and become a little wild maybe if he suddenly felt trapped? Somehow I really couldn't picture him being at all difficult; he would be as gentle, trusting and obliging as he had always been I was sure of that.

Funnily enough, while my mind was working through all these future happenings, I did not feel that old, and very familiar feeling of restlessness and urgency of the need to keep doing more, threaten to take over this wonderful feeling of achievement. I was surprisingly quite content to just sit and savour each moment of our sweet success. All the loving help we had received from the Bob-page coming together to raise enough funds to get our kitten back to the UK. Wonderful Sonia in Jersey for offering this kitten a forever home and the Ark in the meantime agreeing to take him in and get him ready to leave the island of Corfu. I had this immense feeling of satisfaction. Now I just wanted to enjoy the build up to this remarkable and quite miraculous once-in-a-lifetime experience which was fast becoming a modern-day fairy tale that we had ahead of us. So who was I to want to rush these last few hours of this momentous and quite unbelievable journey?

I let my mind wonder and found myself thinking about all the recent posts on the Streetcat Bob page. I had had several private messages from Sonia and Lisa where we had been discussing the finer points of our rescue mission, now that enough, more than enough, funds had been raised for our kitten and his transfer to the UK. It seemed that money was still trickling into the Go Fund Me page which was quite overwhelming. I felt that I was suddenly establishing some very true and loyal friends here along the way and I had the kitten himself to thank for that. It seemed we were helping each other and I marvelled at how this was exactly the same principle and ethos that James and Bob had found themselves in. How fantastic that such a true story with its happy ending was about to spawn another one. It seemed to mirror the love shown between human and feline, and that symbiotic partnership was a real force to be reckoned with.

Now, if my eyes were starting to fill up then it was just through being overwhelmed with all these kind and hitherto unknown supporters having risen to the occasion and coming to the rescue of a stray kitten in another country, instigated by a complete stranger's cry for help. It wouldn't be until I had actually met up with Louisa from The Ark that I'd be able to discuss how we allocated the funds raised, and how we distributed it between vet's fees, passports and transport. I was confident however, that now I had the two sensible and clear thinking women, Sonia and Lisa on board, that between the four of us the path would be a lot smoother and straightforward, and myself a little bit more enlightened with how to proceed with the business-affairs of such a task.

I snapped back to the present as I realised that the café was beginning to fill up now and our table looked as though it was going to be needed. We had long finished our meal and so I caught the waiter's eye and signalled to him that I'd like to pay the bill. Lucy was ready to leave now; I could tell by her body language that she had enough of just sitting there watching her mother gazing into the middle distance, dreaming away.

I left the payment for our food in the dish that gallantly landed on our table and a tip for the very attentive and beautiful waiter. Standing up and reaching down for the cat carrier I could again see heads turn towards my booty, was there or wasn't there something inside? Soon, I thought to myself smugly. Very, very soon. We left the café and everyone there guessing. It was only a short walk to where our boat had been moored and already I could see it was being boarded so we tagged on the end of the little group of holiday makers. Again, the surreptitious glances at what I was carrying, which was not surprising seeing as when I'd previously left the boat, all I had then been carrying was a rucksack.

Nobody said anything about it to me and I wouldn't have known what to say anyway if anyone had ventured to ask why I had a cat carrier with me now. It would be forever shrouded in mystery and I often wonder to this day if our fellow passengers recount the tale to their friends and family about the strange lady they saw on their holidays with a cat carrier on board the boat!

Chapter 17

The journey back out to sea was peaceful and as we sat at the very top of the boat we watched Paxos diminish gradually, for the last time that holiday, until it became just a hazy blur in the late afternoon's heat. There was definitely a feeling of being homeward bound now, in all senses of the word. I closed my eyes against the sun as I leaned back in my seat, enjoying the feel of the sea spray on my face. I could hear a song being played on the radio and for a moment I just couldn't place it, although it sounded familiar enough. It seemed to take on the rhythm of the boat though as the music crescendoed and mirrored our movement up and down over the waves. Then it came to me. It was John Denver singing his *Calypso*.

It was the perfect soundtrack to our journey over the waves. As the music swelled and then came back to earth, so did the boat as it bounced over the surface of the blue, it's rhythm mimicking every subtle change of the musical notes. I will never forget this journey I thought to myself, and I knew that if and when I heard Calypso again, I would instantly be taken back here in my memory. It would be as vivid then as it was now, and I would be transported back to the sites, sounds and the smells of the boat ride from Paxos to Corfu; with a cat carrier at my feet on our way to collect our kitten.

We sailed on. It was hard to believe that it was Tuesday already and that this time in 48 hours we would probably be back home in Glasgow. There was so much that we had to make happen in those few hours for us and the kitten. I wondered what Louisa would be like when we finally met her face to face. We had arranged to meet at the Messonghi taxi rank tomorrow morning at 10am when I would be handing the kitten over to her. How strange that will feel, not only parting with him, but also handing over all responsibility when for the past couple of weeks or so he had been solely mine and Lucy's to keep fed, watered and loved. To be kept *alive,* more the point. It would only be a short walk for us from the hotel to our meeting point, only about five minutes and I knew it was going to be a momentous occasion, to put it mildly.

Louisa had sounded very kind on the phone, but also businesslike and almost brusque. It augured well. Of course it had to be like that; she would only do what was best for the animal, always having their best interests at heart and putting their needs first before anything else. She knew exactly what she was doing, and where I felt I lacked, well, I *knew* I lacked any experience of the deed ahead. I felt she would be the perfect knowledgeable guide. This was completely new territory for me, whereas she had done hand-overs and all the subsequent form filling many times before.

I sighed, and for the second time this holiday wished that Alan could have been with us. I tried to recall him as I had done a few days ago when I'd had that very vivid daydream about him. He had really seemed physically next to me then and I wanted to get that back. I wanted so much for him to just materialise like he had done in my imagination before, but this time it just wasn't happening. Maybe I was just trying too hard. Anyway, whatever the reason, I had my memories and his love and now it was time to stop daydreaming and really concentrate on the job soon to be in hand. The Great Kitten Rescue: a mission which we had chosen to accept quite readily. There were enough compassionate mortals helping me. As for Alan's ghost, I would just have to be content to have him visit me when I least expected it, as all ghosts do.

The sound of the boat's engine changing made me open my eyes and I squinted against the sun. We were already pulling up into the harbour, the journey back seeming to have passed by in mere minutes rather than a couple of hours. I had almost been on the point of dozing off as now I suddenly felt very tired indeed. Exhausted in fact. Strange, after having such an exciting and exhilarating day with a clear and happy conscience, but I suppose it had all just suddenly caught up with me at last. It seemed like it was a different day when the kitten had seemingly gone missing and was then luckily found again, but that particular adventure had only been this morning. Time was playing tricks.

Hauling myself up from my seat, Lucy followed me to the little steps that would take us down to harbour level. The water slapped against the boat's sides as it very gently rocked against its mooring and I thought, quite poignantly, that I would miss that sound. I never thought that I would be so filled with such fondness and heartfelt connection, not ever, about this holiday. An unforgettable one, yes, but not one to ever become sentimental about. I felt I was a different person from the one that had boarded the plane in Glasgow two weeks ago. If I could have a crystal ball, and gazed back then and been able to foresee how events would unfold for us, I wondered what I would have done, and how I would have felt.

I was stronger now, more confident, that's for sure. More resilient. Most of all though, because of all these compassionate people out there in *Bob the Big Issue Cat-land*, I felt part of a huge, albeit unknown family. It felt good, and if I might have felt just a little lonely and lost at the beginning of the holiday, then everyone I had met, both virtually and in person since, had more than made up for it by the end of it. And as I said, I felt I was a different person now. Lucy and I made our way to the bus stop where our bus was already waiting for us and found enough seats for the three of us, her, me and the cat carrier. The. Cat. Carrier. I suddenly froze to the spot, panic setting in and gasped. Lucy looked at me in surprise.

"Lucy! The Cat Carrier!"

I exclaimed frantically, trying to get her to understand, and not being able to keep the wild panic out of my voice now either. I went on.

"How are we going to get past the reception with that? We're going to have to hide it!'" Lucy then cottoned on to the whole situation, realisation flooding her worried face.

"But Mum, how? It's so big!"

"I haven't got a clue. Oh help!"

As the bus pulled out very suddenly into the road, it swung us and our belongings sideways. I had to grab the carrier quickly to stop it falling off its own personal seat. However, I didn't get to my bag in time and that did land upside down on the floor. I cursed the driver under my breath. Luckily most of the contents didn't fall out as I had earlier just rolled up very tightly and squashed the big beach towel on top of it, jamming all the bag's contents underneath. It was just the towel that I had to retrieve off the floor.

"Ahh! Yes!" I scooped it up and gave it a good shake, for the floor was none too clean. "It's a sign Lucy! We can wrap the carrier in this and smuggle it through the hotel that way."

I do believe in 'signs'. White feathers as messages from angels, and those strange little chances and coincidences that happen to us along the way. I was sure that it was Alan's friendly spirit that had prompted that particular item to fall out of my bag and present itself in this desperate hour of need.

"That's perfect Mum," Lucy squealed excitedly, the relief spreading all over her face.

This little episode had me wide awake by now, which was just as well because I really needed to keep my wits about me in future. We were so close to success and I couldn't let anything jeopardise our chances. I exhaled loudly with sheer and utter gratitude for the bus drivers of this world who saw fit to swing their buses about all over the place without a thought for their poor passengers and their wares. And also to a playful and friendly ghost? I wonder.

We composed ourselves again and a little while later were dropped off outside our hotel. Luckily we were the only Nasos Smartline guests on board the bus with no one else alighting here and so anyone that might have witnessed the earlier débâcle of the swift wrapping of the towel around the carrier was left behind on the bus to form their own conclusions. So far our secret was safe. However, I did need to stock up on cat food so we nipped back to the supermarket quickly. I had left Lucy outside with the strange bundle so that any attention to it would be minimised. I was having another of those, this-will-be-the-last-time-I-do-this, feelings. It crept up on me suddenly as I queued up to pay at the till. Not that I would miss this part too much, I thought to myself as I walked out of the supermarket to join Lucy again: the feeding of the kitten at the drain, and then later Misty on the balcony, always wondering and worrying about her too, as well as the kitten. Tonight would be the last time we walked down to the drain for the evening ritual of giving food, water and love to the little white and ginger baby that we had grown to love with such ferocity that it gnawed away at our very cores.

"Come on Lucy, let's go and show the kitten his new present." Lucy was excited at this prospect and told me she wondered what his reaction would be.

"Well we'll see tomorrow right enough; we'll just let him sniff it a little tonight. I'm sure he'll be fine."

Lucy nodded her head and said out loud what I had been thinking earlier.

"I can't believe it's his last night at the drain. Do you think it's gone quickly or slowly Mum?" She was in a pensive mood, I could tell that.

"Well I think that sometimes time's sped by and at other times it's gone really slowly. It's always like that though isn't it, when you look back at things" I replied, seeing her in profile as she walked next to me, looking happy and thoughtful at the same time.

What a dear, kind-hearted and brilliant young woman you are turning into, I thought to myself, and I realised that in the last two weeks, Lucy had suddenly grown up so much. Whether it was just a natural course or it had been exacerbated by all that had gone on, who knew. Whatever the reason, something had been a catalyst but I wasn't going to stand around questioning it. I was proud of her, oh so hugely proud of my incredible daughter

All of a sudden we were at the drain. I had been so wrapped up in my thoughts that I hadn't really been aware of our journey, being too busy reflecting I suppose. The kitten was tucked so far back into the drain that at first I couldn't see him, and my heart gave a silly sort of leap with that old familiar feeling of dread at finding the drain empty. He was so far back and in the shadows that we could have been forgiven for thinking that he wasn't there, when in fact he was.

Lucy called to him gently, and he woke, giving one luxurious stretch, yawned and crawled out into the still bright sunshine to say hello. She brushed some of the debris of dried twigs and dust from his coat with the back of her hand and he stood there enjoying the sensation of this impromptu massage. I was still carrying the cat carrier and so now I placed it slowly and quietly at my feet.

He ignored it completely, being far too interested in Lucy who was starting to rip open a food sachet. His little tail was quivering with delight and he seemed to rock unsteadily on all four legs now, as if he wasn't quite awake after all. He seemed so tiny and vulnerable just then, much more so than usual and I thanked his lucky stars that this would be his final night left alone under the stars. I prayed they'd be lucky anyway. I stroked him while he ate, which he never minded, just enjoying all the attention he got before, during and after his meal.

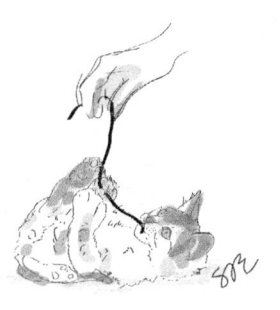

"One more sleep for you little fella", I murmured.

It was a serene moment just then as neither Lucy, nor I, felt like using our normal speaking voices. It was hushed and almost ceremonial this particular meal, and we were just enjoying watching him eat, both of us deep in contemplation. Once he'd finished his bowl, licking it clean one way then turning and licking it the other way, he sat back and washed his paws. Lucy tempted him with an old shoe lace she kept in her bag and he started to bat it playfully, rolling over onto his back exposing his little pot belly and kicking at the lace as Lucy dangled it over him.

He looked like all the playful kittens I had ever seen just then. Take away the Grecian background, the heat and the dust, and he could have been any other pampered kitten from home, the play was identical for kittens all over the world. Endearing, captivating and completely charming. Despite his grubbiness and his still sticky eyes and fairly crusted nostrils he played like a healthy spoiled and loved little kitten. Lucy would dangle the lace just out of reach above him, and he'd then sit back on his haunches and lunge at it, clasping it tight between his fore paws. Then she would let go and he'd start all over again, rolling over onto his back and kicking at it like a kitten possessed. It was good to see. He was going through the motions of playing and attacking prey and even if his mother had abandoned him quite young and not showing him how to hunt, his natural instinct to grab, claw, pounce and attack was inborn.

Meanwhile he still hadn't given the cat carrier a second glance, not even a sniff. And why should he have really, I supposed. My own cats at home flee at the very sight of it in the house, knowing that it spells entrapment and, more than likely, an imminent trip to the vets. Of course, our little kitten didn't know anything about all that; in fact he really didn't know anything at all for that matter. His existence was simplicity itself in that regard compared to our own pampered puss-cats. This suited us of course, as we both knew that it boded well for a smooth transition to the Ark tomorrow morning.

Lucy wanted to keep playing with the kitten but it really was time for us to head back to the hotel for our evening meal. It took us another ten minutes to finally say goodnight to the kitten because tonight, of course, it was a very special and meaningful parting. At last though, after we had put down more biscuits and water for him, and Lucy had reluctantly taken the shoelace away from him, he crept back into the safety of the drain. Playtime now over, and with a tummy full of food, he was a tired little kitten. He bedded himself down once again at the very back of his nest and now it really was time for the final goodnight and the penultimate goodbye. I gulped with the shock-horror realisation of this moment...that this really was it. We would never be able to say goodnight to him again. But that was the whole idea wasn't it? I chided myself?

I had always imagined that when the final moment came, as it had now, that it would be a joyous and celebratory occasion, the culmination of great and miraculous things having happened. I would be relieved that this was his final night when at last he had the safety of the Ark to go to and then a forever home waiting for him. But now it hit me that all these good things planned for his future were for a future which didn't include Lucy and I, in the practical sense that is. Hell! I thought. I had stupidly, naively forgotten how poignant and emotional this parting would be, and we still had the final one to go through tomorrow. It was more than I could bear to drag it out any further now so I had to shrug and bravely say to Lucy that it really *was* time to go now. Lucy seemed to cope with the business of saying goodnight better than I. I had to turn away quickly to hide the tears which were threatening to spill at any minute.

We walked back with no backward glance. I felt tired now, the cat carrier's handle feeling sticky with sweat and I could feel blisters forming where it had continually rubbed today as I had carried it around with me. Oh boy, did that seem a long time ago now when we'd first purchased it. I felt strangely irritable and quite fractious too, but I was just exhausted I suppose. I now took a firm line on my behaviour. I scolded myself for feeling so miserable. Stupid girl! I admonished. This is meant to be a glorious occasion, the happy ending that you have been praying for.

We Did It! For heaven's sake Bev, be happy!

This good talking to by my better self, seemed to do the trick and as we made our way back, passing the supermarket once again, I began to feel more positive and had put things into perspective. I was back to my practical self and thought for the second time that day that, although I'll miss the kitten, I wouldn't miss the constant worrying about him any more. Or Misty. Hang on a minute. In all the musings and ministrations at the drain wrapped up in all that self-pity and procrastination, I had temporarily forgotten about our other little friend, Misty.

I stopped dead, feeling suddenly pole-axed. Lucy turned to look at me and cried,

"Now what's wrong Mum?" I shook my head trying to regain control of my emotions once more and just quietly said:

"Lucy, let's see if The Ark will take Misty as well. I mean, how can we possibly leave her here?" She just continued to stare at me, and I could see her working things out in her mind. Then a sadness as she too had the same epiphany that I had just experienced.

"But Mum, she needs to have a proper home to go to, otherwise The Ark just won't take her. You told me that yourself. She hasn't *got* one has she, it's all so hopeless for her."

She looked miserable then as I felt about the whole situation. I let out a long deep sigh. I knew that all Lucy was saying was true; Louisa had indeed made it quite clear that she only took in animals as a temporary measure whilst the formalities were dealt with for their forever home. I suddenly realised that was exactly what we needed to do; we had to find someone who would give Misty a home as well. Wouldn't that be fantastic if both Misty and the kitten, because I was still convinced that she was the mother cat, could travel back to the UK together? Would it be too much to ask for help from the beautiful big hearted Bob fans I wondered. There was only one way to find out, and that was by putting the call-out. Again.

In the meantime however, we had still as yet to negotiate getting one very large cat carrier through the hotel to our room. I wondered what the penalties would be if they could have guessed our intentions. If I was stopped, how was I going to explain our mission and what would they think about my dealings with the Ark; how was I going to adequately explain *that*? Had I known then what I know now of course, that it was an acceptable practice for dogs and cats to be adopted from abroad then I might not have been so timid but I just didn't know this at the time. I didn't know anything. Was it a crime I wondered, taking a kitten off the streets when we were meant to be just tourists here on a simple holiday? I had learned by now that the hotel staff could be a bit hot-headed about their residents feeding the stray cats, and in my ignorance and naivety I firmly believed that we would have been thrown out of the hotel on our ears had they known what I was carrying in my arms, even though it was empty. Lucy broke into my thoughts and in a hushed voice said to me,

"Mum, we won't get into trouble with what we're going to do, will we?" Lucy was reading me like a book. She went on, "I mean, it is alright to help the animals isn't it?"

Yes, it's all quite ludicrous looking back when I think about it now, but at the time, such was the extent of my guilty conscience and paranoia that I thought we might seriously be contravening some strange law that Corfu had in place that I wasn't aware of. We had to be bold and make our move. Lucy had handed me back the carrier by now and with my rucksack draped casually over the top of a now square and bulging towel concealing the carrier, we managed to sneak through the reception area without anyone noticing our odd-shaped goods that we were carrying. I tried to keep a nonchalant expression on my face, which wasn't easy because my conscience was pricking me, but with Lucy walking just about level with me holding her rucksack in her arms and trying to conceal as much of what I was carrying as possible, it worked. Not one person looked up as we passed the front desk in the foyer fully laden with a somewhat large and mysterious object and anyway, it would only be natural for guests to make big purchases of gifts and the like when nearing the end of their holidays to take back home to family and friends. Although perhaps not a cat carrier.

Chapter 18

We arrived back at our room and once we were safely inside both breathed a sigh of relief. I had been holding my breath all throughout our passage and now, with the door firmly closed behind us, I knew that I'd never make a good burglar – or cat-burglar even. You'd need nerves of steel. Although actually I wasn't taking anything away from the hotel; rather my intentions were to add, but this was just as contraband. I placed the carrier on the bed, taking the towel off it in one swift move in the same way a magician might perform the great reveal at the end of a trick.

"Ta-dah!" I laughed, as Lucy looked on, seemingly unimpressed.

"Phew Mum! That was scary, I thought we were going to be stopped any minute."

She flopped down on her bed and started kicking off her sandals. I was hungry again by now so I chivvied Lucy into action before she got too comfy and back we went to the restaurant. It didn't seem as busy tonight as it usually was at this time, maybe because it was nearing the end of the holiday fortnight for a lot of the package guests, and they had decided to dine out in the town. We lingered at the buffet counter, piling our plates high with all sorts of tasty fare which was definitely more in abundance tonight, some dishes so beautifully prepared and as yet untouched as so few of the guests were eating in.

I will miss this nightly feast I thought to myself, as I helped myself to the ever present olives and feta salads, the locally grown lush plump tomatoes and all the different cold meats. Despite the other shortcomings here, not least the hotel's attitude towards cats, we had actually been very well looked after by the hotel. The staff, especially in the restaurant, were always pleasant, and gave us first-class courteous service, and the building itself was very clean, bright and colourfully modern. It had been nice not to have had to make the meals for the last couple of weeks, to not have to do the shopping and continually have to plan ahead and think of something new and different to cook every night. Although having said that, I'd certainly spent much of our holiday in supermarkets choosing what to dish up to the local feline residents. It *was* possible that I had actually spent as much time and devotion in deliberating over their next meal, despite the scant selection, as I would have done at home for mine and Lucy's. I was doing that gazing into the middle distance again when I suddenly realised that I was being spoken to, and it wasn't by Lucy.

"Excuse me Madam, may I speak with you please for one moment?"

It was the lady from the reception desk. Now, because I don't think that I'd completely managed to shake off the guilty feelings of earlier over bringing a cat carrier into the hotel, I felt as if someone had suddenly put ice cubes down my back. I was rooted to the spot and I could feel my heart starting to race, my face turning red and the thrumming of blood pounding in my ears. The look of fear and guilt on my face must have been so patently obvious. I couldn't find my natural voice at first but eventually managed to stammer out an 'Er, yes?' My tongue and mouth felt dry and I felt paralysed, like a bunny in the headlights and unable to move.

Her whole stance just felt confrontational and it seemed an age until she replied, and now it felt as if the scant few guests at dinner had suddenly stopped eating, had put down their knives and forks and were avidly watching the whole conversation take place. She eventually cleared her throat and continued with what she had appeared to be collaring me for. She looked so stern.

"I have received some information."

Yes, she was definitely stern. I could feel the blood hammering around my body and in my head it started to pulse and pound, threatening to break into an instant migraine at any moment. I swallowed hard, the panic taking a real hold on me now and nearly strangling me. I stood there motionless, caught-out, my palms sweating as I was still trying to hold my very overfilled plate of food, all appetite having left by now and a feeling of nausea creeping through me. She made me feel helpless and exposed, vulnerable and ashamed. My imagination was running riot remembering everything we had done. All that work that we had accomplished, and all those trips to and from the drain, the calls to the charities, the hundreds of people donating to our cause, the home in Jersey. All a complete waste of time and energy. I couldn't speak now. All I could do was stammer out another 'Uh-huh?' Still the stern-like expression, austere and unforgiving and coldly businesslike with her matter of fact accusatory voice and posture. She had more to say it would seem.

"I saw you going to your room. I try to stop you but no you keep walking. You do not hear me."

I felt like a petty criminal. I wanted to put my hands up in supplication and didn't dare try to catch Lucy's eye for I was far too terrified to see her expression. And still I couldn't speak properly, but just stuttered 'Oh?' with a very thin voice.

"Yes, I try to stop you and you walk away quickly. Too quickly for me." She paused for a moment and then she laughed.

"Why is that, I wondered? Then I see you have much to carry and you do not listen and go on!"

Hats off to her, she was really spinning this one out now. Oh please, I thought, just spit it out. Please just put me out of my misery and stop these shenanigans. Get on with it woman! OK, I admit it, I've done wrong, well, about to, I've broken the rules (*were* there rules?), but I'm just trying to save a kitten's life. What's so wrong with that? Tell me! What is so very wrong with that? These were all unspoken thoughts of course, and I could feel a pain in my temples now from clenching my teeth together so hard, my neck muscles tightening and my jaw aching from feeling so locked. I could have cried. I *wanted* to cry. But suddenly I just felt too tired to care. It wouldn't have made a difference anyway whether I cried or not, the result was still going to be the same. A death penalty for the kitten; and for us? Most likely relegated to perhaps a hostel tonight. If we were lucky. But hang it all! It's not as if we had actually smuggled in the kitten himself! All these thoughts, the dialogues and the scenarios that I was playing out in my head were just synaptic microseconds of course. In real time they had taken no time at all. I waited for the sledge hammer blow. It finally came.

"There have been slight changes to your departure time." Ms Stern informed me. Oh well, nicely put. You are so witty, we'll leave now then shall we? Is that what you mean? Out with it damn you! Again, synapses fired out my unspoken retorts.

"But do not worry. Still you will be in plenty time for your flight to the United Kingdom. The bus will just leave at an earlier time but has now to make extra stop on way to airport." She smiled, her mission accomplished, the great missive having been successfully delivered.

I wasn't sure what she meant.

"What?" I managed to squeak, holding my breath, still not quite believing that I might have got her all wrong. I wasn't sure of myself or anything just then. "What does all that mean then?" I asked.

She looked at me almost kindly, and spoke to me now as if I was the strangest and possibly the dimmest person she had ever had the misfortune in her line of duty to meet.

"Your new departure time is on the notice board in the reception. Please take time to read it."

She held her smile still as she gazed at me, then turned round and, with her back ramrod-straight, marched back to the front desk.

I'm sure she was by now feeling quite sorry for me, as if I wasn't quite right in the head and obviously the sort of tourist that needed things explained in loud, capital letters. It was too laughable for words really, although at that moment I didn't know whether I should be laughing or crying. The mounting hysteria of earlier now quashed in its prime suddenly had nowhere to go. Breathless wasn't the word; I wanted to vent steam out of the top of my head, if my cranium could have just opened up to do the job. Fireworks seeing in the New Year on the London Embankment would have been a poor show by comparison.

Apart from feeling like I'd gone through a mangle, been thoroughly chewed up and turned inside out with all that rising panic and self-condemnation, it had all been quite imaginary on my part. It was as if I'd learned the lines for a play only to find I was on stage but in the wrong production. I cannot tell you how long I stood there afterwards, watching her retreat. Perhaps it hadn't quite sunk in yet because as I stood there motionless still it was as if I was waiting for her to turn round in a sort of grim film-noire way and tell us to get out!' Stupid I know and why would she do that anyway? But she didn't of course, and all of a sudden we were back to where we had been five minutes earlier, in the normality of the restaurant, the other guests seemingly unaware of the earlier dramatic interlude. In my fevered imagination we had been playing to a fascinated audience but at last I was coming back down to earth, and back to the present. The gentle chink-chink of cutlery sounds, murmured conversation at tables and glasses being clinked together was reassuring, and like coming out of a strange dream. It had all been quite surreal but gradually everything around me was taking shape and form again. Lucy looked all done-in now and although the colour was returning to her cheeks, she too had gone a deathly pale. Finally, she spoke at last, hushed and still scared.

"Mum, I feel a bit sick." I put my arm around her.

"Do you really, or is it just the shock, do you think? Do you want to go back to the room?" She shook her head.

"No, I think I'll be alright, I just need to sit down. I don't want my supper though." She was looking less ashen now. I felt the same really, although I could feel some of my old self coming back.

"Come on," I said to her, "let's go and sit at that nice table over there in the far corner by the window and take our plates and I'm sure we'll feel hungry in a little while." So that's what we did and sure enough, as we regained our equilibrium once again we were indeed able to start picking at our still laden plates.

A quarter of an hour later these were surprisingly clean. We'd resumed the Status Quo and it was Lucy who got up first to help herself to the desserts. Our original lack of appetite had now been replaced by a renewed feeling of being ravenous. I think all that adrenalin we had used in the earlier confrontation had consumed a lot of energy, so now we more than made up for it. We needed to in fact as we had drained all our resources. It was by now half past eight in the evening. Lucy, I could tell, was fading fast from both exhaustion and, unusual for her, her sheer indulgence at dinner. Having gone from not being hungry at all to eventually demolishing a huge first course (albeit a meat-free one), and then gone back twice for pudding, she was by now fully sated, as I was too, and so we fairly stumbled back to our room. Lucy lay on her bed having at last the opportunity to finally kick off her sandals and just relax. She did look happy as I stole a glance in her direction, plugged into her iPod listening to whatever her favourite music happened to be (which did change on a daily basis), her eyes open but with a far away look in them.

As for me though, I had a strange feeling which was stirring up inside, which had been fighting the battle of tiredness and won, and a new sensation had taken over. I couldn't put my finger on it exactly, but I just had a sense of bristling energy, of agitation bubbling away and to put it bluntly, it was making me feel fired and totally wired. It was all about the kitten. I just suddenly got a kind of stubborn wilfulness in me, call it what you will, but I had to go and do something important. I had to go and bring the kitten back here. The weight of responsibility of collecting and taking the kitten to meet Louisa on the morrow was making its presence felt more so than ever now, you see. In the last couple of days I had been chatting to Sonia, the lady who was giving the kitten his forever home. We had just been messaging each other and firming up the arrangements for him. She had already been in touch with Louisa to assure her that she was indeed organising his onward journey after his temporary stay at the Ark.

Sonia had sent me pictures of her own cats at her wonderful looking home in Jersey and had told me all about where she lived and the freedom and safety that the new arrival from Corfu had to look forward to. Through our messages, I could tell that she was an extremely warm, kind-hearted and compassionate lady and immensely excited about giving the kitten a home. She had certainly done her homework about what she needed to do from her angle and although she'd come up against a few headaches and gone down a few blind alleys on the transport side of things, she was indeed making incredibly good progress now with the logistical planning of the operation. So much so that she had set up a special Facebook page called 'Corfu Kitten to the UK'.

Between us all, we were able to keep everyone who had donated and joined the page up to speed on what was happening, almost on an hour by hour basis. It felt incredible, almost inconceivable, that more members were joining all the time and genuinely wanted to help in whatever way they could with the safe transfer of the Corfu Kitty. Little did this little scrap of fur know what was happening on his behalf. Thinking about this I gave a rueful smile. The Go Fund Me page was still climbing and although we had exceeded our target we had agreed that any surplus funds should go directly to the Ark to help secure their future in helping animals on the island.

Lisa was proving to be the most brilliant business woman managing the crowd funding; I was bamboozled and struck dumb with the legalities of it all but between her and Sonia, they were trail-blazing alright, moving things along for the kitten. I'd had theirs and our Corfu Kitty members' support 24/7 ever since; and now the kitten's final few hours at the drain was my full responsibility until being taken to a place of safety. My thoughts were also harking back to that dreadful morning when on my arrival early at the drain the kitten had been nowhere to be seen. The panic and desperation then was something I just did not, *could not* risk. This seemed much more detrimental now more than ever, the earlier contretemps and my feelings then, when I thought we'd been found out, paled into significance. It made me feel cold all over. Supposing, just supposing I found the drain empty tomorrow morning I thought to myself? It was all in my hands now, and my hands only; I was fully responsible for him and the successful handover tomorrow morning. Yup, it all depended on me. I felt I was on a precipice; this was a pivotal moment. The time to act was now, not another minute could be wasted just thinking and ruminating about it all.

Now, you may be thinking, and quite rightly too, that after all the earlier panic and fright that my guilty conscience had stirred up by smuggling an empty cat carrier into the hotel and consequently what I had put ourselves through, that to go and bring the kitten back here would be the last thing on my mind. Hell no, not now, not after all that soul-searching harking back and dwelling on things. Yes, I'd had a complete shake up and scare, but now putting it all into perspective, the pros and cons and the risk of not finding him at the drain tomorrow morning, well, I was feeling quite bold. Bold enough to do exactly what I *thought* I had to do. A cliché kept going over and over in my head, about lightning not striking twice in the same place. Hmmm, I wondered, but it was too late now, the seeds had been sewn. I had the devil in me and as I say was feeling bold, very bold indeed. Stupid and foolhardy? Quite possibly.

"But lightning doesn't strike twice," I said, reasoning with myself. The words felt, tasted even, good to say out loud and I felt another frisson of excitement and, I admit it, a sense of daring surge through me. Wired and fired indeed. Lucy, still on the bed, propped herself up on to her elbows and looked my way, puzzled.

"What Mum?" I hadn't realised that she had taken her earphones out by now and was watching me closely, trying to define my expression.

"Huh?" I answered, realising that she'd heard me rattling away to myself.

"Nothing. Well...something," I murmured knowing that my answer just wasn't going to be a good enough explanation for my intrigued daughter. Should I or shouldn't I? I paused. Sheer devilment got the better of me then.

"I've just *got* to go and bring the kitten back here. Now! This very minute!"

She looked back at me in wide eyed amazement, speechless. Good, because I didn't want to discuss it further, and nor did I have time to because I needed to act fast before I lost my nerve, and my belief in the foibles of where lightning does and doesn't strike.

"Seriously?" She asked incredulous.

Lucy watched me intently while I bundled my string mesh bag into my haversack. I was fully expecting her to continue with protests because of our imagined run-in with the front desk lady earlier, but she didn't, she remained silent. I didn't want to be told I was mad, or scolded by my daughter for taking such a huge risk after what I'd put her through this afternoon. After all, I was meant to be setting an example. I was meant to be a responsible parent and here I was about to take the biggest risk of all, and doing exactly what I'd said we mustn't do earlier. I concentrated on the job in hand with the packing of the bag in silence. I couldn't make eye contact with her just then, feeling mildly sheepish but at the same time still very determined. I could still feel Lucy's eyes on me, watching me closely as if she was waiting for me to say something, at least.

I looked up at her at last. I couldn't really read her expression just then. She was sitting fully upright on her bed by now, hands in her lap, her hair all tousled and tumbling over her shoulders. She was beautiful and adorable and I wanted to hug her and hold her close just then but I had to leave immediately before I started having second thoughts about my possibly foolish actions. I just didn't want to disappoint her at the same time as truth be told, I didn't really know *what* she must be thinking of me by now. I couldn't falter. I had to admit my fears.

"If I don't bring him back now, suppose he disappears overnight like he did before? It's too much to risk. He *has* to stay with us tonight."

I walked over to the door then turned round to look at Lucy. She was smiling.

"Good!" she said. So I had her complete approval. Of course I did; why did I ever doubt that I might not have. I opened the door and sketched a small wave but just as I was about to close the door she called out to me. I put my head around the door.

"I'm so proud of you Mum."

If I had needed a shove of encouragement now, that was the one I had been looking for, but really, I was seeking reassurance that my convictions were right. Relief flooded through me. I blew her a kiss and gently closed the door behind me and now I was truly on my way. I smiled to myself, not feeling at all sheepish any more in the eyes of my sensible daughter. Out in the corridor I was completely alone now, the hotel seemed very quiet but I guessed that was because the guests were still out on the town enjoying their last night here.

Chapter 19

Isn't it strange how life pans out I thought to myself. Here I was walking down to the drain for the second time that evening, when earlier I'd thought I'd never be doing that at night ever again. It just goes to show how things can suddenly change, I reflected, because had it not been for the earlier issues and then later the soul-searching about my responsibility of it hanging in the balance, then who knows I might not have been doing this. And now look at me! I giggled out loud just then, unsure whether I was quite possibly certifiable in this mission. But my motives were honest, I told myself. Yes, the whole set-up here was quite laughable with my skulking about the place and I was almost catatonic (no pun intended but a more suitable word I cannot think of), with excitement and confidence.

So I walked on. It wasn't quite dark yet, but daylight had given way to a beautiful twilight which settled over this strange, bewildering island. It felt romantic tonight. The warmth was still there, as I could feel it rising from the ground and radiating off the crumbly old walls that banked the pavement every so often. I could feel a little breeze too, and every now and then it would waft the earthy scents up to my nostrils. It was mingling with whatever the local tavernas were serving up to their al fresco diners, and it was utterly divine. I caught the vibe of this serene and exotic atmosphere tonight and it filled me with a stab of pure happiness. Not a euphoric, ecstatic sort of sensation but, more in an inner sense of completeness and contentment.

I asked myself the question: was that all down to the earlier fright and then flood of relief? Had some weird endorphins been released as a reaction to all that emotion and rush of adrenalin? Because if so I decided, I like this feeling. Although I'd never want to repeat the earlier scenario in the dining room, I reminded myself about the risk of not finding the kitten in his rightful place in the morning and that would have far more disastrous consequences. So here I was doing something about it. Never mind the rules and regulations I might flagrantly be about to flout. Perhaps this is how criminals feel when they are complacent enough to think they'll never be caught and continue to take bigger and bigger risks. Oh stop it Bev! I told myself. You are *not* a criminal. I refused to go down that route, that way of thinking. I was happy and that's all there is to it. We will succeed. Positive feelings about things generate positive outcomes, I reminded myself. Wow, I was feeling super-charged and super-energised and if I could have bottled that feeling and taken it home with me, I could have made millions.

I was by now in sight of the drain and I could see our little fella actually sitting outside it. I wasn't exactly shaken at the sight but I was a little stirred I must say. It was just such a relief to think that had it been any other night on one of our usual night-time feeding forays, then I would have been filled with anxiety that he was so vulnerable outside. Tonight however I was extra, extra pleased to see him there because when I finally got to the drain it looked as if he had already been waiting for me to arrive, as if he'd somehow been able to tune in to my thoughts across the ether and knew I'd be coming for him, earlier than we'd both anticipated (had he anticipated?). He had got himself ready and was just waiting for me now, eager to start the beginning of his journey, in all senses of the word. My love for this little animal, and also for all the compassionate Corfu Kitten fans who had Go Funded us, flooded through my whole being at that moment. It was a very humbling feeling too.

Whereas in the past I hadn't wanted to attract anyone else's attention to the little kitten in case he was shooed away, I actually called out 'hello little one!' fairly loudly to him this time. I placed my bag on the ground as I drew level with the kitten and crouched down beside him. I would never ever forget this moment, I knew that for sure.

"Hey little guy, d'you fancy an adventure, yeah?" I gently teased him with the strap of my haversack as he proceeded to lie down and apparently want to play. I let him bat and tug at the bag for a little while then thought, right, it's now or never.

"Right little one, there's something you have to do for me. I'm not sure if you're going to like it but believe me, it's for your own good." I prized his little paws off the strap, he acquiesced and then I opened up the bag and got the mesh hold-all out.

"Here we go then little one."

I reached out for him and held him in my arms just to get him used to giving up his independence just ever so slightly. Then I took the bag in my other hand and opened it up for him to have a sniff at. He found it very interesting and then, in one fell swoop, I placed him inside it. Thinking that this was all part of a new game, he was quite content to just sit and find out what was going to happen next. The bag was large enough for him to have the freedom of movement and airy enough for him to see exactly what was going on around him and he didn't struggle in this strange new state of captivity. I grabbed my haversack off the ground and then with that over my shoulder stood up holding the kitten in the bag in the crook of my elbow. He was as light as the proverbial feather, and as mute as one too. I was completely upright by now, the strange sensation of actually holding the kitten with the intent purpose of taking him away from his hell-hole forever threatening to overflow and making me want to jump up, punch the air and shout with joy. Of course I couldn't do that right at this point in time and so I just had to keep my head. I had to try to be as nonchalant as possible, like this was an everyday occurrence, the most natural thing in the world. It was a hard emotion to keep in but needs must. He was at last coming back with me and he'd be sharing mine and Lucy's room for the night. I hoped that he would be quiet and I had a feeling that all was going to go swimmingly well from now on. My happy and positive epicentre was firing on all cylinders still and I must have been radiating good vibes as the kitten seemed content to snuggle down and close his eyes and doze off. I walked slowly so as not to make him, well, travel sick perhaps? I'd never carried a cat in a bag before so who was I to know how he was really feeling about it, apart from outwardly being fast asleep and not caring at all about this new and bizarre mode of transport.

It was the most beautiful and incredibly surreal walk that I think I have ever taken, or ever likely to take probably. Just me and the kitten, him not knowing where he was going or what was happening to him and putting his complete trust in me, and me in a trance-like bubble of excitement and walking on air. Foolhardy, after the events of earlier? Not a bit of it; in fact it never even entered my thoughts, which for me as a self-confessed worry-wart is really saying something.

The kitten nestled safely and warmly in my arms in his little mesh hideaway bag. The holes in it were large enough for one little front paw to dangle through it as I held him close and still no signs of any struggles or whimpering with fright. I held him up closer to my ear and could just make out a tiny purr despite him seemingly being fast asleep. Being so incredibly tiny I was able to hide him very well. Nobody would have noticed a little ginger and white kitten stowed away in a bag as I neared the hotel, but now I stopped and completed the last part of the subterfuge. Luckily there was no one in the hotel grounds at this time, and so all I had left to do was to place the kitten very gently, whilst still in his sleepy mesh cocoon, in the fold of my haversack. He made no attempt to struggle after I'd disturbed him in his sleepy state, and I wondered what sort of dreams he must have been having to keep him so peaceful and blissfully unaware of his relocation.

He settled very nicely into the bigger bag now that it had been folded over to completely conceal him and so I made my move and entered through the main hotel doors into the reception, praying that he would stay silent. It occurred to me then that for as long as I'd known him, neither Lucy nor I, had actually heard him meow much, if at all. The only sounds he'd made was his mighty rattling purr.

So far so good I thought to myself as I walked through the reception area. It was completely empty and devoid of anything human, except for myself. I was still holding my breath however and cautiously gave the office door behind the reception desk a wide berth in case someone should suddenly burst forth from it. Not at this time of night though I reminded myself but I still had to be very careful indeed. As I walked past this potential danger zone I pretended to be busy with the haversack straps, as if I was having trouble with the clasps in some way, so I would appear intent on mending the bag that I was carrying. I let part of the haversack kind of flop over my arms as if to prove there was absolutely nothing concealed within it, and painted a picture of innocence. I marched onwards to the room eyes down, still pretending to mend my wretched bag. I thoroughly deserved an Oscar for this because I started to believe that there really *was* something wrong with it by the time I got to the door of our room, so absorbed was I that I didn't even notice the door opening at first and Lucy popping her head out of it.

"Good timing!" I told her as at last I was able to fully exhale, leaning against the other side of the, by now, shut door.

"Oh my goodness Mum, he's here at last! And I was getting so worried, you seemed to have been gone for ages!" she whispered excitedly.

"Sorry darling, but I had to be very careful and not rush him. Actually he's been as good as gold, not a single mew or anything. He's as quiet as a mouse." Lucy laughed out loud then at the ambiguity of that last statement.

"So you didn't let the cat out of the bag then? Ha ha!" This attempt at a joke was good to hear coming from Lucy, as any worries she'd had earlier about our longer than usual absence were now completely forgotten.

I removed the haversack from underneath the kitten who was now waking up and, as I could see through the mesh, was clearly taking stock of his new environment. Very gently I handed him over to Lucy, still in the bag, and she placed him on my bed and allowed him to free himself of his own accord from it. He was quite unphased by his journey and relocation, and had it not been for the fact he was obviously still very pleased to be with us and purring away, I might have been worried about his quiet and trouble-free transfer. But no, and now here he was padding away at an old fleece hoodie I'd left lying on my bed, in that lovely way cats do, all four feet massaging and gripping it and obviously enjoying the texture between his feet and claws.

At the same time he really did seem to be blinking in disbelief at this new state of affairs, of comfort and quiet, but I realised too that his blinking was also to do with the fact that his eyes were very gummy and sticky indeed. They'd turned to slits in his reverie of kneading the fleece but they really didn't seem to be opening much wider now that he'd tired of that particular comfort and wanted to explore the rest of the bed.

Lucy was in absolute raptures over him, fussing and stroking him and talking to him in a gentle cooing voice, as I was too, but now I had to be a bit sensible and make plans for the next few hours. Firstly, I realised that he really did smell very bad indeed in this enclosed room. At the drain we had never really noticed his pong, what with all the other outdoor scents vying for attention all the time; the smells then had been such a heady mix of hot tar, sizzling food, charcoal and diesel in equal amounts that it masked our little friend here's particular odour well. Now it was patently obvious that I needed to do something about it, if we were to live harmoniously together for the foreseeable next few hours. It was a struggle but I did have to tear myself away from him, get up from the bed and tell Lucy that I thought it might be a good idea to give him a bath.

"He'll be fine in the washbasin, he's so small...in fact I better put a plug in it," I told her jokingly.

"Yes, we don't want you disappearing down it now, do we, not now that we've got you here at last!" Lucy told the kitten, giggling and cooing at him still and pretending to hold her nose whenever he came close to her.

By now they were playing a game where he'd pounce on her hands wriggling under my (poor long suffering) hoodie and when he leaped, Lucy would cry 'poo!' and he'd leap away again, only to come back when she wriggled her hand under another part of it. I left them to it, with their new little game of, quite literally, ping-pong (more pong than ping of course), and went to run the taps in the washbasin. Once full of a mix of hot and cold water, I tested the temperature with my elbow like I had done years ago when bathing Lucy as a baby. This sudden jolt of memory from the past made me turn just then, and I just wanted to watch Lucy and the kitten playing together. Quietly, without either of them realising, I stood at the doorway looking at them both lost in this funny little game they were playing. Just one of those very sentimental moments looking back on motherhood from the distant past when Lucy was a baby. Where on earth had the time gone? It seemed like yesterday that I was getting a bath ready for her and now here we are on holiday, Lucy now a young woman and being all motherly herself to this tiny kitten.

"Come on you pair of reprobates, it's bath time", I said as I joined them both now.

Lucy caught the kitten up from the now very untidy bedclothes and with me leading, brought him into the bathroom. I wondered how he was going to react to water, cats and baths not known for being the best of friends. I knew that much, but I was about to be surprised. He was no trouble at all and was allowing me to take such liberties that most other cats would bitterly, and bitingly complain about. Before I placed him in the water I had an idea.

"Lucy, just turn the television on, could you please? Just for a bit of background noise. If he meows in the bathroom then the telly will mask any sounds I hope."

This was the one and only time this holiday it had ever been used. I remembered thinking that when we'd first arrived here I'd thought to myself, why on earth would anyone want to watch television when they're on holiday in a place like this? Little did I know it would have its uses after all. Lucy turned back and clicked the remote control and all at once the TV burst into life. It was some sort of news programme from what I could gather, seeing as it was all in Greek but sounding serious and was all be-suited people round a table having a heated conversation. Anyway, I didn't know what was being discussed but the hubbub of voices that now filled the room was ideal for our purposes.

"Ready?" Lucy asked me as she joined me once again. The kitten had meanwhile felt tired after his raucous game and was quite happy just being held while all this to-ing and fro-ing was going on.

"Ready," I replied.

At first I just showed the kitten the water and waggled my finger in it thinking he might think there was another great game afoot which he just had to be a part of. I had already put a thimble full of very mild baby shampoo into the water that I had found in my bag, and now we really were ready to see if he didn't mind a gentle bathing. I held him over the water and very gradually let him down into it, his back legs and tail first and then the rest of him. It was shallow enough to only come up to his tummy but honestly, you'd think I'd just plunged him into thin air. He just did not react! This non reaction was almost spooky really but then, as he had never complained about anything we had done to him so far, I thought that this was all part of his trusting nature. I think I was right because he let Lucy bath him very gently with a little make-up sponge and he took it all.

As he was enjoying the sensation of the water and the massage over his back that she was lavishing on his tiny body, his expression was that of interest more than dislike, and once Lucy had completely soaked him from head to foot, it seem to become actual enthusiasm, as he would deliberately rub his head into the palm of her hand as if it was little more than just being stroked, ignoring the fact that he was partly submerged in water. Needless to say that the water was turning a rather dubious shade of brown and the odour seemed to be getting worse rather than better until I realised that actually, he was suffering from chronic wind too!

"Oh my goodness, you stinky kitty!" I laughingly told him and Lucy, who is much more polite than me, told him he was a soggy-moggy.

Neither insults offended him as he continued to look at us both with such love in his eyes, bless this little creature. He was transfixed by the whole experience as he patiently and obligingly let Lucy make sure he was really clean all over. At last we were able to get the worst out of his fur and now, as I lifted him out of the sink, he seemed to be even more diminished in size. Lucy placed her own hand towel over him and took him from me and walked back into the bedroom with him. His little ears were just visible in that ruff of towel and were still flicking back and forwards taking in all that was happening to him as if it was the greatest adventure he had ever had. Which actually it probably was in his short life so far.

Lucy sat him in the towel on her lap and started to very gently towel him dry. She was meticulous, and every part of him got a little rub. Gradually he started to lose the drowned little waif and stray look and started to resemble once again the little kitten that we knew and loved, albeit a rather cleaner, whiter and less odorous one. Ten minutes later he was completely dry and still he sat on in

Lucy's lap and started to wash himself, his little tongue flicking over his smart new coat. I wondered if he thought he tasted a lot better now, which was a silly anthropomorphic thought, but seeing as he really did seem to look like a different cat, it did make me wonder. There had been parts of him which I thought had been ginger markings. That had apparently not been the case, unless it's a little known fact that ginger markings can come off in water! No, he just seemed to have more white on him now than we had originally assumed and he smelled much better, to boot.

Lucy let him have a little exploration around the bed again and he seemed happy to just stay near her, not even attempting to jump down onto the floor at all. I had never known a cat to be so clingy and it was a joy to see that we had not upset him with all that we had so far made him endure.

"I think we should put him in his cat carrier now," I told Lucy.

It seemed a better option than letting him have free run of the room, just in case he escaped or if we had to open the door to anyone, heaven forbid. I couldn't risk that. I set about putting some paper towels down in the carrier to line it. It was actually quite cavernous inside, and would be a luxury room for a kitten, after the life he'd spent so far at the drain. As he was so small he would have plenty of room to have both a toilet area and a watering area quite set apart from where he might want to sleep. The former was praying on my mind a little as so far he had yet to go to the loo. We had never witnessed him doing that anywhere so far and I did wonder that maybe he was holding it in for now. Cats are so well known for their scrupulous toileting arrangements that I was sure he might be being polite in that regard and would soon need a quiet area to perform something.

He was watching all this preparation of new sleeping arrangements going on with great interest, the rustle of the paper I was putting down seemed to fascinate him. He had settled down into Lucy's lap, his little fore-paws folded neatly underneath him, his tail wrapped around his minuscule frame. Once I'd completed his new bedsit with en suite facilities Lucy cradled him in her arms and very quietly and gently got up from the bed and, kissing him goodnight, placed him for the first time ever into the cat carrier. He didn't resist. He gave its interior a good sniff and once he'd satisfied himself that we had indeed done a remarkable job in it's renovations and interior furnishings, plonked himself down at the very back. Lucy closed the door on his new abode and now that he'd resumed the earlier pose of neat fore-paw arrangement, stared back at us through slightly cleaner eyes. His gaze was of love, adoration, and trust and it truly melted both our hearts. We had put him through so many new and potentially harrowing experiences which might have made another cat go berserk. Being taken out of his familiar territory, bathing and then incarceration, and yet he had taken it all in his stride. A little wobbly kitten sort of stride. He should have hated us by now and yet no, he just didn't seem to have the capacity to hate or resist.

We had positioned the carrier between mine and Lucy's beds so that if anyone should come to our door or even walk past our balcony from the outside then he'd still be completely concealed from any nosey passers by. Not that I'd ever seen anyone pass us from that way before, still I had to be vigilant. Also, it gave him more personal privacy and quiet, and both Lucy and I would be as close to him as it was possible to get during the night should he become fretful. I couldn't see that happening but I just wanted to make sure we'd catered for all eventualities. He had a bowl of biscuits and some water at the front of his cage and so all in all it looked to me like a top-notch, self-contained luxury apartment. That is, compared to what he had been used to.

"I know, I'm going to make a short video on my phone now and send it to Sonia," I told Lucy as I reached out for my phone.

I turned the video app on and, getting down on my bent knees and really close to the front of the carrier, I pressed record. The light wasn't great but through the viewfinder I could see the kitten looking back at me, purring away loudly now. I was watching and listening to what Sonia would soon be able to see and hear; her new kitten at the very beginning of his journey. I wondered how she'd be feeling when she watched this little film. Enraptured no doubt, and it would be the first time she would have been able to see him properly, and in a better state than any previous photos had captured him. The pictures I had sent of him at the drain now bore no resemblance at all really to this new cleaner, brighter looking kitten I now had staring back at me through the camera's lens. I ended the short film and looked up suddenly as I heard a faint tapping sound. It was coming from the patio doors.

"Mum look! It's Misty! It looks as if she's trying to get in" Lucy cried out in surprise.

I couldn't believe my eyes or ears just then, but sure enough there she was standing on her back legs pawing at the glass and looking very determined in trying to get our attention. Clever cat! I had lost track of time by now. When we'd bathed the kitten earlier I had taken off my watch and forgotten to put it back on again. I got up, blood rushing to my head too quickly and had to steady myself against Lucy, who in turn nearly fell over, it was almost comical.

"Mum, what *are* you doing?" She laughed, looking a bit perplexed too.

"I'm trying to get up, what do you think I'm doing? And ouch, I've got pins and needles in my legs. You might be more sympathetic to the older generation!" I pretended to scold.

It was funny, but this wasn't getting Misty fed and watered so I almost limped to the patio doors feeling a bit stupid by now. As soon as Misty saw me approach from the other side she leaped back to her usual place of safety on the balcony wall, her mission having been accomplished. She sat there gazing at me through her beguiling blue eyes now and as I opened the patio doors just a sliver I called out to her, to see if she might perhaps come to me. Not a chance. Now that she had got my attention, she was clearly going to stay at her polite distance and see if her every wish was indeed my command, as it always had been on previous occasions and an evening meal might at last be forthcoming. Was that after playing second fiddle to a seemingly 'new kit' on the block I wondered; had she been watching all these goings on from the other side of the glass?

On my way to get her supper I picked up my watch which was still lying on the edge of the washbasin. I couldn't believe the time. It was coming up to ten o'clock at night. Goodness, where had the time gone? Heaven knows how long poor Misty had been sitting outside waiting for her supper. If her usual internal clock was anything to go by and she'd arrived at the dot of 9pm, then she had been waiting for nearly an hour. Had she been watching us then from the other side of the patio windows whilst we had been tending the kitten's ministrations unbeknownst to us? We had been so busy and distracted by our little feline room-mate that the evening had just flown by, and poor Misty had perhaps got utterly fed up of waiting in silence. So she had taken it upon herself to come closer and, seeing us in the room and seemingly ignoring her, wanted to get our attention.

Had she sensed that we had the kitten in the room I wondered, and more, was she the mother cat? I had told Sonia all about Misty and how I'd been feeding her as well, but because I'd had scant internet of late and been so busy with the kitten I had not yet been able to put anything official out on our social media page. This would have to be something I would give all my concentration to once I'd fed Misty I decided. So back to the job in hand. Tonight I treated Misty to two sachets of wet food, chicken variety in one bowl and tuna in another. I think I did this more through guilt than anything else, feeling that maybe I had ignored her a little bit in the last twenty-four hours. I hadn't really of course, it just felt like that because I'd really had my work cut out with all the other goings on all throughout the day. A day which had started with my finding the drain devoid of kitten, the panic, then our final trip to Paxos and buying the cat carrier, and all the shenanigans with smuggling that into the hotel and then the ensuing 'confrontation which wasn't'. It all seemed like days ago now but it had in fact been only a few hours.

Lucy came out onto the balcony with me tonight, shutting the door firmly closed behind us just in case the kitten suddenly decided to make a bid for freedom and try and open the carrier, albeit Houdini style. It would have actually been impossible for him to get out but we were being extra-super cautious now. Lucy echoed my thoughts of earlier and said:

"Mum, I do wish that Misty also had a home to go to. What on earth is going to happen to her when we've gone? I mean, we leave the day after tomorrow." She looked so sorrowful, as sorrowful as I was about Misty's plight.

I told Lucy that I would do my utmost best to see if someone out in our feline social media world might come to all our rescues and be able to offer her a forever home. That was all I could do for now but if we'd been lucky once, then perhaps we could be lucky again and share this good fortune that the kitten had with another lonely little soul, which Misty really was. I gave Lucy the plates for her to put down for Misty and then she joined me at the picnic table. Not surprisingly, Misty didn't waste any time whatsoever in getting up from her safe corner and running over to her full to brimming dishes immediately. I was sure that she was becoming much more trusting now, less feral, tamer. We watched her tuck into her supper with great gusto from our seats, both lost in our own private thoughts but both thinking exactly the same. Would someone be willing to give this enchanting little cat with the eyes of bewitching blue a home?

I cupped my chin in my hands and just drank in the moment. It was, it goes without saying, another balmy evening, the sky not at all dark, not in the sense we know it at home anyway. Deepest indigo blue with touches of lapis lazuli where the hotel's outdoor lamps illuminated it. In the air there was the usual sensual and heady tang of warm earth and a new scent of rosemary bushes which I hadn't really noticed before. It was a lovely musky smell of the land having been scorched by day and now breathing out as it radiated its scent almost like incense; a herb-infused, sandalwood fragrance. What with that and the usual cooking smells it was tangy, delightful and a feast for the nostrils. It was starting to make me feel hungry again. At the same time Lucy asked me if we had any snacks left in the snack bag.

"I was just thinking the very same thing," I told her. "I'll go and get some crisps and biscuits and we can have a late night picnic out here if you like?"

Lucy said that would be exquisite. I laughed at the somewhat quaint and old fashioned description from one so young, watching her stretch and yawn happily, and got up myself to cobble together some sort of little feast. Back inside the room it was cool now. I checked the kitten in his carrier. Not a peep out of him. How wonderful that he's safe with us, I mused. This time last night he'd been in his rusty, dusty drain, a few shades greyer and fending for himself. And now look at him. He had curled himself up into that familiar tight ball of his with his tail wrapped around him and his nose tucked into it. The epitome of peace and contentment. I left him to his slumbers and went to find food for Lucy and me.

We had drained much of our snack resources but with a bit of imagination I managed to assemble a fair spread of peanuts, crisps, crackers and cream cheese, and for dessert, Greek yoghurt, a few grapes (which had not yet turned to raisins), and some very sweet and sugary looking biscuits. Adding a couple of cans of coke into the equation the tray certainly did look nice and tempting by the time I was back with Lucy and laying it down on the table.

"Wow!" cried my hungry daughter as she took a dollop of cream cheese with a spoon, slopped it onto a plate and mixed it with a few salted peanuts.

It looked such a tasty combination that I copied her; it did indeed taste rather good. Misty had since departed in my absence making this late supper but she was on my mind still. I mentally started to compose a Facebook post about her and with my phone in my free hand, well the one free of gooey cheese and greasy peanuts that is. I started trawling through my photos to find some good pictures that I'd previously taken of Misty during our holiday. I found a gorgeous little photo of her looking up at me from the rough lot behind the balcony. She had such an appealing expression in this particular photo and I thought it would be a very good one to use as it really did show off her pretty markings well and not least her namesake blue eyes. Lucy interrupted my thoughts by getting up and kissing me on the cheek.

"I'm going to bed now Mum, I'm knackered" she said, stifling a yawn with her hand and walking over towards the patio doors. She didn't open them immediately though but just turned round and stood taking in the scenery one last time. She spoke:

"I never thought I'd say it, but I think I'm going to miss this. Well, part of this holiday that is. The you and me bits, like this at night." I turned around to look at her then.

"Oh darling I know what you mean. Me too, I was thinking that earlier. Some parts I would never want to repeat but other parts of the holiday have been really lovely haven't they?"

It wasn't a question really, it was a statement.

Lucy looked exhausted, and I told her to go get a good night's sleep. We needed to be all fresh for tomorrow for the hand-over of the kitten. Oh dear. The hand-over. Our lives were going to feel suddenly exceptionally empty once that had been done and we'd met up with Louisa. What on earth would we do with ourselves for the rest of the day? Relax and enjoy our holiday I suppose, which had been the original intention before all this business ever started. It's what's *meant* to happen after all. Sun, sea and sand, remember? Except of course it had been sun, sea and sand and cats and kittens. I heard the patio door shutting quietly. Right, time to use social media in earnest again and see if we can get Misty sorted as well. Firstly though, as I knew that everyone would be wanting to know how our Corfu Kitten was I put the following out:

'Corfu kitten now safe and settled in cat carrier ready to go to Arc and vet tomorrow. I'll be sad to see him go but know he's going to have a brighter future. He's such an adorable little kitten and he's purring happily now x Thanks so much everyone for all your generosity and support xx Good night all xx.'

It felt so strange now posting things like this. We had so many people supporting us, just dying to know how we were getting on and thinking about us. I knew that from all the well wishes, which filled us with hope, and I realised that people hungrily devoured any information about our kitten that I could give them, such was their devotion to the cause.

It was a pretty responsible position to be in and I did want to let everyone know how we were getting on, but at the same time I had to summarise so many aspects and couldn't answer every question that I was being asked a lot of the time, solely because my internet access was a bit hit and miss and also, I just didn't have any answers sometimes, like how long would the kitten have to stay at the Ark; what was the Ark like? What's going to happen to Misty? The latter of course I now did have to address and so started to write a short post about Misty. Would it be possible to find a home abroad for her as well? I knew I was sticking my neck out a bit here but nothing ventured and all that. I added the photo of her by the balcony and sent that off into the ether.

'This little cat has been visiting me every day. He appears quite thin so I got some cat food for him and fresh water. The poor wee soul ate the food and drank the water very quickly. No one seems to know who he or she belongs to. What should I do?'

Within a few seconds I was receiving comments ranging from 'Awwww' and 'Oh what beautiful eyes' to ''bring her home with you' and 'don't let her stay there to end up being poisoned'. I read and re-read that last comment. Poisoned? What on earth does that mean then? Who would deliberately poison a cat? Hell, they must surely be wrong, or it was a typing error or something. Seriously? I replied to this particular message and apologised but said I didn't understand what they meant by poisoning. An answer was soon forthcoming.

Apparently, it was common practice by some unscrupulous locals, and not just in Corfu, but in Greece as a whole, to put down poison to the cats and dogs at the end of the tourist season as a way to deal with the problem of the number of strays. This was carried out once all the tourists had left the island so that no one witnessed this mass inhumane cull. Various poisons were employed, the most common being rat poison which was of course readily available, and actively encouraged, for the purpose. It would be a slow and excruciating death, sometimes taking days for the animal to die in fear and agony.

It made me almost wretch when I read about all this and by the time I had read it through more than twice, I was sobbing quietly to myself. How naive and stupid was I then? Of course, it all made sense now. Was that why I'd seen all those dishes of food out for the cats? Would they soon be filled with poison now that the locals had successfully lured the cats into thinking that a tasty meal awaited them? How naive I had been to think that the local felines were living the dream with meals placed wherever they seemed to be in abundance.

I couldn't believe that anyone could be so cunning and evil as to lay traps for the animals; traps in the guise of food so that the poor innocent and hungry cats and dogs would of course eat whatever was put out for them, and then crawl away to die somewhere. I wiped my eyes on the back of my hand and put my phone down beside me. I really couldn't see, to read any more anyway. I thought about our little kitten, probably sound asleep in his little carrier by now. What would have happened if we had never been able to find him a home? It was now quite obvious what would have been his fate. But Misty! What's going to happen to her then?

Of course, she'll be lured by some bowl of tasty looking morsels and then within a short space of time she will start to feel very unwell indeed. I didn't let my mind venture any further than that now; I couldn't. I just had to try and get Misty off the island as well. I wished that I could get all the animals off the island, come to that, but waging a one-woman war against this mass slaughtering system that was in-place, well, how could I possibly do that? It would take more than just me. As it was, I wondered how many other people were completely ignorant to the fact that this sort of thing went on behind their backs once they had left this seemingly idyllic country? It can't be just me surely. Me, who had gone around earlier in her holiday seeing all these bowls of food left out for the stray cats and thinking, how nice that they all seemed to be being looked out for. Naivety indeed on my part.

It was time to be practical; however, I couldn't let all this miserable news lull me into inactivity by making me feel so helpless; and where there's life, there's hope. I determined that Misty would now be top of my agenda for finding a home and, even if it meant that we did have to leave her behind here, then I would continue to make it my mission to find her a home so that she could somehow fly back with our kitten when the time came for him to be transported to Jersey. I knew that he would be staying with the Ark for at least another two weeks while all his documentation and vet checks took place, so that might just give us time.

It did occur to me though that the only way for that to happen was for someone from the Ark to capture Misty on our behalf, because Lucy and I were due to leave Corfu the day after tomorrow. In that case, would the Ark be willing to do that, if we could guarantee that a forever home had been found for her? How feasible would it be for them to come out here though; they would just have to keep a vigil until she turned up, and that would all be a bit hit-and-miss. Perhaps they had their own ways and means to capture a cat but for the life of me I hadn't a clue as to how. The only thing in our favour was the fact that Misty always seemed to turn up at the same time and place each night. Would she still return however once she realised that Lucy and I weren't there to feed her any more, or might a new guest take on the responsibility of feeding her? It suddenly all seemed quite impossible that anything could be arranged, and after having had such a wonderful and triumphant day which had ended up with my bringing the kitten back to our room, I felt deflated now and as miserable as I had been before we had found a home for him.

The only real solution was to speak to Louisa about it tomorrow, after all, we were going to have to leave it all in her hands. She would be Misty's salvation then, although that was only if we did manage to find her a home; she had still to be caught. I had a feeling this would be a difficult task as she was both very feral and timid. Being that bit older than the kitten, she'd had time to grow wary and street-wise and was so suspicious of people that I knew it would not be an easy ride for either The Ark, or Misty. I just hoped that Louisa would be able to suggest a way to help her. That was in the event that we *were* able to secure her a home. So much depended on the latter.

It really *was* time for bed now. Lucy had long gone, as had Misty, and I realised that it had actually started to turn quite chilly. Of course, I was incredibly tired by now so that would have made me more sensitive to the cold, it always has done. It was no matter, and actually quite refreshing. I stretched in my chair and slowly got up, being careful not to make a scraping sound on the balcony that might wake Lucy- or indeed the kitten. Opening the patio doors as quietly as I could and squeezing through the gap, not wanting to open it too far, I let myself in as stealthily as a burglar, something that I seemed to have developed quite a knack for today strangely enough. A quick wash, teeth cleaned, phone on it's charger and within ten minutes I was snuggled under the covers. I leaned sideways to have a look at the kitten but he was quiet but I could just about make out in the gloom of the night-time room, his little white form giving the odd little twitch. I think he must have been having dreams as he flicked his tail several times but he did not wake up. I wondered what he was dreaming about, and hoped that he wasn't reliving something frightening that he'd experienced in his, so far, very short life. I whispered to him a goodnight and blew him a silent kiss then turned over and I think as soon as my head hit the pillow I too joined him in sleep. For a change though, mine was dreamless.

Chapter 20

A rustling of paper and a furious scrabbling sound awoke me on that Wednesday morning, and at first I couldn't quite place it. However, as the events of yesterday suddenly caught up with my still tired brain, I realised at once what was going on. It was the kitten in his cat carrier taking a lot of care to cover something up! I sat up in bed and leaned over to get a better view of our little guest.

"Good morning little one," I called softly to him.

He ignored me as he was still determined to rip up every single paper towel until it resembled confetti, scattering some through the bars and into the room. I smiled and thought how lovely it was to have him here with us now like this, all of us waking up together. Lucy was stirring and rolled over in her bed to face me. Then she had the same dawning of memory from the night before and looked down at the kitten who had now stopped scrabbling and was sitting the other side of his cage door looking up at us both as now two sets of human eyes were peering at him from above.

"Ooooh, I think he's been!" Lucy wrinkled her nose as the rather unlovely fragrance started to permeate the room, but still we stayed looking down at him and loving every inch of him, from the tip of his nose to the tips of his toes.

However, I really did need to make him more comfortable in his little house again (and actually for us too for that matter), so I swung my legs out of bed now and got up to find some more paper towels so that I could re-line his house. It also needed a good clean so I asked Lucy if she would take hold of the kitten whilst I did some spring-cleaning for him. I opened up the carrier and he was more than willing to join us up on the bed. Lucy cradled him in her arms and he broke into rapturous purrs, nudging his little nose into her hand as she started to stroke him. He settled quietly and seemed quite happy to stay put now, watching me from afar as I set about cleaning the carrier. It wasn't a pleasant job, not having the right washing facilities around me here in the room but I managed to make it clean again, disposing of all the soiled and shredded paper that was fast beginning to dissolve into a gooey pulp, into a plastic carrier bag. The days were long gone when I'd always carried a plentiful supply of nappy bags around with me, those days when Lucy was still so tiny. I thought of my grandmother's old saying, 'make do and mend'; I was certainly making do with what I could lay my hands on now in this room. I had used up all the paper towels and so I placed an old holiday brochure that wasn't needed anymore underneath the paper and prayed that this would see the kitten through the next few hours as comfortably as possible for him.

It felt strange not having to take my early morning walk down to the drain, where it was just myself and the waking world. Those days were also a thing of the past now. A good thing. The kitten's breakfast could be prepared and served up here within the safety and confines of our room. I started washing his food and water bowls, and now Lucy was lying back on her bed with the kitten resting on her chest. It was such a sweet tableau just then and it reminded me of a painting I had once seen in an art gallery, a long time ago. The feeling that it had given me then as I had looked at it, was the same feeling I was experiencing now, protective and maternal. It was a picture of absolute peace and adoration, a private moment between human and animal, and to me it epitomised the ultimate in that loving and special bond that we can form with them. It made the room feel quiet and blessed and I realised, not for the first time this holiday, how lucky Lucy and I were to have each other and a shared love of animals; and now the shared love of this tiny, scrappy little feline as well.

I turned away from this little scene of contentment and something else caught my eye. Misty was sitting on a chair on the balcony gazing at me with that inscrutable blue eyed stare of hers. She seemed to be watching all the goings on inside our room intently, and it made me wonder whether she had been there all night. I carried on washing and scrubbing the cat bowls and decided to take Misty's food out first so that she didn't feel she was being completely ignored.

"Lucy, have you seen who's outside?" I called as I went to open a sachet of wet food for our al fresco diner. She stood up and walked over to the patio windows now, leaving the kitten snuggled in the warm dent of her pillow.

"Mum, do you think she's been there all night?" Lucy asked me as she gazed back at Misty, who was still sitting on the chair, and didn't move when Lucy appeared at the windows.

"Well that's what I was just wondering," I told her, bringing a heaped bowlful of food out to our other breakfast guest.

Lucy went back to the kitten just then and scooped him up in her arms so that he wouldn't escape whilst I slid the patio doors back. He didn't realise we were all being watched by Misty and was happy to just flop in Lucy's arms until I'd shut the doors behind me once on the balcony. I placed the dishes down for Misty in the usual place and withdrew to the other side of the picnic table. This was too much for her now, my proximity had infringed on her feline rights but then she realised that her breakfast had been served. She jumped down off the chair and almost ran hell for leather to her feeding station. I sat down on the chair she'd just vacated and it felt warm, which again made me think she must have been there some time to have made it so.

I had to press on and make breakfast for the kitten so I didn't stay outside for too long this morning. The bombshell news from last night of poisoning was still playing heavily on my mind of course but I didn't let on to Lucy about this, and I couldn't let it drag me down and hinder the important work we had to do today. I was still confident that Louisa would be able to help with Misty and as time was really not on our side, that was the most I could hope for. I went back through the patio doors and Lucy was already making the kitten's breakfast. It was a sight to behold, as Lucy stood with the kitten under one arm, while with her free hand she was preparing his bowls. The wet food pouch was gripped between her teeth as she tried to tear it open, the kitten wanting to help.

"Mum, he was getting desperate for some food," she told me when I went back in. I took the kitten from her and let Lucy get on with the job in hand.

"Well I did think you were trying to sample his food first!" I laughed as she was now able to finish opening the sachet with both hands and not her teeth this time.

The kitten had apparently sussed the situation but having had his offer of help in tearing the sachet open declined, had started to get impatient. He was wriggling in my arms now but at last Lucy placed his food bowl in front of him and he dived in straight away. It was all gone within a few seconds it seemed and now he started to push his bowl around the floor trying to find any bits that he'd missed under his dish until he succeeded in turning it upside down.

"Shall I give him some more?" Lucy asked me as I turned his dish up the right way.

"I think just a little more, yes, but we'd better go easy as he's going to have a lot of stressful things happen to him today," I told her.

There was caution in my voice because I was anxious about the next few hours as they had the potential to be quite frightening for him as he was taken in his carrier on foot and then on a car journey to the Ark. With a very full tummy I just didn't want him to have any accidents on the way as that would upset him even more. On the other hand, he still seemed so hungry. I guessed, probably correctly, that we were also feeding a belly-full of worms. Not a pleasant thought, but soon he would be treated by a vet so that at least would address any parasite issue.

This time Lucy just gave him a little food out of the sachet and he ate the further offering more slowly this time. When the bowl was once again licked clean to within an inch of its life, he settled down beside it to start his morning ablutions. Although he was so much cleaner since he'd had his bath the night before he still insisted on washing himself in the minutest detail. I left him to it and Lucy stayed watching him whilst I went around gathering up the empty food pouches and bowls and generally trying to tidy up around them both to get a head start on making the room look a little more presentable to us all.

I knew that once we'd returned from meeting up with Louisa and handing over the kitten, coming back to a now empty room would be quite a strange experience, it would be so quiet and poignant. I was mindful to keep any sadness to a minimum by tidying away all kitten-related detritus now. Much as I would have liked to have kept things as they were, I needed to make it look as if he'd never been with us in the first place. I sighed at this thought then had to check myself too; don't forget, this is what you had prayed for, *begged* for, not so long ago. This little kitten rescued, and on its way to a proper home. *Remember* that. I had to remind myself of this, otherwise I might just have caved in with the whole business.

Lucy managed to peel herself away from the kitten and took herself off to shower, leaving him on her bed playing with her trusty old shoelace. He seemed more than content to stay put chewing the end of the lace and so I was able to get on with sprucing up our room. I dragged my suitcase out from under the bed and started to unzip it. I had the strange sense of deja vous as I opened it up. It seemed like only yesterday that I'd been packing it, dreaming about the holiday that we had ahead of us and the adventures we might have. I smiled to myself. Adventures indeed! This was one particular adventure we certainly hadn't bargained for. As I knelt down beside the case now, I heard a plop as the kitten half fell, half jumped off Lucy's bed to join me on the floor. He sat beside me, upright with both forepaws neatly arranged in front of him and put his head over the side of the case. He stared down into it, as if to say 'what's that for then?'

I tickled his inquisitive little head, and then in one awkward bound he jumped from his sitting position into the depths of the case. It wasn't a very deep one but because he was so small it did seem to swallow him up as he retreated to the far side of it, giving it a good sniff.

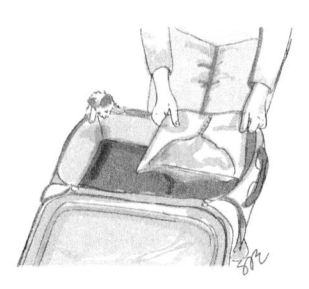

"Now little one, if that's how you'd prefer to travel back with us!" I cajoled, thinking if only it was that simple.

I stroked his back, but he had other ideas. So dipping his back so that his tummy touched the ground, he slunk away from me, determined to carefully examine all four corners of the case, making sure that it was safe for me to pack things into it. He gave his tail a little flick every time he seemed satisfied that there were no demons lurking and then moved onto the next corner. I wondered if he could detect my own cats' scents from home, as it was always a favourite of theirs to jump inside it as soon as it was open. Typical empty box syndrome; cats just cannot resist diving into them. He started to turn small circles in one corner of the case, the precursor to a little feline snooze-time and this provided the perfect distraction to my not packing just yet as I looked on. I reminded myself of the saying that 'time spent watching a cat is never wasted' and so there I sat, watching this peaceful little creature now settled down for sleep, his purring still very audible and in time with the rise and fall of his body.

By the time Lucy came rattling out of the shower, accidentally dropping her wash bag so that the contents tumbled to the floor and clattered against the tiles, I was still under this slumbering kitten hypnosis. The sudden noise jolted me back to my senses however. It did not disturb the slumbering kitten though. He must be tired, I thought. What little dreams was he having I wondered, as his paws and nose twitched and his back legs started kicking, still fast asleep and oblivious to Lucy now crouching over him, her wet hair hanging loose over her shoulders as she studied the kitten in sweet repose.

"Mum, don't you think we'd better go and get some breakfast soon?" she whispered. I knelt back on my knees then and, looking at my watch which told me it was now past eight o'clock, realised that the morning was flying by.

"Oh help! Just let me have a quick shower then we can go and eat." I got up slowly so as to avoid a dizzying blood rush to the head.

I could already feel the pins and needles in my feet which were threatening to render them useless if I wasn't careful. I struggled to get upright without waking the kitten. Reaching full height again I grabbed my own toiletries bag and hopped into the shower, leaving Lucy towel drying her hair, still on her knees next to my suitcase. She never took her eyes off that little mite and as I closed the door of the shower behind me, I could hear her talking very softly to the kitten, telling him how much she loved him. It brought a lump to my throat. My better, more sensible self had to reprimand and remind me once again that morning; this is what you *prayed* for.

By the time I was out of the shower, Lucy was dressed and now we had to wake the kitten up so that we could place him back in his carrier, while we went to breakfast. There was no way I could risk allowing him to sleep freely in the suitcase while we were out, just in case he awoke and started meowing for us or scratching at the door. I wasn't completely convinced that he had it in him to do that just yet, but I still wasn't prepared to take risks either. Well not today anyway.

Lucy brought the cat carrier over to me and I tried to very gently wake him up with a soft cooing and gently stroking his back. He opened one eye, gave an enormous yawn and stretched out a fore paw. Lucy took it in her hand just then and they really did look like they were holding hands. He curled his claws into the palm of her hand and got up unsteadily on all four feet now. I lifted him up, feeling the warmth of this incredible little soul in the crook of my elbow, and placed him back into the carrier. He was unphased by this sudden change of location and settled down immediately, gazing at me while I closed the door and put the catch on into it's locked position. Was there *anything* more trusting than this beguiling kitten I wondered? So far he had made no attempt whatsoever in fighting against anything that we put him through. He was the most biddable little creature and, for the first time that morning, a frisson of excitement went through me as I thought about the day when he would at last arrive with Sonia in Jersey. We were changing his life forever.

Collectively, we had indeed saved a kitty's life between us.

* * *

Breakfast tasted especially good that morning. No longer did I have that little niggling feeling of guilt that always accompanied me after I had returned from feeding the kitten at the drain, and the subsequent 'and now here we are stuffing our faces, whilst out there…'. Lucy and I tucked into our fruit salads and croissants with great gusto and all the while I knew that the kitten was full of good food and now probably fast asleep within the safety and confines of the cat carrier in our room. Having said that however, we were both eager to spend as little time as possible away from the little chap and so, after glugging down one more cup of rather good strong coffee, I wiped my lips on the serviette and pushed my chair back. Lucy gathered up her bag and looked up at me.

"So. Now it begins," she said. I could see that she was trying to be, so very brave about what lay ahead of us in the next few hours; the handing over, the final goodbyes and all the other in-between scenarios that we might have to encounter.

"But look at how far we've come darling," I said softly, reaching for her hand. "This is what we could only have dreamed of a few days ago. We Did It. Never forget that, eh?" She didn't speak but just nodded her head. I waited a beat.

"Come on then, up and at it" I replied and ushered her gently out of the dining room.

I didn't want to go down the same path that Lucy's mind was about to journey down. I didn't want any stirring of those thoughts and feelings of earlier. We had an important job to do and now it was time to see it through to its conclusion. I certainly couldn't afford to get emotional over it just now; there would be plenty of time for all that afterwards and it was a dead certainty that it would happen. For now, we had to stay strong, I told myself.... OK, I answered back in my head, but just for now.

We made our way back to our room and I unlocked the door. Opening it slowly and quietly we let ourselves in. We spoke in hushed voices as we put our bags down and I locked the door behind me. I heard a gentle rustling of paper and could see through the bars of the carrier that the kitten was awake and sitting up watching us with great interest. He opened his mouth as if to meow but nothing came out, no sound at all. A silent meow. Lucy knelt down and unlocked his door to let him out. He gave a slow, languorous stretch, his back legs almost parallel to the floor which made him appear twice as long and sinewy as he climbed out of the carrier. That by now, oh-so-familiar rattling purr of his, seemed to fill the whole room and ricocheted off the walls. It was so loud. Low resonating and deep, it droned on in perfect time with his breathing, akin to someone snoring, guttural and nasal.

Lucy wanted to play with him and so of course he acquiesced. She reached up for the chewed and frayed shoe lace that was still lying on her bed and dangled it above his nose, tantalisingly just out of his reach. He leaned back on his haunches and then stood up on his back legs to grasp it with both paws. Then he'd lunge at it baring all his tiny, immaculate porcelain teeth and then he would try to pull it out of her hands. She would then of course release it and let it drop and he would grasp it and fall over onto his side and start chewing it. Still tightly grasped between all four paws he would kick out against it with one end clamped tightly between his jaws. Then she'd playfully try and reclaim the lace, tugging it gently from between his paws and then the whole pattern of play would be repeated. Bat, claw, fall over; chew, kick, release. He loved it.

I had to keep an eye on the time now and was shocked to see

that it was already nine o'clock. One hour to go until we had to leave for the hand-over. Of course, from now on the minutes started to pass like seconds and as 10am drew nearer and nearer, I could feel myself savouring every nanosecond of his company. The feeling of time passing was palpable. I had the strangest notion that it was like going to the gallows and yet it shouldn't have been like that *at all*. The fact of the matter was, I was just dreading the final goodbyes. I wanted to hold on to it for as long as I could, in suspended animation, paradoxically never wanting to reach the much longed for conclusion. Time, however, does not stand still and at a few minutes to ten I had to start pulling myself, and the rest of the world around me, together. It was that time.

I got up off the bed and started busying myself in practical ways. I lifted the cat carrier onto the bed and replaced some of the paper towels with a few serviettes that I had had the presence of mind to grab from the restaurant earlier during breakfast. Over those I laid a soft hand towel that I had brought from home and flattened it down with my hand. Little did I know what I'd be using *that* for I thought to myself, when I'd originally packed it. How strange this life is. We never know what lies around each and every twisted and convoluted corner of our journey, what we're going to be blundering into as some days we seem to lurch from crisis to crisis and on others, everything we touch seems to turn to gold. It was gold now. Gold all the way.

"Right then little guy. Here we go." Lucy let him grab the shoe lace for one last time and then picked him and his prize up, and held him in her arms. Don't cry sweetheart, I said softly to myself.

I watched silently as she buried her face into his coat with her cheek resting against his. There was no struggle from the kitten as he just returned the love that she was giving him. No tear drops spilled onto his fur as she closed her eyes, not saying anything. She was utterly composed. I couldn't say the same for myself unfortunately as I was by now swallowing hard and trying to fight back the tears which were on the point of spilling down my cheeks. I sighed and it came out as a gulp. A gulping back of tears. Pull yourself together woman, I sighed to myself.

Lucy lifted her face up from the snuggling little heap of white and ginger and passed him to me. Very gently she put him in my arms, not taking her eyes off me for an instant, as if willing me to be as composed as she was. What a sensible girl I have raised, I thought. Then the next thought was, don't you *dare* spoil this moment and lose it completely. The roles had suddenly been reversed though, and I was being coaxed and mothered, and being encouraged to be brave and bold in the face of adversity and all that. Her eyes were shining now, not through tears, but with a strange sort of happiness and hopeful expectancy I think. That's what it looked like to me anyway. It was as a mother watching her child trying to take its first steps and, although she would of course be there to catch them if they fell, she had the absolute faith and belief at the same time that they wouldn't fail. I was that child now. So how could I possibly fail her? It was as simple as that. She gave me the courage to overcome the tears and to become as rational as she was being.

The kitten, who had remained absolutely oblivious to all this role reversal in motherly ministrations, buried his nose into the crook of my arm. I concentrated on him so fiercely, trying to memorise each and every detail of his fur, the whorls and the way his coat lay around his shoulders, the ginger ears with their light sprinkling of frosty white around the edges, the ginger spot on his back. I studied him in the minutest detail, lest I should ever forget a single marking and the way his fur laid on his little body. I tried to absorb every feature and absolutely everything about him into my very soul. But now it really was time to go.

I spoke to him as I tried to uncurl his body from my arms and

Lucy held the cat carrier door open for me so that I could place him gently inside it. As soon as his feet touched the mattress of all the soft towelling inside he started to open and close his paws, kneading it and, like the lovely description goes, 'making biscuits'. Of course the purr became even louder now. Lucy and I were both satisfied and reassured that he was comfortable and very happy just padding away on his new luxury carpet. So once again we had to try and disguise the fact that we were in possession of a cat carrier, and this time it was one that *was* inhabited. I slung the huge beach towel over it for good measure, and then began to put my large hold-all on top too, when I suddenly had a flash of inspiration and I changed my mind on this last item.

"Lucy! I wonder if your lilo would be better over the carrier, if we deflate it first of course."

It didn't take long for her to squash all the air out of it and once flat, lay it over the carrier. I took a look at the effect in the mirror to see how we were looking and believe me, you really couldn't tell that there was a cat carrier at all in my arms. We definitely looked as if we meant business and all set for a serious day on the beach, laden down with all the necessary accessories. I gave a triumphant smile at my reflection and Lucy gave me the thumbs up as she started to unlock the door to let me and my chattels out of the room. I glanced over her head just as she was locking it behind her and took in a very bare sight indeed, the room now thoroughly devoid of kitten and all associated paraphernalia. So far so good.

We continued on to the reception area and as the desk had already attracted a large group of people making enquiries there, it was all to the good and to our advantage. So engrossed in earnest conversation about something, no one noticed one woman and one teenage girl trundling through the hotel with an oversized assortment of beach goods, holding their breaths. Once we were out through the main doors I had a sudden sense of relief and freedom. Now we really *were* on our way.

Chapter 21

We made our way down the hotel's driveway and then once we reached the road side we stopped to catch our breaths. I was anxious that our little kitten wasn't going to overheat in his carrier with the lilo draped over it. There was a kind of pull-in bay just a bit further up so we carried on up the road and there we were able to reassemble our things and gather our thoughts. We were also able to give our little boy a better circulation of air around his carrier now that we were well out of the way of the hotel.

I placed the cat carrier at my feet now and Lucy stooped down to check that he was alright but as usual he seemed completely indifferent to this new situation and was just lying down taking in all the new sights and sounds of the roadside. We had plenty of time on our hands so we didn't have to rush and we didn't have to go far now either, the taxi rank being only another five minutes walk. However, the heat of the day was beginning to make itself felt and the straps of my haversack were already making me feel hot and sticky so I loosened them to relieve the discomfort. It didn't help much at all.

Cars and mopeds swept by but no one took the blindest bit of notice of us as we stood there in the lay-by, me clutching the cat carrier in one hand and fanning myself with the other in the ever climbing heat. It was good being able to feel quite anonymous at last and not have to skulk around a hotel with the secret and somewhat guilty feeling that we were breaking all the rules by harbouring a kitten. As things stood now, we could have been anyone and it didn't matter a jot what we were doing and where we were going. I could have almost luxuriated in that guilt-free sensation had it not been for the fact that, any minute now, we would be handing the kitten over and unlikely to ever see him again.

"Right then. Are we ready?" I said to Lucy as she straightened up from her crouching position next to the kitten.

She nodded, swung her bag back over her shoulder and told me she'd like to carry the cat carrier this time. She carefully picked it up off the ground and now the kitten was sitting right at the very front. I poked a finger through the bars playfully and he gave one of those cat 'smudge' kisses as he rubbed against it, bearing his little fangs and purring, forever purring. We walked slowly in the part shade afforded by the overhanging trees on the road side. The cicadas were noisy this morning and I remembered what one of our tour guides had told us, that the hotter it gets, the noisier they become. This morning was no exception. I hoped the kitten wasn't feeling the heat too much, as we certainly were by now, but of course it would have been foolish to have carried him in my arms; temporary incarceration in his box it would have to be, for all our sakes. At last, the taxi rank in Messonghi came into view. I could see just the one vehicle pulled up at it but this wasn't Louisa yet. The driver was leaning against it languidly drawing on a cigarette. When he spotted us he put his hand up and called out.

"You take taxi to Old Town? I drive you!" He threw down his cigarette and started grinding it underfoot in the road. I shook my head by way of a reply and he just raised his hand again, and lit up another smoke.

Lucy and I found a convenient place to wait, so that other taxi drivers didn't keep thinking we were wanting a lift somewhere! We waited for Louisa to arrive. My watch told me it was twenty-nine minutes past ten. We had made it in such good time to our appointed meeting place. Now I hoped that we wouldn't have too long to wait. Soon the taxi that had been waiting at the rank started up its engine and, without a backward glance in our direction, pulled out into the road leaving a trail of acrid blue smoke behind it. And then we were quite alone. With endless blue up above, it would have been quite a pleasant wait on any other occasion just not this one. Every time a car approached and looked as if it was making to turn into the taxi rank, I jumped a little inside thinking, 'here she is', but then it would keep going and I'd think to myself 'a few more moments with just the three of us together' and then it was almost a relief, a reprieve.

The minutes ticked by. At a quarter to eleven Louisa had still not arrived and I was beginning to worry now. I did have the right day, the right time and the right meeting place, I knew that much; but where on earth could they be? The road wasn't busy so they weren't stuck in traffic I thought to myself. Should I try to call her, I wondered. No, I'll wait for a while longer before I do that. All these thoughts flitting in and out of my head and still the kitten sat contentedly, not minding in the slightest this rather unusual day out for him. Lucy was happy enough waiting but had by now sat down and was leaning against the wall, her hand resting on the cat carrier so that the kitten could still feel our protection, that was how she explained it anyway.

More minutes ticked by and when it got to five to eleven I decided to call Louisa. The familiar ring at The Ark's end pinged back in my ear but after hanging on for over a minute there was no reply. Perhaps that was a good thing I told Lucy, and that it meant that she was on her way. And now it was eleven o'clock.

"Oh please come soon," I muttered under my breath, shifting my weight on to the other leg now with impatience and restless at being stuck in one position for so long, craning my neck so far that it was getting painful.

I walked over to join Lucy by the wall not knowing what to do now, or say for that matter, as we really were in a rather hopeless situation. Do we just wait for another hour or what? Before I even had time to answer this difficult question, I noticed a small Greek lady who was making her way towards us. When we made eye contact she broke into a run and waved at me. I wasn't sure if she was Louisa or not because I had been expecting her to arrive by car but by the time she had reached my side, slightly breathless, she pointed at the cat carrier and said,

"Please, you are Beverley with the kitten from the drain yes?" I said hello then and told her that yes, and was she Louisa?

"I am Spiridoula, I work with Louisa. She busy with sudden emergency and cannot come now."

I didn't know what to say then, but I must have looked a bit shocked and struck dumb because she reached out and put her hand on my arm and went on to say:

"But is OK, is alright! She then will come now at two o'clock." There was an instant recovery on my part as I straightened up again, having visibly wilted in front of her. Spiridoula then glanced inside the cat carrier.

"He is very lucky drain kitten but his eyes are not nice and his nose is same." At first I thought she was describing his appearance in terms of aesthetics but then I realised it was quite literally broken English. She meant of course the 'state' of his eyes and nose which were quite gunked up with discharge, despite last night's bath and his own personal and very vigorous cleaning programme.

"This we see in Corfu cats and is great problem," she went on to tell me and I replied that yes, although I had tried to clean them earlier it seemed it wasn't doing much good. She looked me straight in the eye then and spoke, very kindly.

"But we will have doctor to see him so that is very good, yes?" I nodded.

"Yes, that is very good. We really do thank you so much. So will Louisa definitely be here later on then?" She laughed then.

"Yes she come this afternoon of course. But this morning I come instead to tell you this and why." She was a sweet lady and I liked the way her eyes crinkled when she smiled.

She was smiling at Lucy and I now and her laughter was infectious. What on earth was there to worry about I thought. We had her word that Louisa wasn't going to let us down and I believed her.

"So that is all good and I see you later on again too. Bye bye!" and with that she sped away again on foot and we were left gazing at her as she got smaller and smaller in the distance. I wondered if she had ran all the way from The Ark? Or maybe she had a car parked up somewhere unseen. Either way, and however she had travelled here, now it was just me, Lucy and the kitten again.

"Mum, what are we going to do now then? We'll have to go back to the hotel with the kitten and try to hide him all over again."

She was right of course, and the logistics of this made me for one feel rather giddy. We had to go through it all over again, the smuggling in and out of the room and the constant looking over our shoulders for fear of being caught, despite the fact that by now we were certainly becoming more adept at it. Then all of a sudden I had a brainwave.

"Lucy! I've got it, I know what we should do. If you go on ahead and open up the patio doors from inside the room, I'll meet you on the outside of them and we can take the kitten in that way." She looked at me sideways then and, slapping her head in that kind of way teenagers do accompanied by a 'doh!' asked:

"Then why haven't we been doing it that way all along?"

She was quite right to ask this question as of course we might have been better doing it this way. Truth be told, it had just never occurred to me and to be fair, it had only just occurred to Lucy too, so I felt I could be partially exonerated. I picked up the cat carrier making sure that the kitten was still alright inside it. By now he'd positioned himself at the front of the cage and sat there staring back at me. He yawned and then pressed his nose through the bars as if to say, 'it's fine I'm still here, but now what's going on?'

"We're going back to the room, little one," I told him and the three of us set off back the way we had come, back to the hotel.

I never thought we'd be doing this again but fact is stranger than fiction and yes, here we were retracing our steps whilst still in possession of one very small ginger and white kitten. Lucy had now run on ahead and I began to dawdle so that it would give her ample time to open up the room and then the patio doors. There never seemed to be anyone on the outside of the hotel grounds where our room was situated and I just hoped that today would be no exception. I knew too that both the neighbouring rooms on either side of us were vacant now as I had heard its occupants saying goodbye to each other earlier when I was making a start on the packing and their voices could be quite easily heard through our closed door. We seemed to have luck on our side then and soon I was at the hotel gates, the lilo already in place over the carrier and traipsing over the fairly long dry grasses that skirted the perimeter of the hotel.

Now it was a good job that Lucy had thought to stand outside on the balcony because, seconds before, I'd suddenly had the awful realisation that from this rather new and unusual vantage point, all the rooms and patio windows looked exactly the same. In my panic, I'd mentally conjured up a future figure of me as I slunk from window to window looking for the right one to gain entry through with my illegal cargo. Again, the miracle of the myriad synapses firing taking mere nanoseconds, and yet seemingly paving the way of how I thought the next ten minutes of my life would pan out as if it had already happened.

I must add though that something very similar had happened to me when I was in my twenties and doing a month's travelling around Europe by train. I had been on a sleeper train bound for Copenhagen and at some point during the night the entire train had boarded the ferry. I had woken up a little later and, still being dark, took a wander outside to watch this strange spectacle of a boat on a ferry, gliding over a jet black sea. Having at last got my fill of this rather novel experience I decided I'd better go back to the sleeper, and then had suddenly realised with horror that I did not have a clue which carriage I had originally got out of. There in my pyjamas I had stood, looking and feeling very stupid, heart racing, thinking, I'm going to be stuck out here all night unless I try and find the right sleeper carriage, but the embarrassment of disturbing a complete stranger's sleep as I went from sleeper to sleeper trying to find my sleeper was too much to consider doing. By some strange piece of luck I *had* managed to find my way back to the correct sleeper in the end, but the experience had clearly left its mark, scarred me for life, and now here I was in a similar situation, albeit it was daylight and I wasn't in my pyjamas.

However, luckily my panic was unfounded as there stood Lucy grinning at me from our balcony and ready to take the cat carrier from my hands. I passed the kitten over to her and then climbed up onto the fairly high balcony wall, shimmied over it rather nimbly (if I do say so myself), and walked back into the room cool as a cucumber. I felt somewhat pleased with my stealth and athleticism albeit in a rather unorthodox method, but needs must.

* * *

I closed the doors behind me and Lucy let the kitten out of his carrier so that he could stretch his legs. It felt good to have been granted a couple more hours with him at the very last minute and now here we were back in the room and playing with the kitten. There was a knock at the door. Luckily we had locked that from the inside but Lucy quickly scooped up the kitten and put him in the carrier.

"Hello, just a minute!" I called out frantically from the other side of the door, and then whispered to Lucy to take the carrier out onto the balcony and hide it under one of the chairs out of view. She deftly did that and once the coast was completely clear I opened up the door. It was the room cleaner. She was one of the nicer ones who always had a smile and a kind face, and on more than one occasion we had passed the time of day with friendly but inconsequential chatter.

"I clean for you yes, or not good now for you when I come back shall be better, please?" she asked me in her sweet, sing-song sort of voice. I racked my brains as to *when* a good time might actually be.

"Thank you, yes, that would be better. We'll be gone by 2 o'clock this afternoon..." I left the sentence kind of dangling in mid-air then but she nodded and replied:

"Of course, you have nice time outside and I come back and you come back to tidy room after I go." Again I thanked her and then she scuttled off down the corridor and on to her next room-clean. I closed the door quietly behind me, locked it once again and called Lucy.

"OK, the coast is clear!" The patio doors slid open from the balcony side and in came Lucy holding the carrier and our trusty old beach towel which she had used to cover up the box.

"Phew, no more alarms like that please, I don't think I can take any more of this."

She was right, it was all getting a bit farce-like really. It was like a comedy with all this to-ing and fro-ing from some sort of mischief; always on the brink of getting caught and then there's a reprieve, then the cycle repeats itself another way. It was as if we were continually being set-up by things outside of our control. I wouldn't have been surprised if suddenly somewhere some orchestra struck up and played the *Looney Tunes* music, it was getting that silly now and cartoon-like. All very Tom and Jerry and yes, cat and mouse indeed. We certainly had the cat and it was Lucy and I that were feeling like mice. Would we be caught before we let the cat go free, I wondered, profound as it may sound, but that summed up the situation nicely. And relax…

However, we had no more interruptions or disturbances after that and so we were able to give all our attention to the kitten. I realised that in all our comings and goings that he would be hungry by now and a spot of lunch, for us humans too, wouldn't go amiss. I had plenty of cat food pouches but not much in the way of food for Lucy and I. Never mind I thought to myself, we'll soon have time enough to fill our faces. Once we had met up with Louisa at two o'clock then we would be free to wander off into the town and visit a taverna. It would feel very strange to have that sense of freedom again, and nothing more to do with the kitten; no more ties to the drain and stocking up on cat-food.

The holiday in that respect was really beginning to feel just about over, and yet in other ways it had only just begun, in that we could do as we liked again. It had been a real roller-coaster ride and now soon that would stop and…and what? Be as profound as you like Beverley, I told myself; it will be like swing boats for just a little while, and then helter-skeltering down to the final hours which will go so quickly, and then homeward bound. I stopped myself then; stopped thinking beyond that aeroplane as it was wasting the moment.

"I think the little chap might want some lunch don't you think?" I told Lucy as I got up from the end of the bed where I'd been idly watching her and the kitten playing with his shoelace.

It was of course a rhetorical question and so I left them to their earnest game and went to open one of the remaining cat food sachets that I had previously thought would all be for Misty from now on. When I returned with his bowl, now full of a tasty tuna variety pouch and placed it in front of him, he needed no encouragement to quit his game. He was at his bowl like a little bullet. I sat down on the bed again with Lucy and together we watched him tuck into his food. Unlike those times at the drain when he had literally wolfed down each mouthful without appearing to even chew it, this time he was taking a much more considered approach as each mouthful was being enjoyed but in a more measured fashion.

It was time for us humans to be fed now and I was loath to leave him and Lucy so instead, I pooled together the few snacks we had left which also consisted of the rest of the cream cheese and peanuts and crisps and a few biscuits. We would eat properly later I promised Lucy, but she wasn't at all bothered with this make-do snack. By the time we had eaten and I had once again cleared up and given the kitten's carrier another good spruce up it was nearly time to leave to meet Louisa, for the second time that day. This time there certainly seemed an air of finality about it. Having already met Spiridoula, it was all becoming very real in that now we could at least put a face to The Ark, and although she was not the main spokesperson, she was our link with the kitten's immediate future, and as we had forged that link earlier this morning, now it felt even stronger. This time, when we left the hotel with the kitten, I knew that we would be coming back without him, but it was going to be OK. One massive mission was about to be accomplished. A mission which had snowballed; in the friends we were making all over the world all rooting for this little chap, and the love and compassion that had been shown. This awe-inspiring propensity of love was overwhelming, and now it was time for us to leave for the very last time. Lucy and I shared a group hug with the little kitten and then I put him in his carrier.

"Lucy, I think I'd better go out the same way as I came in, through the patio." My daughter nodded her head and got up to let us out.

"Can you lock the doors behind me, and I'll meet you in front of the hotel just a little way up the road in about five minutes?" I murmured conspiratorially to her now, should anyone be within earshot.

I placed the beach towel over the carrier and she handed it down to me once I'd stepped back down onto the ground below the balcony. There was absolutely no one about again (had there *ever* been thoroughfare through here I wondered?). It seemed doubtful, with the roughness of the patch and no discernible human tread. I made my way to the front of the hotel and for once I did not feel at all self-conscious about my passage through here or about what I was carrying. I reached the hotel entrance and then walked just a little way up the road. I had beaten Lucy to it but only by a minute or so as soon she joined me and together we made our way back to the taxi rank.

This time we were mindful to stand well away from the rank itself in order to avoid taxis thinking we were a potential fare and unlike this morning, we didn't have to wait long at all. In fact, only minutes. A car drew up at the rank. The driver was a lady; she smiled and waved at us, and pointed to the cat carrier which I was still holding in my arms and so I realised straight away that this was it. She had a passenger with her, an older lady and she now opened her door and got out of the car.

"Hello Beverley? I am Louisa," she told me, as by now I was standing at the kerbside. I smiled at her and she held out her hand to make friends.

"So this is the little kitten, yes?" She put her face up against the door of the cat carrier and muttered something in Greek to him which I presumed was a greeting of some kind. She straightened up and said, "I'm sorry you had to wait long for me this morning but an emergency came and no one else can help."

She looked tired and rather care-worn I thought although she was smiling all the time, with her gentle manner, but her eyes didn't quite catch the smile and I wondered what horrors she might have witnessed earlier. There was a weariness about her but also an indomitable spirit lurking there somewhere too. The other lady who had been behind the wheel now stepped out of the car and stood at Louisa's side.

"And this is Anna who also works with me and also she take care of your kitten while we wait for his Jersey home," Louisa informed me. Anna laughed then and said:

"So this is the famous Facebook cat yes?" Word had obviously gotten around The Ark then.

"Well yes, I suppose he is getting a bit famous now," I replied, realising at once what an understatement that was.

Louisa said something in Greek to Anna which I guessed must be about the state of the kitten's eyes and nasal discharge as she was pointing to his face and Anna, looking worried, was nodding her head in concern and agreeing with whatever it was Louisa was saying. Then Louisa turned her attention to Lucy and said:

"Ahhh, you are looking so sad but it is good, yes? You found the kitten and now you find him home and he will be happy now, yes?"

I looked at Lucy then because, up until this point, my attention had all been directed to the two Ark ladies. I hadn't realised that Lucy was suddenly feeling very overwhelmed by it all. Her cheeks were damp and I realised that she had been quietly shedding silent tears despite appearing to be so outwardly brave. I put my arms around her as Anna had now taken the carrier from me.

"Oh sweetheart don't get upset", I whispered to her.

She leant her head against my shoulder and I pulled her in tightly now. Louisa had also placed her hand on her arm and was saying soothing things in Greek. She was kind and gentle and I could well see then that any animal would be happy, and probably thrive, in Louisa's care. She had a quiet calm and an easy manner, and in the same way that I had seen horse-whisperers in action, she too had that rare quality that animals just seem to recognise and respond to immediately. A calm peace and humility about her. She could talk their language and she could see inside their souls. She could see inside Lucy's well before I had had any inkling that Lucy was quaking, hurting inside. Lucy looked up at her and I could sense something pass between them then; a compassionate empathy that could, and probably would, be able to move mountains. She certainly made an impression on Lucy who was responding well to all her concern and care, and now it was her turn to speak.

"Thank you for being so kind and taking care of our kitten until he goes to his forever home. He means the world to me, and Mum too." She had recovered, and she was looking happier again now, and not so glum. She'd be alright.

"So now I think you let me take some photos of you with the kitten then you always will have pictures of him to keep. That make you not so sad if you have pictures forever yes?"

I passed Louisa my phone and after I'd shown her what button to press she stood back and took several pictures. Then Anna took the cat carrier from me and, with Lucy following her, started settling it very gently on the back seat of her car. I watched her making sure it wasn't going to move about as she was very thorough and talking to the kitten all the time. I could tell without a shadow of a doubt that he was going to be in very good hands from now on.

Turning to me, Louisa became businesslike now as we settled the final details of this transfer. I had to guarantee that should the home in Jersey not materialise for any reason, then it was understood that the kitten was completely my responsibility. She explained about the unfortunate occasions when the well- meaning few who, upon promising a home for a stray, would back out of the arrangement at the last minute; panic setting in, the business of finances, logistical planning of passports, booking travel, etc, etc...it was all too much for some people in the end. Rather like a sort of holiday romance where once the heady first few days were over with, the practical aspects inevitably started to kick in and then one of the parties ultimately regrets their rash decision. I assured Louisa that Sonia over in Jersey would not in any way renege on the agreement, but I was more than happy to act as the kitten's guarantor because I knew one-hundred percent I'd never be needed after the handover, although this prompted me for what I needed to ask her next.

"Louisa can I talk to you about another cat that we have been feeding and sort of looking after? She comes to us every night and is so beautiful, she might even be the kitten's mother. I don't know, I'm not sure," I started hesitatingly, but it was now or never, and so I went on to explain to her about Misty. Louisa nodded in agreement as I told her all about our other blue-eyed baby, and then in a much quieter voice so that Lucy didn't overhear, how I was very concerned about the fact that cats and dogs are poisoned at the end of the season.

"I mean, is that true? Is that really what happens?" I ended, dreading hearing the answer.

"I am afraid that yes it is true. We cannot do much to stop it happening and it is happening many times" she replied.

My worst fears were confirmed then, because if anyone knew this to be fact, then Louisa would. The thought of Misty, and all the other cats and dogs on the island succumbing to this violent end, I knew then that I had to do something about it.

"Look, I know that we're leaving tomorrow, but if we were able to find Misty a home too, would you be able to give her temporary shelter?" Louisa didn't answer me straight away then and there was nothing more that I could add, so a moment's silence passed between us. Then she broke the silence by saying that she could only take Misty under the same circumstances as she was taking the kitten; there had to be an assured and confirmed home waiting for her. What could I do then, but promise to get the word out there on Facebook again to find someone who would take on Misty. This would mean putting a massive amount of trust in whoever did come forward to keep their promise and see it through to its conclusion. It was going to be a very difficult ask, seeing as she was obviously an older cat and was living as a feral, untamed and distrusting of humans. Would there be someone out there willing to give her a forever home I wondered, in light of all these drawbacks? It was a huge risk but one that I was willing to take; but would The Ark?

"You must be asking your friends for to give this little cat a home. Then you tell me and then we bring the cat to The Ark." There was a finality about her tone but it was still gentle and kind; firm but fair. It was for everyone's good. I just hoped that it would be that simple.

"I see", I replied, still trying to work out how I'd go about this. "So to get this clear, if I can find someone who will give Misty a home, then all I have to do is let you know and then you will come and collect her? Because we won't be here after tomorrow. I'll need to give you photos of her and tell you exactly where to find her" I finished. Louisa nodded again.

"Yes, that is what must happen so to get the right cat!" There was one more burning question that had to be asked though. "But how will you get her? She's so wild." I couldn't see her being easy to catch, not even by experienced cat-capturers.

"It is with trappings" said Louisa.

She could tell by my expression just then that I hadn't a clue about 'trappings', so she went on to explain: "We place trap for cat and with food inside. Cats is always hungry so she takes food and then 'bang!' the door it closes and now cat cannot escape. See?"

I began to understand now, and somewhere in my distant memory I remembered having seen something similar in a wildlife programme. It was a lure, as the cat taking the food would release a catch which automatically triggered the trap door to swiftly shut behind it. I just hoped that it would be Misty that walked into it first before any other hungry little passer by did. However, I was getting the impression that Louisa wanted to be off now, the Misty situation having seemingly, for the time being at least, been sorted. The onus was once again back on me.

"OK Beverley, now we go and you have nice rest of holiday, and thank you for looking after the little cat." She shook my hand then, and walked round to the side of the car. Before she got inside it, she called over to Lucy and said:

"I will email you and when we take pictures of the kitten soon then I show them to you in emails. I even make small videos for you yes?"

"Oh yes please, that would be awesome, thank you!" Back to her normal self, Lucy looked much more cheerful and brighter now, the earlier sadness having completely dissipated. All thanks to Louisa's ministrations and instinctive, intuitive understanding.

"Bye bye Lucy, bye bye Beverley!" Louisa called to us one last time from the open window of the car as Anna started the engine.

She turned the car round in one deft movement and then pulled out into the road. Lucy and I waved until they were out of sight and our arms were aching. Despite them being long gone from our view by now we were still looking in their direction, neither one of us wanting to break that moment I think. We both stood there on the curb, our gaze still transfixed on all the cars in the distance; but not one of them contained Louisa, Anna and our kitten any more. It was time to turn around and face the other direction now. Lucy linked her arm through mine and said, more as a statement than a question:

"It's going to be OK isn't it?"

"Yes. From now on it's all going to be OK" I answered.

I couldn't reveal what I was really thinking now though, and that was about a certain other little cat, called Misty. I was also thanking my lucky stars that, when I'd had to broach the subject of poisoning, Lucy had been distracted by Anna putting the kitten in the car, and was thus well out of ear-shot. I must admit that so many times this holiday I had felt like a river-gliding swan; two-thirds of the visible me had to remain calm and serene in front of Lucy, but the remaining and hidden part of me, that I couldn't let her see, was churning turbulently at an altogether different pace.

We decided to walk back a different way to the hotel because neither of us fancied retracing our steps for the second time that day, especially as now it was just the two of us. I kept thinking of our little kitten in his carrier at this very moment being whisked along the roads to The Ark. Was he wondering where his family were, and why we weren't with him any more? It would have been so handy now more than ever if we could talk to the animals and let them know why us humans have to do certain things to ensure their happily ever afters. Even when it means a temporary disruption to their up until now fairly peaceful ones.

Louisa and Anna were kind and they would treat our kitten well; they would have him checked by the vet and get him all ready to fly out to Jersey and we couldn't have asked for more. It just would have been nice to have been able to explain that to him though, and for him to understand what was happening. Having said that though, so far he had been the most uncomplicated little cat to look after, and one who had never objected to anything. There was no reason to assume that he would change this mindset now. He would be fine. It still didn't alter the fact that we both felt a bit dismal and quiet without him though, and seeing as he had been the focal point of our holiday since we had arrived then this was no wonder. Now it was Misty's turn, and I hoped that we would be just as successful with her as we had been with him. Our efforts would now be concentrated on another needy little cat.

Chapter 22

Blue sky. Just an endless blue sky. Sun shimmering and hot but comfortably so, as by now we were getting acclimated to the mid-afternoon temperatures. Lucy walked just a little way ahead of me but we were slow in our pace as we took in the local shop window fronts, the meandering, dusty little alleyways leading off to our left and to our right, and the sometimes quaint, sometimes just downright surreal architecture of this strange and new route back. The ever-present salty tang of the sea that mingled with tasty taverna smells, was making us both hungry and so eventually we couldn't help but be enticed into a little café which stood next to the beach.

Sitting down at one of the tables with its gaily coloured pink and green striped parasol, we were able to take stock of a lovely view of the sea and the even lovelier menu. Lucy kicked her sandals off and stretched out her bare and by now very brown legs. Leaning back in her chair, she looked the picture of health; radiant, sparkly and relaxed. She looked how I was beginning to feel. I got my phone out of my bag, saw that I had a very good signal and found our social media Corfu Kitty page. It seemed there were hundreds of well wishing posts and enquiries as to how we were getting on with the kitten's transfer to The Ark. I was able to answer these mostly and then the waitress appeared at my side ready to take our order. Lucy jumped in before me with what she was having and that gave me time to speed read the offerings on the menu. Keeping it oh-so-simple, in the end it was a Greek salad, a side order of fries and a glass of coke.

The waitress smiled, gave our table a perfunctory wipe down and then ambled off indoors to relay our order. I got the impression that the café was on a somewhat go-slow but that suited me admirably today as I wanted to try and think of a solution for Misty without any interruptions by our meal arriving too soon. I reminded myself that although our holiday was drawing to a close, that didn't necessarily mean all hope was lost in terms of finding Misty a home. Bearing in mind the kitten would be spending several weeks yet at The Ark, then time would still be on our side before the serious business of transport had to be arranged for his, and possibly a second cat in Misty's, flight home to Jersey. While we waited for the kitten's passport and vet checks to be done, then maybe during that time someone might come forward in offering her a home; especially if I was to really put my all into campaigning for her cause when we got back to the UK.

Hmmm, I thought to myself, so let's just suppose someone does come forward and offers Misty a home; then what do we do? Well, we'd have to enlist the help of The Ark again of course, but would they be willing to try to locate and capture Misty? Earlier Louisa had made it sound so straightforward about setting traps and things so I had got the impression that yes, they were willing to do this for us. The question here would be, how would they entrap the right cat when all The Ark had to go on were a couple of photographs of her, and my saying that she just hangs about the Smartline Nasos Hotel. Would that be enough? I hardly thought so, and I couldn't really see how anyone at The Ark was going to want to lie in wait for her for hours at a time on the off chance she might appear. Or would they?

Well Louisa had said they would but now, being away from it all I started to have all sorts of silly doubts. It was as if the time lapse between now and the earlier conversation about Misty had diluted the confidence I'd originally felt when speaking to her about it. I continued to argue this point in my brain- But Bev, that wasn't a false memory they'd said they will do that for us; I just need to continue campaigning and championing her cause from the

UK, it's as simple as that. As soon as we're home I decided I would email Louisa again to keep it all fresh in her memory and reassure her that we are going to do all we can to find Misty a home. Yes, that's what I'll do. Oh, and I'll also take more pictures of Misty tonight so that they can be sure they're trapping the right cat. Lots of photos and taken from different angles so that they are left without a shadow of a doubt who they are looking for. And I'll put all the photos on our Corfu Kitty page too which will show everyone how beautiful this little cat is. A publicity campaign with all the photos and descriptions and -

"Mum, what are you thinking about? I've been talking to you for the last few minutes and I don't think you've been listening to a word I've said!"

I realised that Lucy was indeed speaking to me then. I had been so lost in thought, posing questions in my mind and trying to come up with answers that it was true, I hadn't been listening to anything else apart from my personal Q&A trouble-shooting session that was going on in my head.

"Sorry darling", I said, and then excitedly, "I've been trying to work out how we can get Misty off the island too, and think I *might* have come up with some sort of plan. Or at least the beginnings of a plan anyway."

I was about to reveal all that I'd been thinking but just then our waitress reappeared with our food. She put the two separate bowls of salads and the chips down in front of us, and our drinks, wished us a good meal and then wandered off to chat to some newcomers who had just arrived.

"OK, right, so this is what I've been thinking," I said to Lucy after I had taken the first forkful of piping hot and deliciously salty French fries, and as we ate, I outlined to her my plan, as long as The Ark would still be willing to help once we'd got home.

"Mum, I'm sure that Louisa will keep her word and find Misty for us, she said she would and I believe her." Lucy's earnestness was reassuring and I knew she was right. It was just because I'd allowed stupid doubts to manifest and start to cloud my judgement of our conversation earlier, but as the old adage goes: a problem shared was indeed a problem solved, and Lucy's dismissive reaction to my fears had completely quashed them.

"Anyway Mum, what I was saying to you earlier when you weren't listening," Lucy continued, "was can we go shopping for a present for the lady that cleans our room?"

Clearly Lucy wanted to change the subject but I didn't mind now that she'd reassured me with her absolute conviction about Louisa's promise. I agreed with her that yes, that would be a really lovely idea. Our little lady had been so kind and always made our room look spotless while we were out gallivanting. It would be nice to give her something back.

"OK. Let me go and pay for lunch and then we'll take a wander up to the shops," I told her and leaving Lucy at the table to gather up our bags I went into the relative gloom of the café and settled our bill.

Walking back out into the broiling, shimmering afternoon felt quite luxurious. I could handle the heat now and thought, how typical that was with only a few more hours left to enjoy it. We'd soon have to get used to Glasgow weather again, and after all this wall-to-wall sunshine I wasn't sure if I ever would. Out of sheer curiosity every now and again, I'd had a look to see what the weather at home was doing. Suffice to say it had crept up a degree or so since we'd left, and was apparently in the midst of enjoying a positively balmy 12 degrees celsius. No change there then.

As we ambled back along the streets we window shopped on the lookout for anything that would make a nice present for our cleaning lady. There were plenty of shops selling trinkets, postcards, playing cards with cats on, playing cards with women with nothing on, boxes made out of shells, lilos, and try as we might, we couldn't find anything remotely suitable so in the end we decided to see if the supermarket would prove a bit more fruitful.

"It feels strange being in here not buying cat food," Lucy remarked as we browsed the shelves of the sweets aisle.

"Doesn't it just!" I agreed, taking down a prettily packaged box of chocolates and placing it in the hand basket. Lucy popped a carton of Turkish Delight in too. She glanced up at me, grinning.

"Pudding!" she told me as she turned and made her way towards the next aisle which housed the wine and lager. Studying the various varieties of wine I picked out a bottle of Retsina to go with the chocolates. It was perhaps not the most imaginative of parting Thank-You gifts but it was the best we could do.

"I'll pay for these Mum," Lucy announced once we'd got to the check-out and before I could refuse she'd already opened her purse and was handing over Euro notes to the cashier. When we got outside she admitted that the Turkish Delight was actually for me, as a present.

"I thought you said it was pudding!" I laughed, examining the big box of candies and was surprised to find that these delights were not just the rose and lemon flavours that I was used to at home, but also strawberry, cherry and pistachio. Delish.

"Awww thank you. We'll share it," I told my kind, thoughtful daughter.

"Nah," Lucy replied, shrugging. "I hate the stuff. I just couldn't risk buying something that I liked too!" All I could do was smile at her reasoning. A very thoughtful daughter indeed.

Linking arms we made our way back to the hotel, both of us lost in private thought but most likely thinking the same thing; that our holiday was just about over. All that remained for us to do now was pack and then this time tomorrow we'd probably be back at home. The only thing to look forward to about that was being reunited with Simon, Louie and Mimi again. It would be wonderful to see them, but I was also prepared to have to view them from behind as they turned their backs on us for just a little while, their upright and hurt little bodies just oozing disdain and disgust at our absence until they deigned to forgive us.

It seemed unbelievable to think that everything that had happened, and all the things we'd encountered and achieved had only taken place in the space of a fortnight. Just fourteen little days. Not just finding the kitten and all the adventures and the highs and lows that had ensued, but we'd still also had time to do all the things that the holiday had been intended for. To spend time with Lucy, to see the sights and enjoy the day trips and explore the island. Frankly, I didn't know how we'd fitted it all in and yet, we had.

Unlocking the door of our room I couldn't help feeling a little sense of regret that we didn't have just a couple more days here. Ridiculous after everything that had happened, but there it was, and now I really did have to make a start on the packing. Lucy followed with her suitcase and we spent the next half an hour or so in a congenial sort of silence, wrapped up in reliving some of the holiday memories. This morning I'd had the kitten to help me with this packing lark; was it really only eight hours ago? It was strange, for it seemed much longer. I wondered how he was settling in at The Ark. I knew that Sonia was going to ring Louisa tonight and so in that sense, he really was out of my hands as I had no further involvement with him here on the island. It was just Misty now to deal with and so hurrying on with my packing I called over to Lucy who'd gravitated to the bathroom by now and was collecting the bits and pieces we could pack tonight.

"Lucy, can you help me get some really good photos of Misty tonight?" She stopped what she was doing and came over to me.

"If we go outside together when we feed her then I can just sit at the table and take pictures of her while she's eating," she replied.

It was a good plan, as my taking the food bowls out would be a good distraction while Lucy settled herself somewhere else and snapped away. I had finished my packing by now and was able to zip the suitcase up with the greatest of ease. This was quite a novel experience, as usually I struggle to close it at the end of a holiday, having bought all sorts of mementos and things. I realised that apart from the one little cat ornament that I'd bought at the very beginning of the holiday, I hadn't bought anything else. We hadn't had the time really, and as it turned out it hadn't been that sort of holiday. I was taking back some incredible and unforgettable memories though, something better than souvenirs I mused, but then it occurred to me that in a way, we *were* bringing something back from the holiday, albeit one that would be following along a bit later and bound for Jersey. I just hoped and prayed that we could make it two.

* * *

That evening, we decided to have a dip in the pool for one last time. Strangely enough, neither of us fancied going to the beach, probably because we knew we'd have to pass the drain. I don't think either of us ever wanted to see that drain again; we had closed the chapter on that particular part of ours and the kitten's life. We had no need to say goodbye to that part of town. Our suitcases, now packed, stood like sentinels in the middle of our room as we closed the door on them and made for the pool. As we neared it, we could hear the distant chatter that rose and fell from inside the restaurant as the evening buffet was just about to open. We would follow along later, but for now, all we wanted to do was to be able to jump in the water one last time. After dumping down our bags on the two sun loungers nearest the bar I just grabbed Lucy's hand and without warning her, jumped into the relatively cold pool dragging her with me. Shrieking as together we broke the surface of the still water, the spray surged upwards and each droplet, as if in slow motion, seemed to catch the sun for a fraction of a second before showering us in a cascade of miniature crystal rainbows.

Much later on, after we had enjoyed and savoured the final evening meal of our holiday, and also raised a glass to the kitten, we walked out onto the balcony. Misty hadn't arrived yet so Lucy was able to settle quietly at the table poised with her camera, while I placed an overflowing food bowl in the usual spot and then I too retreated back to the table. We didn't have long to wait as all of a sudden up jumped Misty onto the wall and, spying her bowls all ready and waiting for her, trotted over to them and started tucking into her supper. She completely ignored both Lucy and I and so it was easy to train the camera on her and just silently snap, snap away. Every angle was covered as Misty took her time licking her food dish clean, circling it one way and then the other so that she could clean up every single morsel. Not a crumb escaped that rasping tongue as she made sure nothing got left behind. Tonight she didn't appear to be in any hurry to move on after her supper, as she sat quietly in the corner with her back to us to start her washing routine.

"I don't think she wants to leave us tonight," I whispered to Lucy, who still had her camera trained on her.

It was so quiet and still and peaceful out here now, and all I could hear was my own steady breathing. We were drinking in the moment, and although we were both painfully aware of course that this was our last evening with Misty, we were also quite content that our plan to capture Misty in so many photos was going according to plan. It was a satisfying feeling knowing that we were doing as much as we could for this little lady and as we sat on, the minutes ticking by, Misty was lost in her own reveries of her delicate toilette.

She seemed to be quite oblivious to our sitting there and staring at her until at last, having completed her washing routine but still with her back to us, looked over her shoulder. That inscrutable gaze of hers; what was she thinking? Did her sixth sense tell her that tonight things were a little different for us all? Had she decided to grace us with her prolonged presence to mark the solemn occasion of our final goodbyes and imminent departure from her life, forever? Fanciful maybe, but she made no sign of leaving and so there the three of us just sat in the gathering dusk of our last Corfu night together. Eventually of course Misty tired of our company. She got up, gave a little flick of her tail and popped back over the wall into the night. Lucy and I got up very slowly from the table and looked over the low wall after her. We could hear her stalking through the tall dry grasses as they rustled and crackled with her movement, and in the dark I could just make out the tip of her tail as it swayed back and forwards on her casual meander. And then the darkness just swallowed her up and she was gone, out of our sight.

"Goodbye Misty," I called quietly after her into the night. I heard Lucy give a deep sigh next to me, but she was OK. It was too dark now to read her expression but as we walked back inside our room and turned the lights on, I could see that she was smiling.

"Not goodbye Mum, just goodnight and good luck." I felt her optimism just then. And I just knew that everything, from now on, was going to be alright.

Chapter 23

We flew out of Corfu in the early afternoon the following day. While we had waited to board the plane, I had experienced a little pang of envy as I watched holiday makers coming through the Arrivals area about to start their holidays. I wondered who amongst them might be staying at the Smartline Nasos Hotel and who, perhaps, might even find a little tabby and white cat with blue eyes waiting on their balcony tonight, expecting supper. Whoever had our room next, I just hoped that they were animal lovers.

I sat in my seat just gazing out of the tiny window while we waited for the plane to fill, watching all the activity going on outside against the backdrop of the shimmering horizon. It was cool inside the plane, so cold in fact that actually I was starting to shiver. I'd forgotten what it was like to shiver. Neither of us had been used to such effective air conditioning during our trip it seemed. Lucy pulled her hoodie over her shoulders, glancing up at me as she did so and grinned; her teeth were chattering, such was the contrast between out there and in here. We seemed to sit there stationary on the tarmac for a long time and I could feel the plane give the odd, imperceptible movement every now and again as if it had a mind of its own, alive like a caged beast, it was impatient to be free. Its rocking motion was making me feel sleepy until at last the doors were firmly closed and the cabin crew started to make their way slowly up the aisle to do their head count and make sure everyone had their seat belts buckled up.

There was a change in engine sound now as they whined and screamed almost to fever pitch and then very slowly we started to roll over the runway. I wondered how this great lumbering beast would possibly ever get off the ground, let alone fly. But move it certainly could, and faster and faster now as the scenery beyond the windows started to flash past in a blur. I was waiting for that heavenly feeling of weightlessness which came sooner than I expected and made me draw a sharp intake of breath. It was like going over a humpback bridge too fast. Jarring but sensational. I tried to look down at the ground below but as we were being shot fairly vertically upwards it was impossible to make out any landmarks yet. Gradually we levelled out and now I could see the island of Corfu quite clearly as we seemed to hover over it for a while before reaching the coast. I was in a pensive mood; remembering, reliving, re-visiting it all in my imagination.

And somewhere down there, in all that tumble of gold, blue and yellow, of white, terracotta and green, is Misty and the kitten. I wondered what they might be doing at that very moment as we soared over their home in this incongruous giant bird. My mind was drifting. I thought of the little gifts we had left out ready for our cleaning lady to find. The wine, the chocolates and the note of thanks that I'd written to her. I imagined her opening them and hoped that they would be a lovely surprise for her. While I was having these thoughts, I realised that the island was suddenly receding, and then all at once we were leaving land and flying out over the sea, the coastline gradually becoming just a pale gash against the blue. A misty, cornflower blue. As blue as those eyes.

Farewell you beautiful felines, and be lucky, I mouthed silently to the ever diminishing island. I turned resolutely away from the window now. No more backward glances, or any strange longings to have had just one more day there with Misty and the kitten. We were, at last, homeward bound. I had work to do and now it would be forwards; forwards all the way.

This was just the beginning.

EPILOGUE

It was to be another six weeks until the kitten would leave The Ark and at last travel to Jersey. An eventful six weeks, in which during that time it was Sonia now who kept us all up to date with what was happening back in Corfu. My posts and photographs of Misty had suddenly got the attention of another person, also from Jersey. Her name was Christina and she said that she would love to give Misty a home with her and her family. Needless to say, we were all knocked completely sideways with this incredible, happy news and, as we'd exceeded our target with funds for our kitten, there was some left over which could go towards Misty's rehoming. But like before, when Lucy and I had been on our holiday, we knew that life would of course deal out a mixed bag of fortunes, and some surprises too, during the build up to this double homecoming.

Sonia had rung The Ark the same evening that we'd landed in Glasgow and had spoken to Louisa. She was told that the kitten had settled in very well, and Sonia had already decided on a name for him. For now she didn't want to announce this on the Corfu Kitty page though, but chose to just share it between Lisa and me and Lucy. She had named the kitten *Lucky*. This couldn't have been more appropriate. Two days later, Lucky went to the vet for the necessary health checks and it was revealed that actually, Lucky was a little girl! I'd got so used to referring to the kitten as a 'he' but now I thought, well that's just lovely then!

Meanwhile however, now that Misty's situation seemed to have been sorted out, she was suddenly reported by The Ark as having gone missing. Although Louisa had gone back to the hotel and tried to find her, and to try and start to set a trap, she was just nowhere to be seen. She had just vanished, completely.

I had thought then, how typical for life to throw us a curved ball; a home had at last been found for her and now all of sudden it seemed like that might not happen. What on earth had happened to her? I was beside myself with worry, remembering the poisonings that went on and of course fearing the worst. Louisa had been out several times more, literally scoured the area for her and asked local people if they had seen her, but with no success.

We decided that we should make a poster which Louisa could print out at her end. We would advertise her as being lost and showing a very clear picture of her. It was also agreed that we should offer up a reward for any sightings of her. Greece had recently suffered a devastating financial collapse in its economy which had caused disaster and poverty for much of its population, and so by offering up a reward we thought this would give those in the area an extra incentive to be vigilant and try to help us. From the funds raised with our Go Fund Me page we were able to offer fifty euros for sightings of Misty.

As Lucky's flying date was now all arranged we were working within such a frighteningly tight time-line now. We had to make sure that Misty was caught soon because she still had to go through the quarantine process, plus be given a health check by the vet and have a passport issued before she could leave Corfu. Time really was running out for her if she was going to be on the same flight as Lucky. It was nail-bitingly tense as we all waited frantically, desperate for her to turn up in time. By putting a trap down without definite knowledge that Misty was around was also a risk because it meant that if she *had* completely disappeared, then another cat might innocently walk into it and become trapped.

However, we had no other option but to try everything we could think of, and so a trap was laid out. One week passed, and still Misty had not been found, let alone seen. But then, on the eighth day, Louisa emailed Sonia later one evening to say that at last! They had Misty in the trap they'd put out.

Oh, the relief we all felt at hearing this, at really what was the eleventh hour. Misty had been caught in the trap but she was apparently, and perhaps understandably, very angry about it. Hissing, spitting and clawing she was upset at this incarceration, and from now on we had a new problem. Because she was becoming so stressed at being in captivity, her temperament changed from not only being feral, but being completely wild and actually vicious. The Ark began to wonder whether we were in fact doing the right thing at all in re-homing her abroad. Louisa voiced her concerns to Christina, but only time would tell. We hoped, for her sake, that she would eventually become calmer.

By now it transpired that it was actually the receptionist at the Nasos Hotel who was very helpful in locating Misty and Louisa paid her the fifty euros reward as promised. Misty had now been booked in for a veterinary check-up the following day. Life was about to deal us another surprise. Prior to the vet check, Sonia told us*:* 'Louisa just emailed me saying Misty will be getting spayed tonight. I have asked if Lucky would have to wait longer for Misty's 21-day quarantine to be able to travel together. But as I have just thought, Lucky isn't quite 4 months old yet and Louisa has said that Lucky would be ready at the end of August. So the timing may be OK for both of them to be ready at the same time!' Well this was a relief as we waited to hear how the spay op went. We soon found out, from Louisa, who in her own words told us:

'Hello all, just had the vet on the line. Operating on the cat, asking me about what I know about this cat. So I said once again Beverley thinks might be the mother of Lucky or might have recently given birth and still give milk, so please look well...now he did. Could not find the uterus and then...Find tiny balls...so Misty is Misthos...a tom cat...Surprise surprise. Regards, Louisa, photos later.'

So it was Mr Misty! It was so funny to hear this, especially in that enchanted, broken English way. Delightfully undignified for Misty 'himself' of course, to be announced as such, and so publicly! Of course we all giggled for quite a long time after that revelation, and it was even funnier when we heard from one of the volunteers who had been out with Louisa at the time of the trapping and she'd said she thought Misty had indeed looked very pretty and girlie. Christina told us that she would still keep the name of Misty, and we were pleased. It was the namesake eyes, and the name that I'd got to know her, now him, as. But as time went on, we started to get very worrying news from The Ark, which Sonia told us about.

'Misty is not doing so well; he's growling a lot and doesn't want to be touched by anyone so Louisa has serious doubts and says he is wild. She wants to postpone his flight to Jersey as she's not sure he will be a home cat. I think the stress of being in a cage and being neutered is getting to him unfortunately. I'm really hoping he can fly to Jersey with Lucky as planned.'

And later on that day, Christina told us that Misty had been moved into a private section of the house, having been given natural calming medication. Louisa had agreed he was best going to Jersey, and that hopefully travel arrangements can now start, but that she'd check on Misty in a few days. These were anxious times now as we were all very worried that Louisa would insist that Misty should be released back into the wild. Unlike Lucky, who had settled in so beautifully and was proving to be the most friendliest and playful of kittens, Misty, being that much older, had had too much time living a free and unfettered life beforehand. He was naturally timid of humans and would fiercely defend himself if he thought his territory was being threatened. We were sent the occasional video of his behaviour, which mostly made for unhappy viewing - seeing this lovely cat that I had been so used to seeing turn up on my balcony and want supper and sit with me for a while sometimes, now suddenly turning so aggressive. However, we were convinced that he would become calmer once he realised that no one meant any harm to him, and we just needed to be patient with this altogether different little cat. With tasty treats and good food, and with gentle words and encouragement, plus the addition of some natural, calming medication, we all kept our fingers crossed that he would start to become more relaxed.

On the twenty-fifth August, Sonia announced that at last all the flight bookings had been confirmed; both cats were booked to arrive at Gatwick on the 31st of August and fly to jersey, the final lap of their journey the following day. She had also been given the number of the Animal Reception at Gatwick where they would be staying overnight, so that she could find out how they were after their long flight from Corfu. The day before their flight though, Misty had completely refused to move from his pen at The Ark. Louisa had been having a great deal of difficulty in trying to extricate Misty from his private quarters. Still a rather angry cat, he would not be picked up and placed in his carrier and so he had to be lured into it with a few tasty morsels, which took a very long time. Tuna saved and won the day.

And then the day arrived.

Sonia told us;

'So today is the day Lucky and Misty will be starting their journey to Jersey. What an interesting six weeks this has been. With constant emails, phone calls and organising, the day is finally here! And without the support of this group this wouldn't have been possible. Misty and Lucky's flight is at 1.15pm (UK time) which is 3.15pm Corfu time. So they will be at the airport in a couple of hours. Louisa said she will try and get some pictures and a video of them at the airport. My stomach is full of butterflies and I'll be thinking of them non-stop today as well as tracking those flights continuously! I will be 'phoning Gatwick animal reception at about 6pm to ask how they are and will keep you all updated! Stay calm kitties!'

* * *

That day we all logged onto the Flight Tracker app as we were so eager to chart Lucky and Misty's travels all the way over to England. It was exciting as we all kept up a sort of running commentary via our Facebook page, which had by now been renamed as *Corfu Kitten and Cat to Jersey*. We could see exactly when the flight left, and which countries the cats might be flying over, their air speed, everything. I imagined all our followers, like me, with phones in their hand. I started with;

'Am tracking flight, doesn't look like it's departed yet.' This started the ball rolling, as someone else posted:

'They've just left Corfu, at last,' and then later 'Lucky and Misty are flying over Italy now!' We simply flooded the Corfu kitten and cat page with their progress.

'Oh bless, they've just started going over Switzerland'...

'Look! They've reached France already, wow!'...

'Oh my golly, they're over the see now, next stop England, yay!'...

'Argh! They're nearly there!'

And then it wasn't long before we were able to say, 'Awww, they've landed, they are actually here!'

Sonia announced to us:

'I've just phoned Gatwick animal reception centre! They are safe and sound. Lucky went to the toilet in her carrier so they washed her paws, but all OK and she's happy. Misty is OK, wasn't too happy at first but now nice and snug in his bed for the night. Rest assured they are both going to be very well looked after and will be transferred to Southampton tomorrow via their courier.'

Later the same evening I rang Gatwick's animal reception myself. I spoke to the veterinary nurse that had received Lucky and Misty and she told me that both cats were very well. It was an incredible feeling; these two little cats were now in the UK, and to be able to speak to someone who was actually seeing them onto the final lap of their journey was quite something.

* * *

Day 46
They're Here!
1st September 2017

(Sonia) I just phoned Gatwick to ask about Lucky and Misty and they were picked up at 8.20am by their courier to be taken to Southampton, flight is at 1.45pm.

(Sonia) Right guys, as soon as I see the flight has taken off I will be leaving for the airport. Please keep tracking. I'm very emotional right now and I want to thank you all for making this happen! The next post you see from me, I'll be at the airport.

There was a lull from now on, as we let the girls just get on in privacy with the exciting and truly emotional business of meeting their cats for the very first time, at Jersey Airport. I could only imagine how they, and Lucky and Misty, were feeling, as at long last they had come to the end of their journeys and reached their forever homes. It must have been an extraordinarily strange and unnerving experience for those two little cats, but they were definitely no worse for wear after their long haul from Corfu.

And of course we were all eagerly awaiting news from Sonia and Christina about how they were getting on, but we stood back now and let them have a little peace and quiet from our constant messages. I knew that when the time was right, and Lucky and Misty had been safely settled into their new homes, that it would be then they'd post an update. It eventually came.

Jersey, later the same evening…

(Sonia) Lucky's first afternoon with us has been very energetic. She loves cuddles and I believe she will be a lap cat. When we had dinner she went crazy and was almost jumping onto our plates. I know that in time she will learn not to do that! I'm assuming that's what she did on the streets to survive...get all the food she could? She does love her food indeed!

(Christina) We're home. Misty had a toilet accident so needed to clean him up. He's hiding behind my sofa at the moment. We'll upload other pics and a video. Misty has finally eaten, had some water and cat treats. I have also managed to put my hand near him to smell me, with no hissing.

And then much Later on, Sonia closed the evening with:

'So, as you all know and have seen, Lucky and Misty arrived safely and are now in their new homes. I am incredibly overwhelmed with all the support, advice and generosity we have received over these last six weeks to make this happen. Beverley, for finding Lucky and Misty and taking time out from her holiday to get these animals to safety and arranging for new homes for them, also her tremendous love, support and care she has for these kitties has been absolutely amazing; Louisa at The Ark who has been wonderful at looking after these babies and getting them treated as well as keeping us all updated with their progress. The work she and her volunteers do are just out of this world! A lot of respect to them! Lisa for helping me with the Go Fund Me page to raise the funds to make this possible and for all the advice and support she has given me; Samantha, who has been awesome at starting this book and making Lucky and Misty famous! Christina, who has been by my side since she became Misty's mummy, and just for each and every one of you for being there and following our story! More updates to come of course. Thank you everyone! WE DID IT!'

...and Today

'From that moment on Lucky has been, and still is, an absolute delight. She is so friendly and loves human interaction. I don't think there is ever a moment when she isn't purring! She loves to play with our other two cats who sometimes aren't so keen but hey, she's only a baby still! She does go outside now (at first I was very nervous about this), and she absolutely loves jumping around catching all the flying objects. I am really proud of what I have done to give Lucky the life she deserves. It breaks my heart knowing that the start of her life wasn't particularly great but makes me smile seeing the way she is now. She's an absolute diamond and brings us joy and laughter. If only all the strays were as lucky as Lucky.'

Sonia, Jersey 2021

Misty took a little while longer to become the very sociable and loving cat that he is today. It took many months for him to learn to trust his new human family, and finally come out from hiding in any dark recess he could find in his new home. Gradually he became braver, and as he started to acclimatise to his new way of life, he started to allow Christina and her family to stroke him. Misty needed a family who were patient with the process, and who would allow him to live with them on his own terms until he felt ready to thoroughly trust his humans. Today he is the archetypal lap cat, and twice the size of the sinewy little feline that came over from Corfu three years ago. The unconditional love that Lucky and

Misty receive is reciprocated, but more than that, lasting friends have been made through one simple act of kindness which attracted the support and compassion of cat lovers throughout the world.

The Power of The Paw *is* a mighty one.

The Animal Angels

At the time when Beverley took her holiday in Corfu, the adoption of animals from abroad had in fact been in operation for a good many years and, as is the case with Lucky and Misty, there are many 'Happy Ever After' tales to recount, and not just because of The Ark's involvement. Fortunately for the stray cats and kittens that are ever present in Corfu, there are several charities which are of invaluable help to these animals in being able to secure them a loving home, both locally and abroad.

It was the well-known actress Gabrielle Jacoby and a group of like-minded animal lovers, both Greeks and foreigners, who founded The Ark in 1997. As a Greek Registered charity, it was formed primarily to alleviate the suffering of stray and abandoned animals on the island of Corfu. Back in those days there was no social media, but it's believed that they mainly rescued some street dogs and re-homed them in Germany, and carried out sterilisations. There was also at this time a dog shelter in the South of the island run by a lady with the backing and support of a German charity called Tierhilfe who re-homed many of the dogs to Germany. This shelter is now run by the German charity with people employed in Corfu to care for the dogs.

There is also the Greek registered charity called the Corfu Animal Rescue Establishment (CARE) operating in the North. It is operated by an English lady but she employs a local Corfu resident to run the rescue side of it but they mainly rescue dogs and puppies. However, it is the Agni Animal Welfare Fund (AAWF) that probably has the most illustrious and far reaching reputation of them all, for caring for and re-homing cats and kittens abroad. It is actually a UK registered charity and was set up by Angela Travers.

She explained the background of how it all began:

'The charity began in the year 2005 whilst my husband and I were spending half of the year in Corfu. It became apparent after a short time there that there was a desperate need for help with the feral cat population. Having found a little cat on the beach in desperate need of help we took her in and, after much veterinary treatment, we managed to save her life; without our help she would have died. She remained with us travelling back and forth to the UK and Corfu for several years. She became the inspiration for us to set up a charity to try and help more cats like her, and to begin sterilising as many cats as we could.

Since then many years have passed and we have sterilised thousands of cats and helped many sick ones. We have during this time tried to educate and help the Greek people to understand the advantage of sterilisation of animals, something they had never been familiar with or really understood, which is now slowly beginning to show results in an improvement in the condition of the feral cats. Over the years other people on the island have also begun to help the strays, both cats and dogs, and I do believe that as new groups form, it does encourage others to get involved.

It was after a visit to the South, at the end of the summer season, that I was asked by a visitor that had returned home if I would go and collect a little kitten, and take it to a vet that had promised to take it in and treat it as it was in a very poor condition. After this visit I saw an appalling situation in the South and, after asking if anyone would be prepared to help with cats in the South with our support, we started to get sterilisation started in that area. We started in St. George's South and shortly afterwards, the people living in that resort began to set up many events and fund-raising and started to help the animals. They raise much of the money themselves to pay for the sterilising and winter feeding if the cats. We continue to support the South with sterilisation projects each year, and financial help if they need it. We have some lovely volunteers in that area, and the South is just one example of how we have helped to change things. We also get a great deal of support from the visitors to the South who follow the work of the volunteers, and they are always their to support us.

Many Greek people now come to us for help and ask us to sterilise their cats. This is a huge improvement and also many more people living and working in Corfu are helping to get cats sterilised with our support, and many others without. Visitors are also very much aware of the situation and have been contributory in helping the strays that they find on their holidays, and it is through the visitors that many of the donations come to help.'

It is through Facebook that much of their work is documented and, by the constant posting up of the kittens and cats that they rescue, are able to find homes for them abroad. Many of the kittens that come into their care have been dreadfully abused or starved, and the cruelty cases they see are harrowing. Yet once they are brought back to health, which often takes many weeks with either a volunteer fosterer, and includes regular veterinary attention, they are then ready for adoption.

'Since we began, we have concentrated on the cats, and literally thousands of cats have now been sterilised because of our work. Because we are a UK registered charity, this means we have the advantage of having access to all sorts of grants and support form other larger charities. We are able to claim Gift Aid from HMRC, discount on food and medicines and we have support from various fund-raising groups too. The Gift Aid alone increases our income by 25%. We have just been registered on AmazonSmile too, which means that we receive 0.5% of the net purchase price of goods that people purchase if they choose us as their chosen charity to support.

My personal involvement has changed a lot over the last few years as the charity has expanded, with many more people coming to us and asking for help. Social media has become such an easy way to communicate and has played a big part in making the charity a success. This means I am spending a great deal of time responding to messages and emails, and running the financial side of the charity too. I don't spend as much time in Corfu as I used to do, as the charity can operate from any location due to social media and ease of communications. We are very lucky because we have so many lovely volunteers in Corfu who help with the physical work, and so this means I can concentrate more on the administration and fund-raising side of things. We have great support from so many of these wonderful people to keep us going, although I do need to be in constant contact with our supporters and our Corfu volunteers, and so that of course means I am very busy most days. The charity has grown so much over the last few years, and continues to grow still. This means I can see myself needing more help in the future!'

The full story about Little Cat, who was the inspiration for setting up AAWF can be read here:

http://agni-animal-welfare-fund.co.uk/LittleCatsStory.htm

A Day in the Life of an Animal Angel

Theda Bonetis is one of these quite selfless volunteers for AAWF. I asked her if she could describe her typical day.

'It's pretty difficult to describe a typical day in the life of cat/animal rescue since there are so many different situations. None of us are able to work at it full-time (since we have spouses, families and animals of our own), but definitely the days are more intense during and just after the tourist season. The one thing that is always true is that if there is an animal in need, we do the best we can to help. Most of the time we learn of cats in need from social media: AAWF, The Ark and some others who are major players and all have Facebook pages and websites, plus there are several local Facebook pages where animals in need are presented. For sure, Facebook is the main means of communication. Sometimes the alert comes directly to one of us because our names have become associated with rescue. Many times we reach out to people we know who have other resources, or knowledge, and sometimes we go together to find and rescue. Occasionally it's too late; the cat is too sick to be saved or we can't find it or catch it. Many times though our efforts are successful, and the cat or kittens find homes locally or in another country. Quite often the person who discovers the animals adopt it. I have a great many success stories, and have made good friends through animals.'

So, what is the adoption procedure from abroad?

'It's not really that difficult or mysterious. Firstly, the cat must have a person to go to. Usually this is determined between the person who has rescued and advertised the cat and the person interested in adopting it. Occasionally someone will offer to foster a cat while it finds a home, but almost always it goes directly to the person adopting it. Usually that person pays for the transport although sometimes a charity like The Ark of AAWF will assist. Quite often, the adoption expenses are funded through an online fund-raiser, like Go Fund Me. I did this for a blind cat to travel to England in July 2019.

Once it has been established that the cat will definitely be adopted, the method of transport has to be determined. The cost between air and land transport is really not that much different (around £300), but because direct international flights from Corfu stop at the end of October, land transport remains the only winter option. Of course, travelling by air is much faster, but often the adopter must travel to an airport to collect the animal, whereas the land transporter delivers door to door. Both The Ark and AAWF have agreements with TUI for animal transport. Not all airlines will accept animals and some will only take them to certain airports. There are several land transporters that are very good.

For a cat to travel, there are a few requirement difference between countries, but not that many (although some of this could change with Brexit). First and foremost, the cat must be old enough, usually about 3 months, and healthy, which must be confirmed by a vet. Most Corfu vets know the requirements for different countries. Every cat must have a passport which is issued by a vet and shows that it has been given the required vaccinations and parasite treatment, and is micro-chipped. The passport is made out in the name of the person receiving the cat in the country to which it is travelling to; no one else is permitted to accept it. If it is going to a foster home, the passport is made in that person's name and when it is adopted, the new owner's name will be entered into the passport. Again, this is usually paid for by the person that is adopting, and the funds are sent to the rescuer, but sometimes a charity will pick up the passport costs (usually around 125 euros). If the animal is travelling via air, a proper travel box must be purchased by the new owner.

As for neutering the animal, for sure it's less expensive in Greece than in other European countries, so if the cat is old enough, which is around 6 months, and the new owner agrees to pay, then that is definitely the best option. Costs range from around 100 euros (plus or minus, and definitely less for a male neuter op. than for female spaying), but the charities often have discounted rates with a vet that could help.

So, international adoptions are not cheap and if someone agrees to go forward with this, then it's pretty sure that the animal is going somewhere it is truly wanted. There are some charities that do home checks on the adopters, but I've only ever run into that with dogs and have never had a problem with cats. Essentially I would say that most of the expenses fall to the person adopting the cat.'

What are the typical costs of adoption?

Passport and preparation is around 125 Euros and includes vaccinations, parasite treatment and micro-chipping.
Transport – around £300
Travelling box – around 50 euros for an adult cat, if travelling by air; the land tranporters are already equipped with crates.
Contribution towards upkeep of cat until it travels. This depends on the needs of the cat and length of time.

Do you keep in contact with the new home?

'Most owners are willing and love to stay in touch after adoption, which is wonderful. I feel like each cat that I help is partly mine, and tears are often a part of the departure scene, so it's just great to see (sometimes years after) how the cat has grown and changed. Very often the cat is adopted into a home with other animals, so it's especially nice to see how it adjusts to living with them. One kitten was adopted by a yoga teacher who sends me pictures of the cat attending her yoga classes, and sitting on her back during the session. So cute. Each cat has it's own 'catality' and it's great to see that develop.'

Are there sometimes last minute changes when an adoption falls through?

'Luckily this doesn't happen often, but if it does then usually it's because there have been financial or family developments that interfere; the adopter loses his/her job, a couple split up, etc. I can't think of a single time that there wasn't a good reason (or at least it seemed so), and while it is frustrating, at least the animal is cared for. I then focus on another solution.'

Trap, Neuter and Return (TNR).

TNR is a method which involves humanely **T**rapping feral cats, having them **N**eutered (spayed or snipped), and then **R**eleasing them back into their colonies. This means that these cats will not be able to breed and produce more kittens and ultimately live a healthier, happier life. How does this work in Corfu?

'There is not really an organised programme for this is Corfu, mainly because no local vet is willing to organise one and vets prevent an outsider being brought in. Mostly it's carried out by local individuals interested or involved in animal rescue, and is done in their own neighbourhood (maybe one of the residents is feeding there) or a place where cats are known to congregate, such as at the local rubbish bins. In Corfu, rubbish is not collected from one's house. The municipality provides neighbourhood bins and collection, but citizens have to take their rubbish to the bins. People are not very tidy and lids are usually not put on. This results in many cats collecting here and eating from the scraps. Of course, they soon multiply and so there is a large number of cats, many of whom are sick because they don't have proper care and the kittens don't get good nutrition and are born with medical problems.

The TNR is usually carried out over a period of time when the person arranges with a vet and then traps a cat, takes it for sterilisation and after it has recovered after several hours, it is taken back to the place where it has been staying. Mostly this is done one or two at a time, and often one of the charities or a fund-raising group will help with the vet bill. There are some vets that give the charities discounts.

There are a couple of types of traps used. One is a drop trap which is basically a cage with an open bottom. The cat is given something tasty to eat and while it is eating, the cage is dropped over it. A tray is then slid under the cat, trapping it in the cage.

Another type is the automatic style trap. Food is placed at the end of the trap and inside it is a lever that the cat must step on in order to be able to reach the food. This releases the door to close the trap with the cat inside. I've personally had the most success with the drop trap when there are many cats around, because with the automatic ones, sometimes the wrong cat goes in, and when the door closes it scares away all the rest. However, both are used with good success.

Some years ago I determined to adopt the cats at my neighbourhood rubbish bins, so I set about getting them sterilised, starting with the females. AAWF helped a great deal financially, and now I have twenty-plus healthy cats there with no new kittens. If I find kittens there, which has happened, I know that they have been dumped, because all the cats have been neutered and I monitor them daily when I feed.

I do have quite an amusing and happy story about a TNR I tried to carry out. I live in the countryside and at my neighbourhood bins there lived a large ginger tom cat. He was there when I first began neutering but because I was focussing on the females, I didn't take him to the vet right away. He must be quite old, I call him Papou, which is Greek for grandfather, because he had no teeth, only one eye, his tail had been cut off somehow, and he had ear mites so bad that he had scratched most of his ears off. I treated the ear mites immediately and this stopped the scratching, but otherwise he seems a basically healthy cat who always shows up for his food. He must have belonged to someone once because he is gentle and loves a cuddle.

One afternoon it seemed that there was something wrong with his mouth, so I caught him and took him home in order to be ready to take him to the vet the next morning. As I was transferring him to the cat carrier, he escaped and ran out the back of my large garden and into the bushes. No way could I catch him and I was devastated! Instead of helping him it seemed that I had signed his death warrant. I cried, I mourned, I asked my neighbours to watch out for him but with no luck at all. He'd gone. So I went on with caring for the others at the bins. About a week later, when I went to feed the bin cats, here he came, as natural as ever. He had somehow found his way back from my house – which was several kilometres away – and he is still there.'

Are there are objections to TNR in Greece?

'It's the older generation Greeks that object to sterilisation in general. This is not so much on a religious basis, but more because they say it's not 'natural', ie. it's controlling nature. Or they think it may endanger the animal's life (although of course, allowing your dog or cat to have successive litters and throwing these newborns in the rubbish bin is perfectly natural, and aren't their lives endangered every living hour on the road and trying to survive?) That argument makes no sense at all to me.

However, many of those who might be persuaded to neuter simply don't have the money. The good thing is that the young adult Greeks take a totally different attitude, and are proactive for sterilisation. I've lived in Corfu for ten years, with a break before that and then another ten years during the eighties, and in that time I have seen a huge increase in the number of Greeks who are active in animal welfare. Most, but not all, are young adults and *that* is a great prediction for the future.'

Poisoning the animals – is this true?

'This is something I know very little about so can't really give good information. Some of the poisoning may be as a result of an attempt to get rid of the rats (they proliferate, especially at the rubbish bins where many cats are forced to live). It's important to remember though that Greece is, and has been, a poor country; for many years people could hardly feed themselves let alone have pets, and there are some people with very negative attitudes towards animals, as in any country.

The absolute best help for an animal that appears to have been poisoned is to contact a vet immediately. Many do have out of hours numbers that can be called.'

Local Animal Angels

'As I've mentioned, the situation in Corfu has changed drastically in the past few years, and to some degree all over Greece. More and more Greeks have pets in their homes and there are now many veterinarians and shops that cater for them. There are many younger generation Greeks who are not only active in local animal organisations, but who are leaders in animal rescue. Often these young people have parents of mixed marriages (a Greek and a foreigner), but not always. They take in homeless animals, raise money for food and medicine, communicate on social media, etc. Some do get objections from neighbours (too many cats, a barking dog, etc), but not to an overwhelming number. Probably the biggest fear is to report a neighbour that is obviously being abusive to animals; that bad person may retaliate and poison your own. I'd like to say though that some of my best Greek friends that I have, I've made through animals.'

And finally, do you have a memorable re-homing?

'There are so many and each one is special, but there is one that stands out, not least because it's an example of a bad person, and Karma.

As I've said, I live in the country and, besides my bin cats, there's also a small group of cats about fifty metres from my house that I also feed, next to the road. This is totally legal. However, it was Autumn and rather rainy so I put their food in a more sheltered place on a stone wall. One day when I was there, a very grumpy man - who is well known in the neighbourhood for his bad nature - came out of a house nearby and started to become very abusive towards me, and the cats.

'Take the cats to your house! Don't feed cats here, we don't want them around', he started shouting, waving his fists at me and being very threatening indeed. I was polite and told him that I didn't bring them there, I had found them there and that they were hungry and besides, I wasn't on his property. He left.

A few days later when I went to feed these cats, there was a very young ginger kitten there that I had never seen before. It was in the middle of the road, and as cars were passing it by it wasn't trying to run away, so it obviously had no road sense at all. I thought that someone, knowing there was food being given, had left it there on purpose - which is something that happens frequently. So I picked it up and took it home and immediately advertised it on my Facebook page. Within an hour a woman in the UK wrote to me saying that she wanted the kitten, and that she would pay whatever was needed to get it to her. It was a done deal and so I started the process for sending the kitten.

A few days later, I was back at the bins and doing my usual feeding routine when the grumpy man came out, and this time he threatened to slash my tyres if I came back. And, he demanded to know where was the ginger kitten that he had *bought*?

Obviously it was the little ginger fellow that I had sent to the UK. I made no reply at all and just drove away. That was the kitten who went to the yoga teacher I mentioned earlier, and is king of the house!.'

Theda Bonetis, Corfu 2020

Acknowledgements:

It's important that I give some thank yous to the dream makers, so I'm going to go all Oscar Award-ish now and make sure that their talents and their skills are fully acknowledged and above all, praised.

Thank you SuziSavanah Hogan at Synergy and Light Publishing. When sometimes the writing poured from me in the manner of a burst water main, Suzi with her great patience, dedication and creative expertise turned it into the gently flowing river of a book which you hold in your hands today;

To my Publicist Leah Maloney, for her enthusiasm and skill for all things Social Media and for steering my thoughts and ideas in the right direction with her own creative input;

To my family, past and present, including my Grandparents – Nana, who also wrote, drew and composed but typical of the era just couldn't pursue those talents. I know she had several books inside her. Instead she concentrated on being an exemplary wife and the most fun and loving Grandmother who would write poems and songs for us Grandchildren; and to Papa, who after a lifetime working in Fleet Street would, I know, be so proud to see this book in print;

To my Grandmother Elmhirst - Fleur. It wasn't until many years later that I learned just what a courageous woman she had been, overcoming many challenges that were taboo for a woman in her day. Despite all this, she still went on to become an accomplished Royal Academy pianist - but this was way before I was born. I always knew her as a huge cat lover and having a house full of them. I still remember all their names;

>And so to the great melting pot that explains the next generation…

To my phenomenally wonderful and very Cool Dad, not only for passing on to me his music and cat-loving genes, but also for his immense support, belief and encouragement throughout this three year book-writing lark. In fact throughout my whole life; I am incredibly lucky and I count my blessings every day for having you as my Dad. We are two peas in a pod.

To my Mum, so creative and talented in all the Arts and who taught me so much about nature and beautiful green spaces, that I wouldn't know where to begin, so I'll just say thank you for passing some of these on to me; you're an inspiration.

To Mum-P, overseer of Daddy Cool, thank you for creating order out of some of the chaos which sometimes we leave behind us; you are such a breath of fresh air and rooms really do light up when you walk into them.

To the lil' sis Holly, the third pea in the pod who's also all of the above. You're my soul-mate.

To my friends who have shown much support and encouragement not only for this book, but for animal welfare in general. All with either a cat or a dog sharing their lives, they include Julie, Lozza, Kezza, Emilie, Krista, Dawn, Kat, Tracy, Lizzie, and my very dear, slightly crazy Pink Ladies. All of you have been a constant source of sunshine, giggles, cats, love, and afternoon tea with Prosecco and cheese scones. Please never change.

My grateful thanks and overwhelming admiration to the Animal Angels - Angela, Dawn and Theda and all at Agni Animal Welfare Fund and the solo volunteers in Corfu for your selfless, tireless work that knows no bounds, and which also brought a needy little soul to my attention. Little did I know when I started writing this book, that by the time I was finishing it there would be a little ginger kitten trying to walk all over the keyboard and offer her input. My very own Corfu Rescue Kitty who I named Honeysuckle, arrived here with me on 4th August 2020, after making a 1600 mile journey over land and sea.

Perhaps she will be the next story

To Sonia, Lucky and Beverley. Well, We Did It! What more can I say?

To Christina's husband Martin and her three boys, Ash, Jai and Misty, with much love. I know you are very proud.

And finally, it was difficult writing the Dedication which you see at the beginning of the book. As we are all so painfully aware life doesn't last forever, and some lives that still have so much more living to do can be cut horribly short, in both humans and animals. That is *Life,* and so during the three years writing this book there was always the risk of losing some loved ones along the way. Sadly they included Beverley's three cats Simon, Louie and Mimi, James Bowen's Street Cat Bob and also Misty's Jersey Mummy, Christina. These beautiful souls touched my life and had they never crossed my path, the whole course of history would have been so different; there would certainly have been no book. You, dear reader, will have also loved and lost over the years so I thank you for enhancing and enriching a life with your love. And for sacrificing a piece of your heart which travels over The Bridge along with them.

With love and gratitude,

Sam

x

About the Author

Samantha Elmhirst grew up in North London, surrounded by cats and kittens. When she wasn't painting, drawing, writing stories or reading pony books, she enjoyed fundraising for animal charities and entering 'Win A Pony' competitions. She also rescued cats from her neighbouring streets of Finchley, although, it always turned out they had owners after all. A move to the countryside at the age of 12 allowed her dream of owning a pony to come true. The decades that followed continued to be a mix of art, music, equestrianism and a ferocious love of animals. Sam is still doing all of these things, but slightly better and with more efficiency. In 1995, she set up LivingArt, her veterinary illustration company. She also works as a musician and actress.

Whilst on holiday in Greece in 2007, Sam witnessed the strange and sudden illness of a dog who had been hanging around her hotel resort, the memory of which had always disturbed her. Ten years later, she came across Lucky's plight on the 'Streetcat Named Bob' Facebook group, which opened her eyes to the treatment of stray animals in Greece. It was then that Sam realised that the dog from all those years before had been poisoned. Seeing the kindness of strangers all coming together to help this cat inspired Sam to share Lucky's story. She hopes to raise awareness of the situation and show that help is out there, through the kindness of strangers and charities like AGNI.

Life so far seems to be a constant string of curious, serendipitous events, not least finding out she has ancestral connections with Corfu! Sam lives in Norfolk with three and three-quarter cats, on account of one being three-legged Honeysuckle, who is Sam's very own Corfu rescue kitty.

Synergy + Light

Publishing

Visit: www.synergyandlight.com or email info@synergyandlight.com

Synergy and Light is an independent publisher dedicated to stories. Stories of life, of death, of myth, of legend. Stories from authentic voices and people who have a precious gem to share with the world. If this sounds like you, and you have a completed, edited first draft, please reach out and email us at info@synergyandlight.com. Who knows, maybe we can work our magic and make the synergy and light of your creativity flow out into the world!

Many Blessings,

SuziSavanah x

Printed in Great Britain
by Amazon